MARRY ME IN GOOD HOPE

CINDY KIRK

WAVERLY
HOUSE

ISBN-13: 978-0990716631

CHAPTER ONE

Hadley Newhouse normally didn't eavesdrop. Still, the way she saw it, whatever went on in David Chapin's life was very much her business.

At the moment, Hadley was the only one working in Blooms Bake Shop. After an early rush this morning, business had slowed to a trickle. For now, David and his mother, Lynn, were the only occupants in the dining area.

Hadley was busy restocking the bake case when the conversation between the mother and her adult son turned interesting.

"I can't believe Camille would do something so impulsive." Hadley's hand froze on the pastry she was adding to the bakery case. Slowly, she added a kouign amann to the tray, then even more slowly reached for a Danish.

"She and Allen have been dating over a year, so getting married doesn't really fall into the impulsive bucket." David expelled a breath and sat back in his seat. "I just never expected her to marry him while they were on vacation. Or to quit without notice."

Hadley inhaled sharply. Camille had been Brynn Chapin's

nanny since David and his now ex-wife had first moved to Good Hope.

Lynn, an attractive woman with silvery blond hair, set down her cup. David's mother was a businesswoman and head of the Chapin banking empire. She was a person who identified problems and found solutions. "What are you going to do?"

It was the same question Hadley wanted to ask.

Through the bakery case glass, Hadley watched David's brows pull together. She waited, barely breathing, for him to say he already had someone wonderful in mind. A special woman who would care for Brynn and make the child ridiculously happy.

That's what Hadley wanted more than anything for Brynn. She wanted the girl happy. Losing her longtime nanny was another blow to a girl with a young, tender heart who'd already faced so much loss. First, her mother leaving. Then, the recent death of her best friend from cancer. Now, Camille.

"I got the call from her right before I left to meet you. I haven't had time to formulate an action plan." David raked a hand through his thick, dark hair. "It's too bad there isn't an agency on the peninsula that supplies nannies. But I'll start by asking around. Unless you know someone?"

Lynn's brows pulled together in thought. Then she slowly shook her head. "Does Brynn know Camille won't be coming back?"

"Not yet." David expelled a breath. "I asked Camille to let me tell her."

Hadley frowned and added a cherry Danish to the case.

"This news will crush her." Lynn's voice thickened with emotion. She took a sip of the floral tea she preferred before continuing. "She's been through so much since her mother left."

Mother.

Hadley gritted her teeth at the word. David's ex-wife had never been a *mother* to Brynn. From the moment Hadley had first set foot in Good Hope, she'd seen where Whitney Chapin's priorities lay.

There were the numerous trips Whitney took, always with friends, rarely with her daughter and husband. Not to mention the programs at school and the Seedlings activities that Whitney had dismissed as mundane and not worthy of her time.

Hadley pulled her thoughts back to the present when she realized David was answering his mother.

"...and no." He leaned back in his chair.

When his eyes flicked to the counter, Hadley dropped her gaze and busied herself shelving the rest of the pastries.

As if suddenly conscious of her presence, he lowered his voice. "It's been a difficult year for Brynn."

He obviously had more to say, and Hadley didn't want to miss a single word. If she went into the back, listening would prove impossible. She couldn't very well ask him to speak up.

Yet, she couldn't stay crouched behind the bakery case without arousing further suspicion. After placing the last Danish on the lower shelf, she stood.

At five feet nine inches, Hadley towered a good foot and a half over the top of the case. Clad in a hot-pink T-shirt emblazoned with the slogan "Baking Up Some Love," there was little hope of blending into the woodwork.

Lynn reached across the table and covered her son's hand with hers. "I'll do everything I can to help you find a suitable replacement for Camille."

Hadley bought herself a few seconds by wiping the counter.

"All I want is for Brynn to be happy."

Hadley refrained from glancing in their direction, but she heard the tears in Lynn's voice.

"I know you do, Mom." David's voice held that comforting reassurance Hadley had often heard him use with Brynn. "We need to remember that, in the end, this will turn out best for everyone."

Hadley forced herself to breathe. David was right. He'd find the perfect nanny, and everything would go back to normal. She reached the doorway leading to the commercial ovens just as the bell over the door jingled. Hadley swung around.

Ryder Goodhue, owner of the Daily Grind, a coffee shop that featured pastries and desserts baked at Blooms Bake Shop, covered the short distance to her in long, confident strides. Though summer was in full swing on the Door County peninsula, Ryder was dressed in his customary black. Black jeans. Black T-shirt. Black high-tops.

Hair and eyes the color of walnut completed the picture.

Hadley offered him an easy smile. "You only needed to call if you needed more pastries."

Ami Cross, the owner of Blooms Bake Shop, had secured several outlets for the shop's pastries and baked goods. While it would be unusual for Ryder to have run out of product so early in the day, because of the high influx of tourists at this time of year, anything was possible.

"We got hit hard this morning, but after upping our order last week, we're in good shape." Ryder halted in front of the bake case. "Is Ami available?"

"She's at Muddy Boots today." Hadley gestured with one hand in the direction of the café Ami and her husband owned. "Is there anything I can help you with?"

Though Hadley didn't have a formal title, she functioned as Ami's second-in-command. Once her boss had become a mother, Hadley had assumed even more administrative responsibilities.

Out of the corner of her eye, Hadley saw Lynn push back her chair and watched David stand.

Though Hadley wanted to listen to any last comments, she forced herself to concentrate on Ryder. "Or, if you need to speak with Ami now, I can reach her on her cell."

"I'll stop by Muddy Boots." Ryder cocked his head and studied her. "Are you working at the Crane tonight?"

Hadley nodded. "I'm there every weekend."

Despite Ami giving her a substantial pay increase, along with the extra responsibilities, Hadley had held on to her second job at the popular waterfront bar.

"I'll see you tonight, then." The wink he shot her on his way out of the shop left her puzzled.

Reaching the door several steps ahead of Lynn, Ryder held it open for her. The two stepped out into the sunshine. David resumed his seat at the table.

Lines of fatigue edged his eyes and sadness filled the gray depths, leaving Hadley to wonder if his confident assertion that he'd find the perfect nanny had been merely an act.

David decided he should have left with his mother instead of brooding over a cup of now lukewarm coffee. Right now, he didn't have the energy to get up. Between his work as a partner in an architectural firm and trying to be both father and mother to a distraught child, his stores were depleted.

Damn Whitney.

His lips pressed together as he thought of his ex-wife. If she didn't love him anymore, so be it. But to run out on her daughter…

David knew the demons that haunted Whitney and the fear that was ever present in her life. But Whitney had made her choice. Right now, she was living it up in Boca. The popular South Florida hot spot north of Miami had been a favorite haunt of his ex and her friends.

His ex-wife could take care of herself. It was Brynn's welfare that concerned him. He and Whitney had adopted the child as a newborn. For him, it had been love at first sight. The day they'd signed the private adoption papers in the Chicago attorney's office had been the happiest of his life.

Initially, Whitney had appeared equally enamored of the baby with sweet features and wisps of blond hair. She'd purchased loads of clothes and paraded the baby before her friends. When the teething started, Whitney had tired of the child.

"Care for a refill?"

David's head jerked up.

Hadley stood beside the table, coffeepot in hand.

"Thanks."

She refilled his mug in silence. It was a welcome change from the servers at Bayside Pizza, Brynn's favorite place to eat. The servers there talked nonstop to the patrons.

Hadley, on the other hand, exuded a calm, restful presence. It was no wonder Brynn adored her.

"Did I hear you say you were working at the Flying Crane tonight?" The second the words left his mouth, David wished he could pull them back. That had been a private conversation between her and Ryder.

Still, she had a voice that carried, and it had carried right over to where he sat.

"I'm there every Friday and Saturday night." She flashed a bright smile. "Stop by. I'll give you a free plate of nachos."

David wondered if she offered free nachos to everyone. He hadn't heard her mention anything about nachos to Ryder.

"Of course, you'll probably be home with Brynn." Two bright patches of pink appeared on her cheeks when the silence extended. "I just thought—"

"Actually, Brynn is spending the evening with Lia, one of her friends from the Seedlings." He paused. "The Seedlings are a scouting organization—"

Hadley laughed. "Oh, I may not have grown up here, but I know all about the Seedlings."

David mentally kicked himself. Of course, he didn't need to explain the Seedlings to Hadley. He remembered how excited

Brynn had been last year when Hadley had helped the leaders with a rock-climbing unit held at the YMCA.

"Yes, well, it's a great organization." David shifted in his seat, wondering just why he felt so awkward. "I was planning to stay home tonight and finish up a project."

Her eyes lit with interest. "Another hospital? Or a surgical facility?"

It surprised him that Hadley knew his firm specialized in designs of healthcare facilities, until he recalled a brief conversation they'd had last year. He'd mentioned that an emergency department he designed for a hospital in Queens had won an AIA/AAH Healthcare Design Award.

Even if she didn't recall that specific conversation—and why would she?—everyone in town was aware he'd designed the Good Hope Living Center. The retirement community project, financed by the Chapin Foundation, focused on independent living for seniors.

"C'mon, what is it this time?"

He flashed a smile, and the awkward feeling vanished. "Another emergency room, this time in Spokane."

"I'm sure it will be both lovely and functional." She waited for half a beat as if truly interested.

David knew he'd been mistaken when she turned and headed back to the counter. He took a deep gulp of coffee, tossed a five on the table as a tip and stood.

Before Hadley reached the counter, she bent to pick up a napkin from the floor.

He couldn't help admiring her toned backside. Hadley had the whole package. Brains, body and personality.

Then he remembered that was what he'd once thought about Whitney.

David swallowed the words he'd been about to utter, the ones that would have committed him to stopping by the Flying Crane that evening.

Instead, he paused when he reached the door and called out the inane, "Have a nice day," before strolling out of the shop.

CHAPTER TWO

David stood outside the Flying Crane. Why had he come? His college days were so far in the past they seemed to be another lifetime. He was a single father with many responsibilities.

He was also lonely. Tonight, in the beautiful house he'd designed, the walls had begun to close in...

It wasn't that the house reminded him of Whitney. His wife, his ex-wife, had spent very little time under the multi-gabled roof of the house he'd designed for them on the stretch of road facing the beautiful waters of Green Bay. The same went for the town of Good Hope. Despite voicing early in their marriage that she wanted to be part of a community, she'd made little to no effort to get acquainted.

No, it wasn't reminders of dreams unrealized that had driven him out on this late July evening.

"Are you going to stare at that door all night or open it?"

David turned and gazed into the amused eyes of Beckett Cross.

Beck's wife, Ami, gave her husband a poke in the ribs. "Be nice."

David smiled. He liked the attorney-turned-café-owner who'd relocated to Good Hope several years earlier.

"I'm surprised to see you here tonight." Seeing their confused expressions, David hurried on without giving them a chance to speak. "I mean, with having a little one at home."

"Prim and Max are watching Sarah Rose this evening," Ami said, referring to her sister and brother-in-law. "The Giving Tree holds a special place in my heart, so I wouldn't miss an opportunity to help raise money for it. Plus, it's nice every once in a while to spend an evening out with my husband."

Ami gave her hand a swing, and David noticed she and her husband held hands. He couldn't recall the last time he and Whitney had held hands. Perhaps if they had…

David shoved the thought aside. Water under the bridge.

Beck reached around him and opened the door.

"Are you meeting someone?" Ami raised her voice over the sound of heavy bass spilling from the doorway.

David shook his head and stepped inside. It had been so long since he'd been here, it was as if he was seeing the place for the first time.

The high tin ceiling added a vintage vibe, while the scarred wooden floor contrasted with the gleaming mahogany of the curved bar. The large mirror behind the bar made the room look double the size.

Music blasted from the back of the room, where the band was set up. David winced. The large open space and hard walls made for horrible acoustics. He briefly wondered if the owner had looked into a sound-absorption system. Even a couple bass traps and sound baffles would help immensely.

"Welcome to the Flying Crane. There's a ten-dollar cover charge tonight."

The comment snapped David's attention from the noise to Izzie Deshler. Tonight, the local artist with massive talent and even more massive hair, wore a black shirt with a red crane in flight.

Izzie stuck out a jar filled with bills. "We've got a band from Chicago playing tonight. Five dollars of the ten will go toward the Giving Tree."

The Giving Tree was unique to Good Hope. Not a charity, but a fund for helping neighbors who'd fallen on hard times.

David reached into his pocket, pulled out a twenty and stuffed it in the jar. "Keep the change."

He didn't notice what Beck gave, but knew it must have been substantial by Izzie's squeal of delight. David shifted his gaze to the bar, searching for an empty stool.

"Fin and Jeremy have a table on the deck." Ami's fingers touched his arm. "We have an extra seat and would love to have you join us."

"It'll be quieter out there." Beck gestured with his head toward the doors leading to a raised deck overlooking the water.

David was well-acquainted with the entire Bloom family and with Jeremy Rakes, the town's mayor. Not only had he and his siblings grown up with them, his mother was dating Steve Bloom, Ami and Fin's father.

"Sure." David spoke quickly, then qualified, "If you're certain I won't be intruding."

"Not at all," Ami assured him. Unexpectedly, her smile widened. "Hadley. Hello."

Hadley looked even more, well, *beautiful* was the only word that came to David's mind. She wore a short black skirt and a curve-hugging black tee with the crane logo. Her hair, instead of being pulled back as it had been at the bakery, hung in thick golden curls past her shoulders.

"Your family is out on the deck." Hadley's tone might have been upbeat, but David saw the fatigue edging her eyes.

"Which is where we're headed." Ami stepped aside to let a couple get past. "I'm afraid we're causing a logjam."

"I have your table, so I can get your drinks now, if you know what you want." Hadley's smile appeared directed straight at David.

He felt the punch. It really had been too long since he'd been out if he could react so strongly to a simple smile from a pretty woman. "Dos Equis with a lime."

"Whatever beer you have on tap." Beck slipped an arm around his wife's shoulders. "Club soda?"

"You know me well," Ami responded with the easy familiarity of a couple in perfect sync.

"And a lime for the club soda," Beck quickly added. "Almost forgot that part."

"Coming right up."

When Hadley brushed past him, David caught the scent of cinnamon, vanilla and sugar. "She smells like a cinnamon roll."

He realized he'd spoken aloud when Ami chuckled.

"Occupational hazard." Ami smiled. "When you bake a lot, those aromas get under your skin."

"I find them incredibly potent." Beck's soft Southern drawl added a nice emphasis to the words.

Ami shot her husband a wink. "Potent is a good word."

The interplay and the fact Ami wasn't drinking alcohol made David wonder if she was pregnant. From what his mother had said, because Beck and Ami had gotten started late on building their family, they were determined not to wait long before working on baby number two.

What would it be like to share a pregnancy with your wife? Because of Whitney's family history, he'd known when he married her they would never share that experience. That had been okay.

What hadn't been okay was—

"David." Jeremy rose from the table and extended a hand.

Good Hope's mayor was blond, with the body of a surfer and

a keen intellect. He was also one of the most good-natured guys David knew.

Delphinium—Fin—Rakes, the mayor's wife, had the polished look of a woman he'd expect to see dancing the night away in a trendy nightclub.

Her look reminded him of Whitney, with one exception. David was sure Whitney had never looked at him the way Fin looked at Jeremy with so much love in her eyes.

Fin aimed a friendly smile at David. "How nice you could join us."

"Thanks for asking." Sensing someone behind him, David whirled and nearly knocked the tray out of Hadley's hands.

Automatically, he reached out, steadying her. For several seconds, his gaze locked with hers.

As if conscious of everyone's stares, she gave a little laugh. "That could have been disastrous. My boss says if I drop one more tray, I'm outta here."

A look of distress crossed Ami's face. "Lyle wouldn't really fire you, would he?"

"Lyle is gone. All the servers report to Jeff now. The owner brought him in from Milwaukee." Hadley's lips pressed together. "He's a real piece of work. I'd quit, but with the bakery closing, I need the income."

Startled, David shot a gaze at Ami then back to Hadley. "Blooms Bake Shop is closing?"

"I'll let Ami tell you all about it." Hadley glanced nervously over her shoulder where a thin man with slicked-back dark hair stood staring. "Jeff doesn't like it if we talk too long with the customers."

Once the drinks—and another plate of nachos—were on the table, Hadley hurried off. Marigold, the youngest Bloom sister, arrived with her husband, Cade, the local sheriff.

"Why is this the first I've heard about you closing the bakery?"

David felt very out of the loop. "Mom didn't say a word about it this morning."

Everyone must know but him, David realized, when the others at the table simply continued their conversations.

"We're not closing, not in the way you think. We're expanding." Ami sipped her club soda and reached for a chip. "The space next to the bakery became available, and we jumped on it."

David visualized the area. "You plan on making the dining area larger."

Ami nodded, chewed and swallowed.

"Why not wait until winter?" David knew he had to be missing something. "Why close during the height of the tourist season?"

"Well, we hope to be pretty busy at home this winter." Ami glanced at her husband, who grinned back at her. "And what we have planned for the bakery is major. We're not just expanding the dining area, we're adding additional commercial ovens, holding cabinets and packing tables. Kyle gave us a very competitive bid, but for his crew to do it, it has to fit between two other projects. Which means the renovation has to be done now."

"Kyle Kendrick does good work." David had been impressed by the man's attention to detail, not only on the Good Hope Living Center, but on the theater renovation project. "You're going to completely shut down?"

"The bakery will be gutted. We have a commercial oven at home, so Ami can still honor her contracts and accept special orders." Beck sipped his beer, then slanted his wife a mischievous glance. "If she gets bored, I can keep her busy at Muddy Boots."

Even before Beck and Ami were married, she'd started supplying his café with pastries in the morning and desserts for the lunch and dinner menus.

"You're so thoughtful." Ami returned her husband's teasing smile. "But I believe I'll keep busy enough supplying the café with desserts and the Daily Grind with their orders. Oh, and spending time with you and Sarah Rose."

"The last is the most important." Beck leaned over and kissed his wife gently on the lips.

David had to look away. The warm glow of emotion between the two only served to remind him just how cold his own marriage had been. His gaze landed on Hadley, who was serving drinks to a group of guys who looked barely old enough to drink.

She was laughing with them, flirting a little without letting things get out of hand. When one of them laid a hand on her ass as she bent over to pick up their empty glasses, David gritted his teeth and pushed back his chair.

Before he could stand, Hadley shot the guy a withering look that had him dropping his hand.

"We were out by your place today, David."

David turned back to the table as Cade went on to talk about the house he and Marigold planned to eventually have built on land down the road from David's property. The next thirty minutes flew by.

Cade had shifted his attention to his wife and her comment about the upcoming Founder's Day celebration, when Ami shoved a chair in between her chair and David's.

"There's more than enough room." Ami's voice brooked no argument. "This is your break. Sit and relax. You've been running all evening."

"If you insist." Hadley dropped into the chair next to David.

The fit was tight. Ami had to pull out her chair for Hadley to get into hers. Though Hadley fit, her shoulder brushed David's.

"Sorry." She shot him an apologetic look.

"No worries." He studied her for a long moment. "I don't know how you do it."

Hadley met his gaze, seeming oblivious to the conversation swirling around them. "Do what?"

"Get up when it's dark to bake, work all day in the shop, then come here and be on your feet all evening." He pointed the beer bottle toward her. "Not many people could handle that pace."

"Women who have families often do all that and more." She lifted one shoulder and let it drop. "All I have to worry about is me."

David set down the bottle. "I still think you're amazing."

For an instant, something flickered in her cobalt-blue depths. Just when he worried he may have mistakenly given the impression he was flirting, she laughed and waved a dismissive hand. "That's nice of you to say."

Ami leaned close. "What are you two talking about?"

"Compliments." Hadley didn't miss a beat. "Sincere ones and some not so sincere. A woman told me she liked my shoes. I was feeling pretty good until she added I'd probably be able to get to my tables faster if I was wearing sneakers."

Ami glanced around as if expecting the culprit to be standing in plain sight. "Is she someone I know?"

The look in Ami's eyes told David that if it were, Ami might have a talk with her. While the bake shop owner might have the reputation for being sweet, she was loyal and fiercely protective of her friends.

"Tourist." With a flick of her wrist, Hadley dismissed the episode. "She and her friends left about twenty minutes ago."

"I hope she at least gave you a big tip." Marigold leaned across the table, telling David there were no private conversations here.

Hadley rolled her eyes. "What do you think?"

Though Hadley didn't seem disturbed that she'd been stiffed, it had to sting. No one worked two jobs unless they needed the money.

"Have you had a chance to look at the plans?" Cade asked David, reaching for a nacho in the center of the table.

Several days ago, Cade had given him the house plans he and Marigold were considering. Though the sheriff had made it clear they couldn't afford to build now, they wanted plans in place when they were ready.

"The house has curb appeal, and the floor plan utilizes the space effectively." David had reviewed the plans as a friend, not as their architect, so he treaded carefully.

The sheriff, a trained observer, picked up on the unspoken *but*. "What issues do you see that might present a problem?"

"Your lot is good-sized, but I don't believe it's wide enough to do this particular plan justice." David lifted his beer. "Now that you know the style you like, I suggest looking for one that contains the features you want, but different dimensions."

"What about if we cut ten feet of width and made the house deeper?"

David wiped the condensation off the bottle with his finger. "That would change the exterior as well as the interior setup."

"Maybe you could draw something up for us?" Cade glanced at his wife and received a nod. "We'd pay you, of course."

"I specialize in healthcare design, not residential." David saw the light in Marigold's eyes fade and felt like a shmuck. "But I'll be happy to draw something up for you. I should have time once I finish my current project."

"We're going to pay you." Cade told him.

"You look at the plans. Then we'll talk." David's tone made it clear the subject was closed.

Cade and Marigold were friends. Marigold's dad was dating his mother. Heck, they were practically family.

Besides, neighbors helping neighbors was the Good Hope way. What better illustration than all the people who'd turned out this evening to support the Giving Tree?

∼

Hadley's fifteen-minute break was nearly over when Fin distracted Ami with a question about the Cherries' plans for the upcoming Founder's Day parade.

At the same moment, Marigold and Cade—who'd monopolized David for most of the evening—pushed back their chairs and headed inside to the dance floor.

Hadley shifted in her seat to face David. "There's always something going on in Good Hope."

"You're right about that," David agreed. "Once we got through the Fourth, the Cherries turned their attention to promoting the Founder's Day events."

The Cherries, originally known as the Women's Events League, planned all the holiday celebrations. Their commitment to fun activities for families, as well as couples and singles, made Good Hope a prime tourist destination.

"From what I hear, there's going to be lots of activities for children on Founder's Day." Hadley cocked her head. "Will your mother be attending with you and Brynn?"

A look of puzzlement furrowed David's brow. "It's a month away. We haven't discussed plans for that night."

"I would think a grandmother would want to enjoy the activities with her grandchild. Mine certainly would have." The second the comment left her mouth, Hadley wished she could pull it back. The last thing she wanted to speak about was *her* family.

Interest sparked in David's gray eyes. "You were close to them growing up?"

No more mistakes, Hadley told herself. She took a few seconds to corral her thoughts. "No."

He studied her, his gaze sharp and assessing. "I believe Ami once mentioned your parents live in North Dakota."

"My grandparents lived there. I mean, they used to live there." After what had happened in Williston, North Dakota was on her do-not-visit, do-not-mention list.

David's gaze turned curious. "They don't live there now?"

Hadley gave a laugh, but it ended up too high-pitched to come across as casual. Still, she had to start digging out. Or bail. "My, how did this conversation get so off track?"

She didn't wait for a response. Instead, Hadley pushed her chair back, scrapping it across the deck with such force it nearly toppled. "I'd love to stay and chat more, but duty calls."

Hadley offered a brilliant smile to everyone at the table. "Thanks for letting me sit with you."

With everyone protesting at once that she hadn't stayed nearly long enough, there was no opportunity for David to ask further questions. Questions she had no intention of answering.

If she left now, there would be zero chance of her putting her foot in her mouth for what felt like the zillionth time.

She'd never been good at off-the-cuff conversation. She did better when her actions and comments were carefully considered.

Which was why, instead of saying something else she might regret, she gave Ami's shoulder an affectionate squeeze and strolled off.

CHAPTER THREE

Hadley had just left when David's phone dinged, a reminder alerting him that it was time to pick up Brynn.

Coming tonight had been a good decision. He wished he could stay longer. Being around friends had gotten him out of his funk. A man could stare at design software and amble around a too-silent house for only so many hours a day.

Ami glanced up as he stood. "Do you have to go already?"

"It feels as if you just got here," Marigold protested.

"Brynn is at a birthday party. It's pickup time." He glanced around the group. "Thanks for sharing your table."

Jeremy flashed a smile. "Now that we know it's possible to drag you out of that fortress you call home, we'll do it more often."

David chuckled, dropped a bill on the table for his beer and share of the tip and lifted a hand in farewell. While it was possible to exit the deck without going through the bar, he chose the longer route.

He told himself it was because he wasn't in any hurry. The alarm had been set with an extra fifteen minutes of lead time. Though the fact that he had time to kill didn't explain why he was pushing his way through wall-to-wall people in a room with music that hurt the ear.

His gaze scanned the room, stopping when he spotted Hadley. She stood near the bar, a full tray of drinks balanced on one hand. A guy about his age, with thinning blond hair and a cocky stance, blocked her.

Though his path hadn't crossed with Clive in years, David recognized Clint Gourley's younger brother. Close in age, the two men looked so much alike they were often mistaken for twins. This guy had to be Clive, because older brother was currently a guest of the state, serving time for burglary, multiple counts.

Clive moved closer, crowding Hadley. She stood her ground.

Anger spurted through David's veins.

Then, in a gesture that seemed just a little threatening, Clive placed a hand on Hadley's arm. Seeing her stiffen was all it took for David to veer off course and approach the two.

Hadley lifted one hand as if to brush back her hair. The movement effectively dislodged Clive's hand from her arm.

Smart woman.

David was ready to turn toward the door when Hadley's eyes met his. The look she shot his way had him continuing toward her.

He hadn't taken more than a couple of steps when Clive cupped a hand around the back of Hadley's neck and yanked her close.

She jerked back with such force her tray of drinks went flying. Beer and whiskey rained over nearby patrons, while glasses hit tables and shattered on the floor. Now free of Clive's hold, Hadley stumbled backward, her arms flailing in an attempt to right herself.

In the commotion, Clive slipped away.

David reached Hadley just as she lost her fight for balance. He wrapped his arms around her. She struggled for a second, then relaxed when she saw it was him.

The same man David had noticed on the deck pushed through the crowd as the band continued their rendition of the rock classic *Layla*. "What is going on here?"

His narrowed gaze settled on Hadley, on the tray at her feet, on the whiskey-and-beer-soaked patrons loudly voicing their outrage. A muscle jumped in the manager's jaw. "Get out. You're fired."

David stepped forward, hands clenched into fists at his sides. "This wasn't Hadley's fault. Clive grabbed her."

The manager looked him up and down. "I don't see anyone but you."

Hadley's hand curved around David's bicep. "It's okay. I didn't like working for him anyway."

She turned and strolled toward the door, head held high.

David glanced at the manager, who was attempting to soothe an irate customer, before hurrying after Hadley. He caught up to her on the sidewalk and fell into step beside her. "I'm sorry you lost your job."

"I'm not. He's a jerk."

"But with Ami closing down the bakery, you need the money."

Hadley hesitated. "She offered to pay me my salary while the bakery is closed."

His worry disappeared. He should have trusted Ami to do right by her employees. "That's nice of her."

"She's a good friend." Hadley gestured with her head in the direction of the bar. "You don't have to cut your evening short on my account."

"I was leaving anyway." David noticed she smelled like beer now, instead of cinnamon and sugar. The scent wasn't particularly appealing, although he did like the way her alcohol-saturated shirt molded to her breasts. "I have to pick up Brynn from Lia's birthday party."

Hadley's lips curved. "I hope your daughter has had a better evening than I've had."

David laughed.

They walked in comfortable silence the short distance to the bakery. When she stepped inside the back entrance and he heard the dead bolt click, David headed for his car.

∼

Thanks to being fired, Hadley arrived home in plenty of time to get a good night's sleep. Unfortunately, sleep had eluded her. Her thoughts kept circling back to David and the way he'd looked when he pushed through the crowd to get to her.

He'd been ready for battle, with fists clenched and gray eyes blazing. Even that magnificent jaw had been set in a determined, hard line. In that instant, he'd reminded her of one of those gallant knights in the books she'd devoured as a kid.

Except, she wasn't some frail damsel in distress who couldn't take care of herself. Hadley knew self-defense, had trained and practiced. She didn't need rescuing.

The desire to have David pull her into his arms, wrap those strong arms around her and tell her he was there for her made no sense. Still, the image of him holding her tight kept circling in her brain, and it was nearly two before she'd fallen asleep.

Thankfully, she lived over the bakery and needed only to walk downstairs to start her shift at eight thirty. She and Karin handled the morning rush, until the college girl left at ten.

Ami stepped from the back and glanced at the nearly empty shop. "It appears we've hit a slowdown."

"More like a five-minute speed bump." Hadley rolled her shoulders. "It's been a good morning. Lots of customers, but in a steady stream. I'll take that any day over getting slammed."

"Are you sure you're okay handling the front alone? I

wouldn't have let Karin off this early, but it's her parents' anniversary, and the family is planning—"

Hadley stopped Ami's words with a squeeze of her arm. "Seriously, I can handle it."

"You're amazing." Ami's green eyes turned suddenly serious. "I don't know what I'd do without you."

Feeling her cheeks warm, Hadley went for the joke. "You'd hire another employee."

"You're not just an employee to me." Ami's soft voice held a hint of reproach. "You're my friend."

When she'd moved to Good Hope, Hadley had been determined to keep it strictly business between her and her new employer. Ami would have none of it.

Over time, they'd become friends, more like sisters. The closeness only complicated matters. Hadley had no doubt that when all of her secrets came out, Ami would feel betrayed. As would everyone else in town.

"I want you to reconsider taking a salary while we're closed." Ami's green eyes beseeched her to agree.

"I'm not changing my mind." Hadley kept her tone firm and matter-of-fact. "I won't allow you to pay me for doing nothing."

"You'll be helping with both contract and special orders."

"Yes, and you can pay me for those hours." When Ami's chin lifted in that stubborn tilt, Hadley knew she needed to change the subject and fast. She pointed to the doorway leading to the ovens. "It's getting late. Katherine Spencer will expect her order to be waiting."

"There's plenty of time." Ami's gaze shifted to the clock on the wall. She inhaled sharply. "Or maybe not."

"She needs them for her mah-jongg tournament. We both know waiting isn't in her nature." Hadley pretended to shudder. "The last thing we need is for her to sic Eliza on us."

Eliza Shaw Kendrick was a friend of Ami's. She was also Katherine's great-niece. Or was she her cousin? Regardless, the executive director of the Cherries wasn't known for her sunny nature.

"I'm not worried about Eliza. Since her marriage to Kyle, the once formidable Ms. Shaw is a changed woman." Ami chuckled. "But you're right. It's definitely brownie-baking time."

After another rush, business in the shop came to a grinding halt. Most families looking for a pie or another dessert for supper had already stopped by. Katherine came and left, happy as a clam with her boxes of heavenly smelling brownies.

Hadley rolled her shoulders to ease the stiffness. When the bells over the door jingled, she glanced up from the table she'd been wiping and froze.

David strolled into the shop, dark hair gleaming in the late afternoon sun. But it was the little blonde with him who had her heart stuttering.

Taking a firm grip on her emotions, Hadley offered a welcoming smile.

"Hey, you two." She took note of David's dark pants and polo shirt and Brynn's summer dress. "You're looking pretty spiffed up for a Saturday afternoon."

David rested his hand on his daughter's shoulder. "Brynn had her dance recital this afternoon."

Hadley switched her focus to the little girl. Brynn's blond hair was pulled back into what Hadley recognized as a ballet bun. Her pale blue dress made her eyes look extra blue. "I bet you did fabulous."

"I don't like ballet." The nine-year-old scrunched up her face. "I don't want to do it anymore."

"I said we would talk about you quitting," David reminded her. "Your mother thinks dance is important."

"Mommy's not here." Brynn's tone held a hint of defiance, but her eyes were sad. "I want to take rock-climbing at the Y."

"Dance and rock-climbing are both fun." Though she could understand where Brynn was coming from—Hadley had also hated dance as a child—the last thing she wanted to do was come between a child and her mother. Even if that mother was fifteen hundred miles away. "What can I tempt you two with this afternoon?"

"I heard from one of the grandmothers at the recital that Ami was baking brownies today for a tournament at the Living Center." David's smile eased some of the stress lines around his mouth. "Would there happen to be a couple left for a hungry dancer and her dad?"

Basking in the direct heat of his smile, Hadley felt her earlier fatigue vanish.

"We're going to eat them on the way home. Before dinner." Brynn spoke in a hushed whisper, then touched a finger briefly to her lip. "You can't tell Gram."

The tips of David's ears reddened, like he was a small boy whose hand had been caught in a cookie jar. "It's, ah, a special occasion."

"My lips are sealed." Hadley made a zipping motion across her mouth.

Brynn giggled.

The sound, so pure and innocent, brought a smile to Hadley's lips. "The only ones left have chocolate icing. If you don't like yours frosted, I can scrape it off."

Brynn's eyes went huge. "Don't do that. We like frosting. Don't we, Daddy?"

"We sure do, Sweet Pea."

While David reached into his back pocket for his wallet, Hadley put on gloves, then pulled the tray out from behind the glass bakery case. After nestling the brownies in a small white box, she dropped napkins and forks into a sack. "Is this to celebrate your dance performance?"

Hadley glanced up from the cash register in time to see the two exchange glances.

"You don't have to tell me." She waved a hand. "Not my business."

"We're celebrating me starting my History Fair project."

Hadley must have looked confused, because Brynn continued. "For the Founder's Day celebration."

"I'm looking forward to it." David handed Hadley a five. "I like projects about family."

Hadley pressed the bill back into his hand. "On the house. For last night."

For a second, he looked as if he might argue, then he smiled and put the five back into this wallet.

"We're going to have brownies tonight." Brynn spoke in a singsong tone as she danced around the dining area.

David pointed at the white bakery sack dangling between her fingers. "Just remember, one of those is mine."

It did Hadley's heart good to see the closeness between father and daughter. When Whitney left, she'd worried David might withdraw from his daughter and drown himself in work. It was what her own father had done.

"What did you mean when you said the project is all about family?" It might not be any of her business, but they'd opened the door by bringing it up, and Hadley was curious.

Brynn stopped dancing to answer.

"The Chapin family is one of Good Hope's founding families." Pride infused the child's words. "My History Fair project is all about my family."

The child's eyes sparkled as she outlined what she had planned. Hadley thought of her own history.

Her father had been a highly decorated police officer killed in the line of duty. His family had been early settlers in North Dakota. Would any of that history ever be included in a family tree?

Hadley returned her attention to Brynn and smiled at her enthusiasm. "Sounds like fun."

"We're also making pizza." Brynn leaned close as if imparting a secret. "We're not going to order it. I'm going to make it myself."

"Hey, I thought you said I could help," David protested.

"You can, but I get to put on the pepperoni," Brynn told him, then leveled her blue eyes on Hadley. "Do you like pizza?"

"I like pretty much everything," Hadley admitted.

"You could help us."

Though Hadley had no plans for the evening, a child's casual offer didn't an invitation make. "It's been a really long day. I'm looking forward to going home and putting my feet up."

Impulsively, Hadley reached out to tousle the top of the girl's soft blond hair. It was a mistake. An ache of longing swamped her.

"You can put your feet up at our house." Brynn shot Hadley a winning smile. "Since I'll be the one making dinner."

"Really, I don't want to impose—"

"You won't be imposing." David's gaze met hers. "Join us."

Hadley hesitated. "If you're sure—"

"Are you going to make us beg?" David's smile turned wicked. "Or perhaps I could sweeten the deal with anchovies."

Hadley grimaced.

Puzzlement filled Brynn's eyes. "What are those?"

Hadley's shudder had David's smile widening.

"Join us." His tone turned persuasive. "I promise we'll stick to pepperoni."

With her teeth biting her bottom lip, Brynn carefully spread the sauce onto the premade crust.

"Looking good, Sweet Pea."

Brynn looked up. "I wonder when Hadley will come."

As if in answer, the doorbell chimed.

"I bet that's her now." David covered the distance to the front door in eager strides.

She'd changed from her Blooms Bake Shop tee into a sleeveless summer dress. The white dress covered with blue flowers brought out the blue of her eyes. Her hair hung loose to her shoulders.

"Welcome to Casa Chapin." David stepped back and caught the scent of vanilla as she glided past him. "I hope you didn't have difficulty finding the place."

The houses on this road weren't well marked, most sitting far back from the twisting road that hugged Green Bay.

"No, I knew—" Hadley paused, appearing to rethink her response. "No problem."

"I should have told you that GPS isn't always accurate for houses along this road."

"When I heard you'd designed and built your home, I expected something...modern." Hadley stopped in the center of the foyer and glanced around. "Not this."

"Surprise." David's eyes had turned watchful.

"It was—is—totally not what I expected." Hadley made a sweeping motion that encompassed the room. "Not only the outside, but this lovely interior gives the impression the home has been here since the 1920s."

"You have a good eye." David found himself pleased by the keen observation and obvious approval. "That's exactly the era I aimed for, as that was when the first cottages appeared on this road."

When he and Whitney had first discussed building in Good Hope, David had been surprised his wife left the entire matter up to him. He'd tried numerous times to involve her. After all, this was her home, too. But she'd insisted whatever he designed would be okay with her.

David had embraced the freedom, positioning the home on an

angle in a wooded area at the end of a winding drive. The location allowed a perfect view of the bay.

"It's stylish but homey." Hadley's gaze shifted from the gleaming hardwood floors to the large stone fireplace.

"We like it." David motioned for her to follow him. "Brynn's in the kitchen. I'd give you a tour, but she'd have my head if I didn't bring you right back."

Before she'd gone three feet, David's hand was on her arm.

"Thanks for coming tonight. It means a lot to her." His smile turned rueful. "She didn't give you much choice. For that matter, neither did I. I put you on the spot, and I apologize."

"I had a choice." Hadley's gaze met his. "I wanted to spend the evening with you."

Their eyes locked, just as they had at the Flying Crane.

"Was that Hadley at the door?" Brynn called out just as he took a step closer.

Hadley turned in the direction of her voice. "I'm here."

It was relief he felt, David told himself as he escorted her to the back of the house.

Hadley paused in the doorway, and her eyes widened as she took in the modern, yet made to appear vintage, kitchen with its gray Venetian plaster walls and white cabinets. He wondered if she noticed the cook-friendly layout.

At the time he designed the home, Whitney had expressed an interest in gourmet cooking. Long before they moved in, she'd lost interest.

"Hi, Hadley." Brynn waved from the work space where she was carefully adding pepperoni to a pizza.

"Hi back." Hadley gestured with her head toward the pie. "That looks good."

Brynn grinned. "Pepperoni is my fave."

"Sweet Pea, while you finish up, I'm going to tell Hadley about our kitchen."

"Go for it." Brynn popped a pepperoni into her mouth.

David rolled his eyes and exchanged a smile with Hadley.

"The kitchen is laid out for the serious cook. The design allows cooking, cleanup and storage without needing to double back. I had two sinks installed so cleanup and wet prep can be separated. There's also a separate dry area for storage of baking items."

Hadley moved to the range and studied it for a long moment. "This is a high-output gas unit."

David nodded. "Commercially adapted."

Her fingers stroked the island's white Calacatta marble countertop, and his mouth went dry.

"Nice." Her gaze shifted to the separate double electric ovens, then moved to the dishwasher installed between the dual sinks, before rising to cabinets that went all the way to the ceiling. "You did it up right."

The comment pleased him. When Whitney had seen the finished product, she'd merely shrugged and said she supposed it would do.

"Hadley, look at the pizza. I made a happy face with the pepperoni."

The blonde immediately shifted her attention to his daughter and the ready-for-the-oven pie. She delighted Brynn by moving to the pizza and stunned her by snatching a piece of pepperoni from the nose.

Brynn squealed with mock outrage, and the two laughed.

Everything in David relaxed. Brynn seemed happier and more herself than she had since her mother left. He'd worried needlessly.

The night was off to a stellar start.

CHAPTER FOUR

"Wow." Hadley gaped. After they'd polished off the pizza, Brynn guided them into a room at the back of the house. The massive table could easily seat a party of twenty.

The table wasn't the only surprise. The windows spanning the length of the wall afforded a primo view of the bay.

"This is all the stuff for my project." Brynn waved a hand, her tone cheerful. "Camille helped me get it all together before she left on vacation."

Hadley jerked, but the girl's focus was on the stacks of paper at one end of the table. Brynn's expression gave no indication of any stress. Did she know her nanny wouldn't be returning to her?

Hadley glanced at David. He gave an almost imperceptible shake of his head before he shifted his gaze out the window.

"Where do we start?" she asked Brynn.

To her surprise, the child pondered the stacks for several seconds. "With the questions."

Hadley saw David wince. She thought she heard a soft groan, but couldn't be certain.

Lifting a sheet of paper from one of the stacks, Brynn whirled and fixed her pretty blue eyes on her father.

"I'll ask you the questions tonight. Then, when Mommy calls me back, I'll ask her." Brynn's bright smile dimmed. "If she has time. She might be too busy."

"Did you call or text her?" David asked in a casual tone that Hadley guessed was forced.

"She doesn't like people to call her." Brynn spoke matter-of-factly. "So I've texted her—twice—and asked her to call me."

"You have a phone?" Hadley couldn't hide her surprise.

"A flip one," David explained. "Not a smartphone."

"I want an iPhone." Brynn cast a glance at her father. "But—"

"Not until you're older."

"How many questions are there?" Hadley asked, more to change the subject than out of any real curiosity.

"Five." Brynn pulled out a chair and plopped down.

When Hadley started to round the table so David could sit next to his daughter, Brynn grabbed her arm. "You sit by me. Daddy, you sit there."

Brynn pointed to the chair opposite her. "'Cause this is an interview."

David hesitated for only a second, then moved to the chair indicated. "I thought we'd work tonight on something Hadley can help with."

"She is going to help." Brynn shot Hadley a sunny smile. "She's going to write down your answers."

"I am?"

Brynn's smile faded. "If you don't want to, I—"

"I want to." Hadley closed her hand over the child's small, almost delicate one and gave it a squeeze. "Since you're the one asking the questions, you have more than enough to do."

"Okay." David sat. "I see I'm outnumbered here."

His tone was easy, his smile indulgent. The brightness from the art deco light fixture played on the dark strands of his hair. He was a nice man. A wonderful father. So different from Justin.

With long practice, Hadley shoved the unpleasant memories

into the rusty file drawer in her head and turned the key. Tonight was a treat and too special to ruin with past pain.

Hadley experienced a surge of pleasure when her eyes locked with Brynn's and they exchanged a conspiratorial look.

"Out of curiosity, who gets to answer these questions?" Hadley inclined her head. "You mentioned your mother and father. Anyone else?"

"Gram." Brynn beamed, obviously referring to David's mother, Lynn. "I already told her about the questions. She can't wait to answer them."

"What about your mother's parents? Are they—?"

David's eyes shot a warning.

Hadley fell silent, not finishing the question.

"My mom's dad is dead." Brynn spoke matter-of-factly. "My mom's mother isn't into kids."

"Oh," was the only response Hadley could summon.

"What's the first question?" David redirected the conversation with an ease that told Hadley he'd had practice.

Brynn pushed a notebook and a couple of pencils in Hadley's direction. "Are you ready?"

Hadley lifted a pencil. "Ready."

When she'd hopped out of bed this morning and considered the day ahead, Hadley had planned to spend the evening figuring out how she was going to afford the basics on a drastically reduced income.

Instead, here she was, with David and Brynn.

Brynn lifted the sheet and read, "What is your full name?"

"David Robert Chapin."

Hadley wrote it down, glanced up. "Robert?"

David flashed a smile. "My father's name."

Brynn looked up from the paper. "How did you get your first name?"

They moved swiftly through the rest of the questions, with

Brynn doing the asking and Hadley recording David's answers in her best penmanship.

Hadley smiled as she handed the paper to Brynn, recalling David's pained expression when he'd reluctantly admitted his grandfather had given him the nickname Davy.

"Davy." Hadley mouthed the word, while Brynn slid the paper with the answers into a folder.

"Don't go there," he mouthed back, and she stifled a chuckle.

"What's next?" Hadley asked, as if it was understood there was more to come. She hoped there was more. She wasn't ready for the evening to end.

"It's my turn." David snatched the paper with the questions from in front of Brynn. "I get to ask my daughter these questions."

The look of pleasure washing over Brynn's face had Hadley's heart swelling.

Looking very grown-up, the child straightened in her seat and placed her hands on the table. "I'm ready."

David's gaze shifted to Hadley. "You'll record her answers?"

Hadley twirled her pencil like a baton. "Ready when you are...Davy."

Stifling a chuckle, David focused on Brynn. "What's your full name?"

"That's easy." Brynn tossed her head, the gesture sending her blond hair rippling down her back. "Brynn Elizabeth Chapin."

When her grip faltered, Hadley tightened her fingers around the pencil. "Elizabeth was my grandmother's name. It's mine, too."

The words popped out before she could stop them. Hadley reminded herself this wasn't about her. This was about the Chapin family and Brynn.

"A pretty name." David continued to the next question. "How did you get your name?"

"My mommy liked the name Brynn and chose it for me. My

daddy liked it, too, because it was kinda like his mother's name. Right, Daddy?"

"Exactly right, Sweet Pea."

"Elizabeth." Brynn smiled. "That came from my birth mother."

Hadley froze. She tried to recall if anyone had told her Brynn was adopted. "Birth mother?"

"My mommy and daddy chose me. Out of all of the children in the world, I was meant to be their little girl. They promised my birth mother they'd love me forever."

"It was an easy promise to make." David gave his daughter a wink. "An even easier one to keep."

Hadley kept her voice light. "Have you met your birth mother?"

"No," David answered before Brynn had a chance. "Everything was through an attorney. The birth mother wanted Brynn's middle name to be Elizabeth. It took great courage and love for her to trust us to raise Brynn. Giving her that middle name was a small thing to ask when she'd given us so much."

Tears stung the backs of Hadley's eyes, but she blinked them back before either David or Brynn could notice.

"Back to the questions." David glanced down. "Do you have any nicknames?"

Brynn thought for a moment. "You call me Sweet Pea."

What about your mother? Did she have a special name for you?

"When and where were you born?"

Hadley wished David would slow down. She had the feeling that once they were done with the questions, the evening would be over.

Brynn rattled off her birth date, then paused. "I was born in Chicago."

"That's right." David shifted his gaze to Hadley. "At the time Brynn was born, Whitney and I were living in Lincoln Park."

His expression grew thoughtful.

"There's much about the city to like." He smiled at Brynn. "It will always be special because of you."

"Camille was born in Chicago, too," Brynn added.

It was a perfect lead-in to a discussion about the nanny. Hadley wondered if David would take it. She didn't have to wait long for the answer.

"Next question." David's tone turned teasing. "What are your best memories of your father?"

Brynn's eyes lit up. "That's easy. Reading to each other at night."

The pencil in Hadley's hand paused in midair. "You read…to each other?"

"Brynn picks a book. We read a chapter every night." A look of tenderness settled over David's handsome features. "I read a paragraph aloud, then Brynn reads the next. Then it's my turn again."

"If your part is really small, like just a sentence," Brynn explained, all serious, "you can ask permission to read an extra paragraph."

Hadley could practically see the heartwarming scene. "Sounds wonderful."

"Did your daddy read to you?" Brynn's blue eyes were bright with curiosity.

Evasion had become her go-to whenever anyone got too close. But Hadley was tired of the subterfuge. Besides, she was simply answering a question from a child, not shouting her past from Eagle Tower.

"My father was a police detective." Hadley left out where he'd been on the force. "He wasn't home very much."

"My mom was gone a lot, too." Brynn nodded in understanding. "They can't read to you when they're not around."

"Exactly right." Hadley kept her tone light.

Brynn's brows pulled together in thought. "Did your mommy read to you?"

The kid was like a dog with a bone. Hadley knew she'd need to shake Brynn loose before she gave out too much information. But she wasn't at that point. Not yet.

"My parents were divorced. My mom moved far away. Once she left, I didn't see her much." *Ever,* Hadley mentally added.

Sympathy crossed the faces of both father and daughter.

Hadley's heart clenched when Brynn reached over and lightly touched her hand.

"I have my dad." Brynn eyes were like liquid pools of blue. "You had no one."

"It was okay. Really." Hadley's voice thickened, and she wondered who she was trying to convince.

"We should probably move on." David's deep voice soothed like balm on a raw burn.

Hadley shot him a grateful glance.

"Next question." His gaze shifted to his daughter. "Best memories of your mother."

Hadley hoped, hoped, hoped Brynn had a few happy memories of her mother.

The child opened her mouth, but closed it when a loud barking sounded from outside.

"Ruckus is back." Brynn jumped to her feet and turned imploring eyes on her father. "Can I feed him some roast beef? Please? I bet he's starving."

"Who's Ruckus?" Hadley stood when David reluctantly pushed back his chair.

"A stray German Shepherd." David shook his head. "He came around for a couple of weeks a month or so ago. Then he disappeared."

"Who does he belong to?" Hadley followed Brynn and David into the kitchen.

She watched Brynn fill one bowl with water, while David took roast beef wrapped in cellophane from the refrigerator and cut it into small chunks.

"My guess is he got dumped," David told her. "We checked with the vet and humane society. No one reported him missing."

Holding the metal water bowl carefully in both hands, Brynn sighed. "I was sad when he ran off."

Hadley followed her onto the back porch. "How do you know his name?"

David chuckled. "We don't."

"He barks a lot." Brynn grinned. "When we first saw him, Daddy said, 'Who's making that ruckus?'"

Brynn set down the bowl. She'd nearly reached the screen door of the porch when Hadley touched David's arm. "Shepherds can be high-strung and edgy."

She hoped David wouldn't tell her to mind her own business, but Hadley knew some shepherds were more aggressive than others.

"He's gentle." David leaned close, as if to keep the conversation between them. "He barks a lot, but he's no danger to Brynn."

Ruckus was big, nearly two feet tall. The one Hadley's dad owned had been the same size and weighed close to a hundred pounds. This dog was so thin, his ribs showed.

Hadley studied the animal as he lapped gratefully at the water. "What are you going to do with him?"

"Can we keep him, Daddy? Please?" Brynn clasped her hands together.

David's momentary hesitation had his daughter increasing her pleading.

"I promise I'll feed him and water him and walk him and—"

"I know you would." David crouched down before her, his voice gentle. "We can't keep him, Sweet Pea."

"Why not?" Brynn crossed her arms over her chest and lifted her chin.

"Taking care of an animal is a lot of work, and"—David paused for a long moment—"we'll be undergoing some changes in our household. I was going to tell you later, but Camille is moving to Sturgeon Bay."

Brynn stared. "But Camille lives here. With us."

"She's married now." The cheer in David's voice didn't reach his eyes. "She'll be living with her husband, Allen, now, not with us."

Brynn's bottom lip began to tremble. A glossy sheen filled her eyes. "I want her here. With me."

Hadley sincerely hoped David had more sense than to give the child the platitude that we don't always get what we want. Not when Brynn had already lost much.

"Despite those changes, I think you should keep the dog." Hadley knew she'd stepped from solid shore onto ice that could crack at any moment, but she also knew Brynn needed something to go her way.

David turned slowly toward her, those gray eyes suddenly cool. "I don't think—"

"I know I don't have a vote, but"—Hadley met David's gaze and prayed for the right words—"sometimes little things can make a big difference."

Hadley prayed David understood what she was trying to say. She released the breath she'd been holding when he slowly nodded.

"You're right." David's eyes never left hers. "You don't have a vote. I—"

"But, Daddy—"

David silenced his daughter's whine with a glance.

"Let me finish, please." His gaze shifted to the shepherd, who was stretched out on the rug, licking his paw. "I was going to say, she may not have a vote, but Hadley makes a good point. You and I can make a difference in Ruckus's life. He won't have to be cold and lonely and hungry anymore. He'll have us to love and care for him."

Hadley's heart rose to her throat.

"I love him already." Brynn's body vibrated with excitement. "Are you saying we can keep him?"

David winked. "That's what I'm saying."

Brynn flung herself at her father, wrapping her arms tight around his waist. "Thank you, Daddy. Thank you."

As he stroked his child's hair, David met Hadley's gaze, and no words were necessary.

CHAPTER FIVE

David blocked Beck, spun and let the ball fly. The only sound was a satisfying swoosh as it cleared the net. Oh, and Beck's groan. The buzzer sounded seconds later.

Beck wiped the sweat from his brow with the back of his hand, his breath ragged. "You're on fire today."

"This is what I needed." David, not the least bit winded, clapped Beck on the back. "I'm glad I decided to drive in."

Before the divorce, David had been a regular at the weekly pickup basketball game at the Y. After Whitney moved out, he'd started working out in his home gym.

He'd made Brynn—and his work—his entire focus.

Nothing wrong with that...in moderation. But he needed his daughter to see that life went on.

Meeting friends at the Flying Crane on Friday night had been a good first step. Entertaining Hadley on Saturday had been another. Now, he was out amongst friends again.

"I heard you showed up at the Crane Friday night." Max Brody, a local CPA, grabbed a towel from the bench and tossed one to David. His blond hair dripped with sweat. He was nearly as tall as David, with a lean, muscular build.

"It was a last-minute decision." David swiped the towel over his face, then slung it around his neck. "The band was good, but loud."

"That's why we got a table on the deck." Beck grabbed a towel off the stack at the sidelines.

"I wish we could have been there. But Steve was out with your mother." Max gestured with his head toward David. "Ami and Marigold were at the Crane. With the exception of Hadley, we only use family for sitters. Unfortunately, she was working that night."

David couldn't hide his surprise. "Hadley babysits for you and Prim?"

"Not often." Max and Prim had twin boys who were Brynn's age and a new baby girl. "Like I said, between Prim's sisters, my mother and Steve, we have childcare covered. On those rare occasions when everyone is busy, Hadley helps out."

"She's watched Sarah Rose a few times for us," Beck added.

"Ever since we moved to Good Hope, we've had Camille." David's fingers tightened around the ball he held. "She's left."

He briefly explained his predicament. "Once school starts, I should be able to handle the before- and after-school hours. But I need someone to get me through the next month."

"Camille was a live-in." Though said as a statement, Beck's tone held a question.

"She had her own suite of rooms." David tossed the ball in a high arc. He shot up one hand and grinned when it fell neatly into the metal bin by the wall.

"I know of someone who'd be perfect for you," Beck said. "She's looking for not only a temporary place to live, but some extra income. Interested?"

"Definitely." David knew Beck would never suggest someone he wouldn't trust in his own home. "Who is this Wonder Woman?"

Beck turned toward the lockers. "Hadley Newhouse."

Hadley?

Her name rolled around in David's head as he showered and dressed.

He discovered from Beck that while Ami wanted to pay her for the month the shop was closed, Hadley had refused. Not only that, her apartment above the bakery would be unlivable during parts of August.

Beck was right.

Moving in with him—and Brynn—would be a perfect solution to both their problems.

"You were on fire today, bro."

David's younger brother's voice broke through his thoughts.

"Some days everything goes your way." David lifted his hands. "Other times…"

"You miss an easy lay-up." A smile tugged at the corners of Clay's lips.

David sometimes had trouble believing the little kid who once insisted on wearing a Batman costume to church was now a principal. "You may have missed the lay-up, but the three-pointer you hit from midcourt was impressive."

"You know me." Clay shrugged. "Always the show-off."

It was something their father used to say about Clay, and not always in a complimentary way.

"You liked to test the limits." David kept his tone even. "Nothing wrong with that."

"Do you have time to grab a quick lunch?" Though Clay was on a year-round contract, his schedule was more flexible when school wasn't in session during the summer months.

David hesitated for only a second. Granted, there was work waiting for him at home, but he was on target with his deadlines. His sister and Brynn were likely still busy perusing vegetables and flowers at the farmers' market in the town square.

"Sure. Where do you want to meet?" David saw the flicker of surprise in his brother's eyes at his easy acquiescence.

"Muddy Boots?"

"Works for me."

As he drove to the café, located in the heart of Good Hope's business district, David thought of unfulfilled hopes and dreams. When he and Whitney had moved here, it had been with high spirits.

Though he no longer had a wife, he was blessed. He had a child, family, friends and a job he loved. And a home that was big enough to share with a huge dog and, hopefully, a new temporary nanny.

Hadley's lunch break usually consisted of climbing the steps to her apartment over the bakery and having a salad. Or perhaps a bowl of soup. Today, she was at Muddy Boots with Ryder Goodhue and determined to keep it strictly business.

They ordered, and while the temptation was strong to simply get right down to contract terms, she resisted. The years she'd spent as a corporate marketing exec had taught her casual conversation came first.

She tucked the menu back in the metal holder on the table and found Ryder staring.

"Do I have something on my face?" Hadley resisted the urge to pull a mirror out of her purse.

"No." Ryder grinned. "I'm surprised to be negotiating this contract with you."

He wasn't the only one. Hadley hadn't known what to say—or think—when Ami had approached her. While she understood her boss wanted to devote more time to her family, this contract could make or break her business.

"Beck drew up the agreement." Hadley kept her tone friendly. "All you and I have to do is agree on the particulars."

"That's all?"

"And enjoy our lunch." Hadley struggled to find common ground. There was none of this awkwardness with David. It was always so easy between them.

It felt good to brush up on her skills, Hadley told herself. A lifetime ago, she'd been frequently complimented on her ease with clients.

Hadley glanced idly around the crowded café. Her gaze came to an abrupt halt when she spotted David. He sat at a table by the window with his brother. Her eyes locked with his for a second before she refocused on Ryder.

"I'm curious." She studied Ryder. "You have a chain of successful coffee shops in the Pacific Northwest. Why come back to Good Hope?"

"Most of those shops are franchises." Ryder smiled at the waitress with the orange hair who brought their drinks. "Only a few are corporately owned. Even those I can manage from anywhere."

Hadley lifted her glass of tea. "That didn't answer my question."

"Boomerang."

She'd heard the term. People might leave Good Hope, but they always returned.

"This is home," Ryder continued, his brown eyes assessing. "Didn't you ever want to go back home?"

Hadley thought of Cincinnati, where she'd grown up. Her dad had tried his best once her mother left. Yet none of the apartments they'd lived in had ever felt like home.

"Not really." Fearing she might have been too abrupt, Hadley smiled and gestured with one hand. "Then again, I'd probably feel differently if I came from a town like Good Hope. There's something special about it here."

Ryder took a sip of cola. "Do you plan to stay?"

"Right now, I have no plans to leave." She lifted a shoulder in a noncommittal gesture. "Of course, that could change."

Ryder raised his glass in a mock toast. "To the master of evasion."

Though irritation surged at the cocky grin, Hadley only chuckled. This was a business meeting. Her duty was to secure favorable rates.

She would not betray Ami's trust.

Deciding the chitchat had gone on long enough, Hadley got down to business. "From information I've gathered, your shops always contract with a local bakery to provide pastries and desserts instead of doing their own baking."

"That's correct." Ryder sat back. "The model for our shops is we specialize in coffee and premium teas. We are not bakers."

"Unlike other national chains, there is no uniformity in the bakery items provided at each location."

"True." Ryder paused when the waitress set a burger and fries in front of him and a salad before Hadley. "That's the beauty of our stores. You can meet the local needs in each shop."

Hadley thought about pulling a few papers from her briefcase for reference, but having food on the table had her discarding the option. "One consistency I noted was your shops on the West Coast all carry coffee cake squares. While I know Blooms Bake Shop has on occasion provided those for your location here, specific items haven't been part of the contract."

"I'm glad you brought that up." The appreciative gleam she'd seen earlier in Ryder's eyes had been replaced by the keen edge of business. "Our analysis shows that, regardless of location, coffee cake is always a top seller. Though I don't have multiyear data yet, it appears cherry Danish and kouign amann are tops on the peninsula."

"That's in line with what we've seen in the bakery." Hadley tamped down a surge of excitement. She thought she'd left the business world when she moved back to Good Hope.

Thanks to the baking skills taught by her Scandinavian grandfather, she'd landed a job at Blooms. Now, Ami was giving her the opportunity to blend her business savvy with her baking skill.

"I'd like you to modify the existing contract and include the proviso that those three baked goods are always included." Ryder swirled a fry through ketchup, his gaze firmly focused on her.

"If you're agreeable, I think it'd be simpler to do a new contract, one that includes your business in Good Hope and the new shop you're opening this fall in Sturgeon Bay."

Ryder popped the fry into his mouth and nodded.

"Of course, the rates we agree upon will apply to both locations." Hadley offered a smile, stabbed a piece of endive.

When Hadley had seen what Ryder was paying the bakery, she'd been shocked. Though she understood Ami had wanted to help Ryder build his business and help hers during the slow winter months, what Ryder was paying now barely covered costs.

That needed to change.

"I'm agreeable to keeping the rates Ami and I discussed last year."

"The previous rates are a good starting point for negotiation." Like a racehorse poised at the starting gate, Hadley felt herself quiver.

She would do right by Ami and Blooms Bake Shop.

By the time she finished, Ryder Goodhue would have his contract, and Ami Bloom Cross would have a fair rate.

Hadley wouldn't have it any other way.

"The difference to the interior since Beck bought the place is staggering." David had spent enough time in the "old" Muddy Boots as a kid and young adult to appreciate the changes.

Gone was the unattractive wallpaper, which had been a coffeepot pattern in harvest gold and mud brown. The scarred and stained linoleum had been replaced with shiny hardwood.

The yellow vinyl on the backs of the chairs and booths was now a bright cherry red.

"The place has a happy vibe." Clay lifted a hand in greeting to Etta Hawley, a teacher at the high school. His gaze sharpened. "There's someone you rarely see in here."

David set his open menu on the table. "The summer months are probably Etta's only chance to eat out."

"Not Etta." Clay smiled his thanks when a waitress dropped off two glasses of water then promised to return for their order. "I was speaking of the delectable Miss Newhouse."

David followed the direction of his brother's gaze. It was Hadley all right, and she appeared totally absorbed in her lunch companion. A knot formed in the pit of David's stomach.

Hadley had spiffed up for the date. Her summer dress, the color of ripe cherries, left tanned shoulders bare except for two thin straps. She'd done something different with her hair, twisting it into a complicated knot at the nape of her neck.

"Looks like she's giving Ryder some serious attention."

His brother's gaze narrowed on the couple. "Nah. It's business."

"How do you know?"

"She's totally focused on him." Clay's tone was matter-of-fact.

"Maybe she's into the guy."

Clay shook his head. "Rumor is Blooms Bake Shop is vying for a contract for Ryder's new coffee shop in Sturgeon Bay. I bet that's what they're discussing."

Perhaps Clay was right. Not that it mattered. David had no claim on Hadley. She was free to date whomever she wanted.

"She came over Saturday night." David cursed himself when Clay's eyes lit up.

"You had a date?"

"Not a date." David spoke firmly, so there could be no misunderstanding. "She helped Brynn with her history project for Founder's Day."

Clay took a sip of water. "Are you interested in her?"

"Didn't you hear what I said?" David fought to keep his tone casual. "Hadley was there for Brynn, not me."

The realization was a punch to the heart.

Clay picked up the menu. "What are you having?"

Instead of looking at the selections, David found his eyes drawn once again to Hadley. This time, her gaze wasn't focused on Ryder.

It was on him.

Their eyes locked.

She smiled before turning her attention back to Ryder. But the brief contact had been enough.

The knot was gone. David was suddenly ravenous.

"You eat here more than me," he told his brother. "What do you recommend?"

CHAPTER SIX

Despite feeling foolish, Hadley had to admit the filmy white dress topped by a wide-brimmed straw hat with a blue ribbon held a certain charm.

Ami had insisted that Blooms Bake Shop get into the spirit of the old-fashioned ice cream social held on Wednesday in the town square. She'd furnished her employees with dresses fashionable young women would wear at the turn of the twentieth century.

"I can't believe I let you talk me into dressing up." Hadley touched the brim of her hat.

"You know you wanted to do it." Ami flashed a bright smile. "You'd have said no otherwise."

It was a true statement. Hadley knew how to say no. Just as she knew the reason for her blue mood didn't have a thing to do with today's event.

Once the setup was complete, Ami and college-girl Karin worked like a well-oiled machine. They stood in the center of two long tables offering a tantalizing display of cookies, muffins and pastries.

Several nearby ice cream stations, manned by members of the

Cherries and the rotary, did a brisk business. Donation-only stands, staffed by Seedlings and Saplings, part of the local scouting organization, served lemonade and iced tea at scattered locations in the square.

Despite the complimentary offerings, the coffee cart directly across from the bakery stand had been busy all evening. Cassie Lohmeier had been working alone since Hadley had first arrived. Color rose high in the tall blonde's cheeks, and perspiration dotted her brow as she struggled to keep up with orders.

Hadley frowned. Where was Ryder? Didn't he realize that one person, no matter how hardworking and experienced, wasn't enough to handle the crowd?

Squaring her shoulders, Hadley placed a hand on Ami's shoulder. "I'm going to see if Cassie needs help."

"Good idea," Ami murmured without breaking stride.

Like most of the adults working the event, Cassie had dressed for the bygone era. Her simple red A-line dress hung to midcalf, accentuated by the red-and-white-striped ribbon woven through her straw hat.

She'd pulled her sun-streaked blond hair back into a messy twist that managed to look stylish.

Hadley stepped forward. "Need help?"

Cassie flashed a smile. "Do ducks like water?"

Working as a barista in college had given Hadley serious skills. Once she found her rhythm, it was like stepping back into Starbucks time.

Thirty minutes later, when Pastor Dan Marshall ordered a coffee, she and Cassie were caught up.

"It's good to see you, Cassie." Dan offered both women a warm smile. "You, too, Hadley."

Hadley couldn't recall the last time she'd been to church, other than for a wedding. She certainly didn't go weekly. The pastor at her grandparents' church in North Dakota had preached hellfire and damnation.

She could only imagine what God thought of the mess she'd made of her life.

"It's nice to see you, Pastor." Cassie filled the cup and snapped on a lid.

"Is, ah, is your sister around?" The minister's voice might be offhand, but the way he gripped the cup told Hadley this was no simple inquiry.

"I haven't seen her." Though a muscle in her jaw jumped, Cassie kept her voice equally nonchalant.

Hadley busied herself making lattes for a couple of teenage girls. Everyone in town was aware that Cassie's sister, Lindsay, had broken off her engagement to the minister at the last minute.

Though Dan and Lindsay had gone on with their lives, it appeared the minister still hadn't fully gotten over the youngest Lohmeier sister.

When he strolled off, sipping his coffee, his gaze scanning the crowd, Hadley turned to Cassie. "That was awkward."

Cassie lifted a thin shoulder and let it drop. "He doesn't normally ask about Lindsay. He was probably being polite."

"Maybe."

"He comes into the shop every Monday to work on writing his sermon for the next week." Cassie's tone remained even. "We talk, but never about Lin."

"That's probably a relief."

The crowd had dwindled to a handful of tourists as the free concert by the Good Hope Brass started in the bandstand.

"Do you enjoy working for Ryder?" Hadley fixed herself a cappuccino and made one for Cassie.

"He's a great boss. Very accommodating." Cassie smiled her thanks and took the drink. "It's difficult to work with a two-year-old, especially during the school year. The older boys watch Axl in the summer while I'm at work. If I have to pay for childcare, it pretty much eats up any money I make."

Hadley knew Cassie had gotten pregnant at fifteen with her

daughter, Dakota, who was now in college. She had two sons by another guy. Those boys were now in high school. Axl's father was in prison, convicted of a string of burglaries in Good Hope.

Cassie's life could have been hers, Hadley thought, if she'd made different choices.

Almost as if she knew the direction of Hadley's thoughts, Cassie flushed. "Ryder gave me a chance when almost everyone else in town—including my mother—had written me off."

"Our past doesn't dictate our future." As she spoke the words, Hadley felt herself steady.

"I've taken many wrong turns." A profound weariness filled Cassie's voice. She gazed into her cup.

"I'd wager we all have things we'd do differently given the chance." Hadley's lips twisted in a rueful smile. "But we can't change the past. We can only change the present and the future. You're making positive changes, Cassie. You should be proud."

Tears filled Cassie's eyes. "Thank you."

"Don't thank me." This time, it was Hadley's turn to let her gaze drop. "Like you, I'm not going to let the past define me. Not anymore."

~

"Looking for someone?"

David turned so quickly the lemonade in his cup sloshed over the rim. "Dan. I didn't see you."

The steaming coffee the minister held looked more appealing than David's lukewarm lemonade. He made a mental note to ask Dan where he'd gotten it.

"I don't normally see you at these events." Dan sipped his coffee.

"Brynn is a Seedling." This fall, his daughter would move up to the next local scouting level and become a Sapling. "Her troop is working one of the drink stands."

"Doesn't Camille usually bring her to these types of events?"

"She used to." *Emphasis*, David thought, *on the past tense.* Though he considered himself to be an involved father, over the past couple of years, he'd turned over more of the parenting to his longtime nanny. "Camille is married now and living in Sturgeon Bay."

The minister's brows lifted. "Will she continue to care for Brynn?"

"I'm afraid not." David finished off the lemonade and crushed the tiny cup between his fingers.

"I imagine that's been difficult for Brynn."

David started to nod, then paused. "I broke the news Saturday night. She was upset at first, but then seemed to be okay. Still, I'm concerned that maybe it hasn't really sunk in yet. She's had a lot of hard knocks this year. First her mother, then Mindy—who she considered her best friend-and now Camille."

"You've built a solid foundation for your daughter in Good Hope." Dan's gaze met his. "Brynn has her grandmother, her aunt, her uncle and lots of friends here. While Camille's absence will undoubtedly be felt, Brynn will be fine."

Thanks in large part to Ruckus. Hadley had been right about the dog.

"Just remember." Dan rested a hand on his shoulder. "God has a plan."

With those parting words, Dan left to greet fisherman Joe Lyle and his wife.

Recalling seeing a coffee cart across the square, David headed in that direction. He paused when his path crossed with Tim Vandercoy's.

A successful real estate agent, Tim brokered most of the deals on the peninsula. Short, with thinning brown hair and a salesman's smile, he held out a hand to David.

Though David wasn't well-acquainted with the man, his mother had dealt with Tim on many occasions, most involving commercial real estate. Just knowing she held Tim in high regard was a good enough reference for David.

"I love these events." Tim smiled, showing a mouthful of straight, white teeth. "An excellent way to touch base with people you don't get to see nearly often enough."

David rubbed his chin. "Do you have a second to talk business?"

"Absolutely." An excited gleam sparked in Tim's dark eyes. "What can I do for you?"

"Tim." The shrill female tone held more than a little exasperation. "I told you to wait for me."

The irritated look on Anita Fishback's face vanished when she spotted David.

David stifled a groan. Anita, owner of Crumb and Cake, mother to Cassie and Lindsay Lohmeier and former girlfriend of Steve Bloom, was one of his least favorite people in Good Hope.

Though he personally didn't know her well, he'd heard enough about her antics from his mother to want to keep his distance.

"David, how lovely to see you." She extended her hand in such a way that he found himself wondering for a second if he should kiss it or shake it.

Anita was a pretty woman in her fifties, with dark hair and hazel eyes in an angular face.

As he shook her hand, a calculating gleam filled her eyes.

"Don't tell me you're thinking of selling your beautiful home on Millionaire's Row." Before he could answer, Anita's voice filled with faux sympathy. "I understand how difficult it must be for you and Brynn to live there without Whitney. I'm sure everywhere you turn, from the bedroom you shared to the dinner table, you see her."

David wondered how she'd react if he told her Whitney had spent so little time in his bed and in their home that he barely recalled her being there.

He kept his mouth shut. Anita was a known gossip, and Whitney was Brynn's mother. David offered a noncommittal smile and refocused on Tim. "I was going through my insurance papers, and I'm concerned the house may be underinsured."

"How long have you lived there?" Tim cast her a sharp look when Anita opened her mouth.

"Five years." David remembered vividly the beautiful spring day when they'd moved in. He'd carried Whitney over the threshold. Brynn had insisted he carry her, too.

"You built it new."

David nodded. "The assessment was accurate at the time. However, a home down the road with less amenities recently sold for a lot more than I have mine insured."

"Home values, especially in your area, have skyrocketed in the last few years." Tim studied David's face. "Are you interested in a market analysis or an assessment?"

"Either works." David inclined his head. "Would you be able to stop out next week?"

"I'll make the time."

Out of the corner of his eye, David spotted Hadley. She slowed when she saw Anita. Apparently, she wasn't a big fan of the woman, either. He motioned her forward.

"When you decide to sell, Tim's your man." Anita looped her arm possessively around the real estate broker's arm. "He's been the top seller on the peninsula for the past ten years."

Her voice carried in the still summer air.

David saw Hadley stumble to a stop. She'd obviously concluded she would be interrupting business. Actually, what she was doing was saving him from a woman the Bloom sisters had not-so-affectionately nicknamed "the piranha."

Slipping a business card from his wallet, David handed it to Tim. "Call me. We'll schedule a time for you to come out."

Quickly saying his good-byes, David hurried over to Hadley.

~

He's having a real estate agent come out.

"Are you thinking about moving?"

David blinked, then appeared to catch the direction of her gaze. He swiped the air with one hand. "No. Just having the home assessed for insurance purposes."

Hadley expelled the breath she hadn't realized she was holding. "Always smart to keep on top of insurance stuff."

"I agree." David smiled. "I've been meaning to call you."

"Why?" she blurted, then flushed.

"If you have time, we can talk about it now."

"Now?"

Amusement danced in his eyes. "If you have time."

"Ah, sure." When he began to walk, she fell into step beside him.

"I like the hat."

Hadley touched her fingers to the brim. "I feel ridiculous."

"The outfits add a nice touch." He surprised her by taking her elbow. "You look thirsty. Brynn is serving up lemonade over there."

He gestured in the direction of a refreshment stand under the branches of a large oak. "I need to warn you. The cup I had wasn't the coldest."

"I'm sure it's fine."

He studied her for a moment. "You're an optimist. I like that about you."

The warmth that surged through her body had nothing to do with the sun overhead. How long had it been since someone had come out and said they liked her? Especially someone she…admired?

Hadley slowed to a stop and lifted her face to the sun for several seconds. Though she was eager to see Brynn, she needed to know what was on David's mind.

"I noticed you helping Cassie with the coffee cart," he said.

"I worked as a barista at Starbucks in college." Hadley spoke absently. What could he have to say to her? "Making lattes and cappuccinos was actually fun for me."

"Where did you go to college?"

It figured he'd latch on to her past, the one thing she preferred not to discuss.

"In Illinois." Hadley kept her answer vague. "That was a long time ago."

"Not so long." David's gaze turned assessing. "You're what, twenty-five? Twenty-six?"

The man had missed his calling. Instead of an architect, he should have been a detective. "I'm twenty-eight. Is my age what you wanted to discuss?"

David only chuckled.

"Then, what?"

Before he could respond, she heard a voice that was robust and capable of reaching the back row of any theater. "Yoo-hoo, David and Hadley. Over here."

Confused, Hadley turned in the direction of the summons.

When she saw who was beckoning, Hadley knew she and David would have to postpone their talk.

She'd lived in Good Hope long enough to know that no one ignored Gladys Bertholf.

CHAPTER SEVEN

David had adored Gladys from the time he'd been five and she plucked a frog from the edge of her backyard pond just for him. While his mother watched wide-eyed, Gladys had identified it as a northern leopard frog. Her lips had curved when she confided its call sounded just like her husband snoring.

After letting him hold it, she'd gently taken it from his hands and placed it back by the water.

Over the years, David had watched the accomplished actress perform in more plays and musicals than he could list. Last year, at ninety-six, she'd formally retired from the stage. It appeared from her current garb she'd taken on a new role.

Always one for the dramatic, Gladys stood at the opening to a tent decorated with moon and stars, dressed like an old hippie, er, gypsy. Her hair, dark as midnight with a bold strip of white, was partially covered by a scarf adorned with gold coins. To the right of where she stood, a placard proclaimed Madame Gitana, Fortune Teller.

David smiled. Trust Gladys to choose her name from the Spanish word for gypsy.

"Madame Gitana."

The slight bow David added to his greeting had Gladys's lips curving.

"What a pleasure to see you together."

Before David could correct the misunderstanding, Gladys took control of the conversation.

"Madame Gitana has been busy, but now she has time for you." Gladys stepped into the tent, motioning for them to follow her.

When Hadley hesitated, David gave her a wink.

"You will sit there." Gladys pointed to a chair off to the side for David, then her gaze fell on Hadley. "You will sit there."

The chair she pointed to was directly in front of the table holding a crystal ball.

For a second, David thought Hadley might refuse. With a wary look in her eyes, she sat.

The smell of sage and cedar hung heavy in the air, and the spiritual music playing in the background only added to the otherworldly atmosphere. It was as if, by merely stepping inside the tent, they'd left Good Hope behind.

"I'm not really into getting my fortune told." Though Hadley's tone was light, her voice quivered slightly.

Gladys, now seated on the opposite side of the table, reached forward and took Hadley's hand in her bejeweled one. The older woman's pale blue eyes seemed to glow in the dim light of the tent. "You need to know."

"If she doesn't want—"

"Silence." The sharply spoken word pierced the air. "Self-understanding is essential for healing."

David fell silent from sheer astonishment.

"It's okay." Hadley appeared to force a smile, though lines of strain edged her mouth. "This might be fun."

Gladys, er, Madame Gitana nodded approval and lifted the purple ball from the black obsidian stand.

David frowned. "I thought crystal balls were supposed to be clear."

"It doesn't need to be clear. It is merely a tool for freeing my third eye." Gladys's voice turned soothing, like water in a bubbling stream. "This is made from natural amethyst quartz. This type of ball is best for answering questions about matters concerning the past, for issues of guilt and blame."

Hadley cleared her throat.

David nearly chuckled. Gladys sounded so serious, as if she believed every word she was saying. He played along. "What will you see?"

"I won't know until I look. Until I ask the question." Gladys turned and fixed those pale eyes on him. "Close the curtains. It's time to begin."

With the outside light cut off, the interior would have been dark except for the two candles flickering behind Gladys.

The old woman's gaze fixed, unblinking, on the ball. A minute, then two, ticked slowly by.

When Gladys's eyes became unfocused, Hadley shot him a worried glance.

David offered a reassuring smile. The older woman was a veteran actress. Gladys knew how to put on a good show. He wondered idly what had made her try fortune telling.

He was about to give in to temptation and check the time when the older woman's gaze relaxed. She blinked rapidly, then picked up a pencil and began to scribble rapidly on a pad.

Hadley leaned forward, resting her forearms on the small table. "What did you see?"

"I saw a name, a man's name, but not one I recognize." Gladys rose, moved to the entrance and flung open the curtains. Sunshine spilled into the tent. "There was a bird in a cage."

"What kind of bird?" David asked.

Gladys ignored the question. "The cage was unlocked, the door open, but the bird remained inside."

The woman's attention turned to Hadley, who was slowly rising to her feet. "The bird didn't realize the door was open."

Gladys nodded, appearing pleased.

"Well, thanks." David paused, not certain how this was supposed to go. He pulled out his wallet. "How much do I owe you?"

"Whatever you want to give." Gladys gestured to a large glass bowl filled with bills and coins. "All is being donated to the Giving Tree."

David dropped in a twenty, then stepped out of the tent, relieved the strange experience was over.

"What name did you see?" he heard Hadley ask the "gypsy" in a low tone.

David didn't catch the name Gladys whispered, and he didn't ask. Right now, he had a more important question to ask Hadley. Was she interested in being Brynn's temporary nanny?

"I can't believe how everything fell into place." With Sarah Rose playing at her feet, Ami neatly folded one of Hadley's shirts and put it in a suitcase. "You not only have a place to stay, rent-free, you have a well-paying job that should be super fun for the entire month of August."

"The offer was certainly unexpected." Hadley looked up from the other suitcase she was filling with toiletries from the bathroom. Ever since her strange encounter with Gladys on Wednesday evening, she'd felt scattered. She hoped packing would settle her. "When David asked if I'd move into his home and be Brynn's temporary nanny until school started, I agreed without taking time to think."

"Do you regret your decision?" Ami paused, another shirt, blue this time, dangling from her fingers.

Hadley glanced around the cozy living room, taking in the

overstuffed sofa with throw pillows of yellow gingham. "I love living here."

"Once the demolition downstairs is done, you'll be back." Ami lowered the shirt. "But you didn't answer my question."

Hadley dropped down on the sofa, thinking of the emotions that had surged when David made the offer. Being under the same roof with him and Brynn would be a dream come true. "I'm excited. Brynn is a wonderful child. David is a good man."

The tense set to Ami's shoulders eased. "He's also a hunk."

"Am-eee." Hadley punched her friend's shoulder. "You're a married woman."

"Yes, and very happily. That doesn't mean I can't recognize a handsome man." Ami's lips twitched. "Don't even try to tell me you haven't noticed the way he looks at you."

Hadley opened her mouth to deny it, then gave a good-natured shrug. "I may have noticed."

"Well, I hope you two have done more than exchange smoldering glances." Ami tucked the shirt on top of the other one in the suitcase. "How does he kiss?"

Hadley rolled her eyes. "I've never kissed him."

"Disappointing, but no worries. You'll have plenty of opportunity to remedy that now that you'll be under the same roof."

The sizzle was what worried Hadley. "I can't get involved with him. He'll be my employer."

"You won't be Brynn's nanny forever." Ami's tone was matter-of-fact as she started on a pile of pants. "Even if you are the nanny, as long as you don't get hot and heavy in front of Brynn—"

"Stop." The socks, rolled into a tight ball, hit Ami in the chest. "I'm not going to make out with David in front of Brynn, or...or anyone."

Ami scooped up the socks from the sofa, tossed them into the suitcase, then grinned wickedly. "You'll wait until you're alone to jump him."

What did it say that Hadley could easily envision the scene? She and David on the sofa, talking and laughing, sharing a bottle of wine...

"No." She blinked the image away. Not possible. Okay, possible, but not wise. Not with everything in her past between them.

Ami lifted a brow. "No?"

Only then did Hadley realize she'd spoken aloud. She thought quickly. "No more talk about David and me."

While she watched, Sarah Rose reached into the suitcase and pulled out the socks, staring curiously at the ball.

"Sarah Rose." Ami held out her hand. "Give those to Mommy, please."

"She can play with them." Hadley tossed several more the child's way.

The little girl squealed with delight and pounced.

Hadley added yet another "ball" to Sarah Rose's pile. "That should keep her occupied."

"For another minute or two," Ami said dryly.

There were a thousand and one things left to do around her apartment. Tonight, she'd move into David's home on Millionaire's Row. She needed to make the best use of her time while she had Ami around to help. But she couldn't tear her gaze from Sarah Rose.

The thought of how Brynn must have looked at that age, wisps of pale blond hair sprouting up from a band at the top of her head, had Hadley's heart lurching. She wondered if Whitney ever thought about Brynn. If she thought about how much she was missing. If she cared...

How could Whitney stand to be so far away from her daughter? How could she not text Brynn back?

"What did you think of Gladys's fortune-telling skills?"

Hadley inclined her head. "How did you know she told my fortune?"

"Lucky guess, but not difficult." Ami sat back. "Everyone and their dog went into that tent. She brought in tons of money for the Giving Tree."

"How did she decide on fortune telling?" Hadley kept her voice offhand, as if the answer was of no concern.

"She was tired of face painting, and there were others who were eager to take over that booth." Ami shrugged. "Grandma Ruby told me that Gladys had been really into stuff like that when she was young. Ruby said Gladys has natural talent."

A cold chill washed over Hadley.

"What did she tell you?" Ami asked.

"Nothing real concrete. An image of a bird in an open cage."

Ami wrinkled her nose. "A bird?"

"Bird," Sarah Rose repeated.

"That's right. Bird." Ami smiled proudly at her daughter before returning her attention to Hadley. "What did Gladys say about the bird?"

"What is there to say?" Since the living room and kitchen were combined in the tiny apartment, Hadley stepped into the kitchen and made a great show of retrieving her favorite teas from the cupboard. She added them to the suitcase.

"I don't know." Ami tapped a finger against her lips. "Maybe what kind of bird? Or why was it sitting in an open cage instead of flying free?"

Flying free.

A shiver traveled up Hadley's spine. "The bird didn't realize the door was open."

"Now *that's* interesting." Ami's eyes sparkled. "So the bird could have been flying free, but didn't because it thought it was still caged?"

"I guess." Hadley lifted one shoulder, let it drop. "Oh, and a name came to her."

"What kind of name?"

"It was a guy's name. A guy I'd been, well, involved with years ago." Though the suitcase was only half filled, Hadley slammed the top shut and latched it. "And no, I haven't been thinking of him, so I don't know what it means."

Though she remained bent over the suitcase, Hadley felt Ami's eyes on her. She lifted her head and braced for more questions. Questions she had no intention of answering.

"Wow. Sounds like your session was loads more interesting than mine."

Hadley shot Ami a look of gratitude. "What did she tell you?"

Ami grinned and patted her flat stomach. "She said Sarah Rose is going to have a baby brother."

"Brynn." Her name spoken in a low warning tone from her father was enough to have the child stopping. "We do not explore Hadley's private living quarters without permission."

"I agree with your father." Hadley shot David a reassuring smile, wanting him to understand she wouldn't usurp his authority. "It isn't good manners unless you have an invitation. Which I'm issuing to both of you now. Please, come in."

Last night, she'd moved into Camille's suite of rooms, which she'd been shocked to discover held more living space than her apartment.

Bright and early this morning, Brynn came knocking at her door. Hadley slipped an arm around Brynn and motioned for David to step inside. "I won't be here long, so I didn't bring everything from my apartment, but I'd love to show you what I've done."

After a glance at her father for confirmation, Brynn stepped inside the small sitting area. The desk now held Hadley's laptop, and the love seat and chair would work in a pinch if she had guests over.

"I love the colors in the bathroom." Hadley spoke over her

shoulder as Brynn followed her down the hall. "Camille had put out gray towels, but I wanted something that would pop."

Walls the color of lemon sherbet were accented with white and gray. Though Brynn stepped into the small room, David only glanced inside.

"Cheerful and optimistic," he murmured, then turned and found her staring at him.

"It's super pretty." Brynn fingered a buttercup yellow towel edged in white eyelet lace. "I can't wait to see the bedroom."

Hadley hesitated for only a second. She'd promised a tour before thinking it through. While she didn't mind showing her bedroom to Brynn, showing it to David felt somehow…intimate.

Which was absolutely ridiculous.

Squaring her shoulders, Hadley pushed open the door to the room that would be her sanctuary for the next month.

"Oh." Brynn's mouth formed a perfect O as she stepped inside.

The comforter Hadley had brought with her was a luxurious peach satin. She'd wondered if it would clash with the décor, but it added just the right splash of color. There was gray here, too, in the form of a stylish rug with a Moroccan-inspired design.

Last night, Hadley had discovered just how soft and supple the pile was under bare feet. Light streamed in through the lace curtains at the single window, the shade allowing for privacy when pulled down.

Brynn stepped immediately to the bedside table. Hadley hadn't been able to leave the lamp behind, not even for a month. It had been an impulse purchase at a tag sale in Egg Harbor. She'd fallen in love instantly with a tree branch-inspired base and crystal beads at the end of each tip.

"It's beautiful." Brynn touched one of the crystals, then turned in a circle, her eyes missing nothing. "I love your room."

"Thank you." The child's approval sent a rush of pleasure coursing through Hadley's veins.

Brynn picked up the book sitting next to the lamp. "I always have a book by my bed, too."

Not trusting herself to speak, Hadley nodded.

"You've made it nice, Hadley." David's tone was easy, his words polite, but something in his eyes had blood coursing through her veins like warm honey.

His gaze dropped to her mouth.

Hadley couldn't help thinking about Ami's kissing comments.

Plenty of opportunity, Ami had said, when you're under the same roof.

Well, no matter how tempting, Hadley didn't plan to take advantage of those opportunities. For the next month, she planned to keep her lips to herself.

CHAPTER EIGHT

David wondered if all nine-year-old girls were as busy as Brynn. Another Saturday. Another birthday party.

Hadley was equally busy. She'd baked nonstop all morning. It had been part of the agreement. There was no reason for her to do her special event baking at Ami's certified kitchen when his house had an almost-new commercial oven practically begging to be used.

The delicious aroma of chocolate, yeast and sugar filled the air. David had to stop himself from wandering into the kitchen—again—to see what magic she was whipping up.

After opening his laptop, David pulled up the program containing the plans he'd been tweaking. He'd been making small adjustments to what should be the finished product ever since Hadley moved in several days earlier. He still wasn't satisfied with the work flow in the ER design. Though he was certain the client wouldn't have an issue, his perfectionistic tendencies had him holding on to the design. Only when the design satisfied all *his* expectations would he submit it.

David relished the opportunity to work in silence. Other than for Ruckus's snoring, that was.

The shepherd lay on the plaid dog bed David had brought into his office. He had quickly discovered if he shut him out, the dog would scratch on the door and whine until David let him into the room.

After a visit to the vet for shots and a flea dip bath, Ruckus had settled in as the newest member of the Chapin family.

David was deep into the design when Ruckus emitted a low growl and then another. When the dog scrambled to his feet and began to bark, David saved his work and pushed to his feet.

That's when he heard a knock on his office door.

Hadley had removed the apron she'd worn at breakfast, giving him a good view of the summer dress and miles of bare legs. She'd twisted her hair into an intricate knot and kept reaching up as if to push back a strand that wasn't there.

She smiled. "I hope I'm not interrupting."

Considering he had work still to do, his full-out delight at seeing her made no sense. "Not at all."

Hadley shifted from one foot to the other. "Are you at a point where you can take a break? I have extra Cherry Garcia brownies."

David wondered if he should mention the dusting of flour on her cheek. He decided not to say anything. It made her look approachable. "I have no idea what a Cherry Garcia brownie tastes like, but I'm up for taking a break and trying one."

"You like cherries?"

"We live in Good Hope." David had eaten—and loved—everything cherry for as far back as he could recall. Understandable, considering red tart cherries were the primary crop on the Door County peninsula. "Who doesn't love cherries?"

"Well, these brownies have cherries, cream cheese and chocolate chips."

"The trifecta of goodness." He grinned. "How about I get the drinks, you get the brownies?"

"Milk for me, please." She stared at the dog who stood at his side, tail swishing slowly from side to side. "I'm glad you gave him a home."

"He's one of the family now." It amazed him just how easily Ruckus had fit into the family. David believed Hadley would fit in just as easily. "Do you want to sit on the porch. Or in the kitchen?"

"You pick."

In a matter of minutes, tall glasses of ice-cold milk and a plate of warm brownies sat between them. He expected her to start talking the moment they were seated on the porch.

Instead, she gazed dreamily over the water. "It's so beautiful here."

"I hope you'll consider this your home for the next month."

"That's very kind of you."

"I'm a kind guy." He grinned, then turned serious. "Not to mention you're doing me a huge favor."

"It's almost as if it was meant to be." Her brows pulled together as if disturbed by the thought.

"That's what I told my mom."

"What did she think of me moving in?"

"She was surprised I'd found someone so quickly."

"I'm surprised, too." Hadley's lips curved. "I fully expected to be eating ramen noodles and sleeping on Cassie's couch for the month of August."

"Cassie?" David cocked his head. "Cassie Lohmeier?"

Hadley nodded. "We got to talking one day, and she said I could bunk at her place."

David set down the glass of milk without drinking. "Both Ami and Fin have large homes. They—"

"They offered. I refused. Fin and Jeremy haven't been married all that long. Ami and Beck, well, they don't need another person underfoot. Things are going to be chaotic enough with her doing so much baking from home."

"You're always thinking of someone else."

Hadley shrugged the words of praise aside. "Like I said, your offer was a godsend."

"I like having you here."

Pleasure skittered across her face. "You do?"

"The house smells like a home." He popped a bite of brownie into his mouth. "And these are delicious."

"I've figured you out, Mr. Chapin."

The teasing gleam in her eyes had his lips curving. "Tell me."

"To get a good reference when the month is over, I simply need to keep your stomach happy."

"Keeping my daughter safe and happy is all I ask."

"That's easy." Hadley bit into her brownie and chewed. "I love making Brynn happy."

David's gaze searched her face, and he watched her watching him. The moment his eyes touched hers, something inside him seemed to lock into place and he couldn't look away.

She was beautiful, both inside and out. Like the flour on her cheek, the smear of chocolate on her lower lip only added to her appeal. Did she have any idea the power she had over him?

Without taking time to think, David leaned close. Even before his lips brushed hers, he knew the feel of her lips, the softness, the warmth, the gentleness.

He started to move back, then realized she was stroking the back of his neck, twining her fingers in his hair. Taking that as a sign she wasn't in any more hurry than he was to have this end, he changed the angle of the kiss and kissed her with a slow thoroughness.

David wasn't sure where this might have gone if the alarm on his phone hadn't buzzed.

"What's that?" she asked, her breath coming in soft puffs.

Dazed and breathing hard, David pulled back, fought to find his voice. "Time to pick up Brynn. I could—"

Two fingers closed his mouth before he could suggest calling Sabine's parents to see if Brynn could stay longer.

"We need to stop. Take time to think. To consider all the ramifications."

Something in her low, husky voice made David look at her, really look at her. A rosy blush stained her cheeks, and her eyes were still dark with desire. No, he decided, he wasn't the only one who wanted, who needed. "Are you saying you don't want this to happen again?"

"Oh, I very much want this to happen again." Hadley gave a little laugh, then sobered. "We just need to be smart about it."

Embarrassed, though not sure why, David pulled to his feet and gave a jerky nod. He hadn't been with a woman since Whitney left. He hadn't been with anyone but her since college.

He had no idea how any of this worked. Though David was normally a planner, he had no idea where his feelings for Hadley would lead him.

All he knew was she was the first woman who'd captured his interest in a long, long time.

"I like you, Hadley. I enjoy spending time with you. I won't take advantage of you living here, but neither will I walk away from the chance to get to know you better." He grinned. "If that includes more kissing, well, that has my vote."

He strode away before he could do something foolish, like haul her up into his arms and kiss her until the only thought either of them had was how quickly they could get undressed.

"I'm happy you could all make it." Lynn's gaze shifted from David and Hadley to her granddaughter. "And my darling girl."

Hadley watched Lynn envelop Brynn in a hug. "Callum and Connor are here," Lynn said. "I set up the croquet game in the back."

"I want to play." Brynn glanced at her dad, a question in her eyes.

Lynn stroked her granddaughter's hair. "You have time before we eat." Then, turning toward David, she added in response to his unspoken question, "Max is watching the boys."

Twins Callum and Connor were Brynn's age. That's where any similarities ended. Hadley had watched the boys fence with badminton rackets at one of Jeremy's summer barbecues and climb to the top of the flagpole in their grandfather's backyard.

While they were nice boys, they were definitely rough and tumble. Max, who'd become their father when he married Prim Bloom, was someone David could count on to keep them under control.

"You can play for a few minutes. Have fun," he called after Brynn as she raced through the house. "Walk."

His daughter slowed her steps ever so slightly, then disappeared from view.

Lynn cast a speculative glance in Hadley's direction. "How do you like being my granddaughter's nanny?"

"I enjoy it." Hadley's smile froze on her face. "I hope I'm not intruding today."

"Absolutely not." Though her eyes remained watchful, Lynn gave Hadley's arm a squeeze. "I'm going to see how lunch is coming. Most everyone has arrived."

Hadley guessed "most everyone" meant David's siblings as well as the Bloom sisters and their husbands. Though she still wondered what Lynn thought of her son inviting the "nanny" to lunch, knowing her friends would be here had made accepting David's invitation easier.

That and the fact she wanted to spend all the time she could with Brynn and David this next month. She'd likely never have another chance to get to know both of them on such an intimate level.

Intimate. Her thoughts kept going back to yesterday's kiss, er, kisses.

Hadley cursed the heat traveling up her neck.

"Mom and Steve make a good couple." David's voice remained low and for her ears only.

Grateful for the diversion, Hadley followed the direction of his gaze. His mother stood beside the high school teacher with the wire-rimmed glasses and ready smile. His arm rested lightly around her back. When she looked closely, Hadley saw that Lynn was leaning slightly into him.

"I remember when he was dating Anita." Hadley's tone turned wry. "I know they'd been friends for years, but I never could see them together. Your mom and Steve are different. They fit."

Hadley never imagined a driven bank executive and an easy-going math teacher would be a good match, but it was apparent they brought out the best in each other.

How lucky they are, Hadley thought wistfully.

She'd learned early on that not every couple was meant for the long haul. Or, in her case, even the short haul.

Shoving the thoughts aside, Hadley concentrated on her surroundings.

The two-story gray stone home, built in a Georgian style, had a warm and welcoming vibe. A sweet scent wafted from spires of violet spilling from a cut-crystal vase.

As if he could read her thoughts, David smiled. "Do you like the scent of lavender?"

Hadley nodded. "Very much."

David's eyes softened. "When Steve found out how much Mom likes the fragrance, he put in a standing order at the Enchanted Florist."

"Is it serious between them?"

A look of startled surprise skittered across his face.

"C'mon," she teased. "Don't tell me you haven't wondered."

David rubbed his chin. "I've never asked about any man she dated. Not that there's been many since dad died. No one ever stuck. Before Steve, my sibs and I used to joke that it was one, two, three dates, they're out."

"I guess it just takes finding the right one," Hadley murmured.

His eyes twinkled. "I never pegged you as a romantic."

"I have my moments." Hadley shrugged. "Seriously, I can see them getting married."

"I know Steve makes her happy." David spoke slowly, as if pieces of conversation were coming together in his head. His brows drew together. "They both had good marriages. I remember Mom saying shortly after my father's death that she'd never marry again."

"How long ago was that?"

"He's been gone ten years."

The pain in his voice had her taking his arm, giving it a squeeze. She understood what it was like to lose a parent, knew well the grief that hit you at unexpected times and stole your breath. "It's been over five for me. Like yours, my dad was a good guy. I still miss him."

The sympathy on his face gave her the courage to continue. "I'm sure your mother will always miss your father and what they shared. But how she felt a decade ago may not be the same way she feels now."

Hadley thought of all the decisions she'd made in the past ten years.

People changed.

Situations changed.

Resolutions made once weren't necessarily ones she'd make now.

Her turmoil must have shown on her face, because David put his hands on her shoulders and turned her to face him. "Is something bothering you?"

Hadley shook her head. "I stayed up too late, then was up early baking."

He seemed to buy the explanation. It was the truth, as far as it went. She was tired, but not from getting up early. Last night she'd lain in bed, troubled by the growing closeness she felt toward him.

The guilt over lying to him had kept sleep at bay.

Wasn't withholding certain facts lying by omission? Even though she had good reasons for not telling him. What was the right thing to do?

"Maybe you can take a nap later." His smile reassured. "I'll be around all afternoon, so you don't need to worry about Brynn."

"Then I'll definitely consider a nap." The door to the back terrace was open, and Hadley stepped out into the sunshine.

Flowers edged the flagstone covered by a green and white awning. The food sat on long tables in the shaded area.

Prim and her baby—a little girl named Adelyn—sat in the shade visiting with Ami and Sarah Rose. Beck, Jeremy and Cade tossed horseshoes with Steve at the far edge of the yard, while Max supervised the badminton net. It appeared Max had recruited Marigold to partner with Brynn in a showdown with the twins.

Hadley assumed David's siblings would be here, but she hadn't yet spotted them. "Are Greer and Clay coming?"

"Right behind you."

Hadley turned. Greer looked as fresh as lemon sorbet in a white summer dress with yellow piping. Her dark hair hung loose to her shoulders.

Although Hadley didn't know her well, she knew that Greer had returned to Good Hope after college. She was following in their mother's banking footsteps, and rumor was, she was a natural.

"I wasn't sure you were back from Milwaukee." David lifted an oversized glass bowl containing lettuce interspersed with mandarin oranges and pecans from her hands. "How was the banking seminar?"

"Very informative." Greer's smile took on a wicked edge. "The Bank Secrecy Act Compliance seminar was especially enlightening. I could tell you about the new beneficial owner rule over lunch?"

"I'll pass." David grinned. "The banking bug that Dad always hoped would bite me...still hasn't."

Hadley watched the interaction between David and his little sister with interest. She wondered if Brynn would miss not having siblings when she was grown.

Greer rolled her eyes, then glanced at Hadley. "Congrats. I hear you're Brynn's new nanny."

"Temporarily," Hadley clarified.

"Well, she couldn't be in better hands." Appearing to shift gears again, Greer turned back to her brother. "Have you heard from Clay? Once this salad is on the table, we're ready to eat."

"He was in church this morning." Lynn strolled up and took the salad bowl from her son's hands. "We can start without him. He'll be here. The boy never misses a meal."

Hadley hid a smile. Clay was pushing thirty. He hadn't been "a boy" for a number of years. Then again, he would probably always be Lynn's little boy, just like Brynn would always be David's little girl.

She shifted her gaze to the badminton area in time to watch Brynn hit a shot that sailed over Connor's racket. The child jumped up and down, doing her own version of a victory dance, then high-fived Marigold.

Her blond hair caught the light, and when she turned, the happiness on her face brought a sweet heaviness to Hadley's heart.

Sometimes, a decision made a decade ago wasn't one you'd repeat.

Even if you knew it was the right one at the time.

CHAPTER NINE

The look of tenderness in Hadley's eyes when they landed on his daughter had a lump rising in David's throat. He couldn't believe how lucky he was to have someone in his household who cared so deeply for his daughter.

David thought of the kisses he and Hadley had shared. He needed to keep his desire for her under control. The last thing he wanted was to affect the balance at home.

He forced his eyes away and caught his sister staring. Before she could ask any questions, he walked to the brass bell mounted on a post at the edge of the terrace.

"Ready for me to ring the bell?" David inclined his head, his gaze fixed on his mother.

The captain's bell, complete with stick, had been an impulse purchase by his mother early in her marriage. Surprisingly, his father had taken a shine to it. For as far back as David could remember, they'd rung the bell before each meal.

As kids, getting chosen to ring it had been a big deal.

Lynn nodded. "Everything is on the table and ready to go."

For a second, David thought about calling Brynn over, but

then Callum and Connor would want to get in on the action. There was only so much bell-ringing he could take.

Everyone was claiming their seats, either in the sun or under the awning, when David heard Clay call out.

"Way to wait for me."

"You snooze, you lose," David joked.

Ami strolled over with Sarah Rose on her hip. The toddler stared at Hadley for a long moment, then broke into a smile of recognition.

Little hands reached out, and Hadley scooped the child into her arms.

"She likes kids," Clay said to David, not bothering to keep his voice low.

"Hadley is wonderful with children." Ami turned to the men. "She'll make a fabulous mother one day."

Of that, David had no doubt. He was only surprised she wasn't already married with several children in tow. But he was glad, for his sake—and Brynn's—that she was still single.

The line formed, and David took his place beside Brynn and Hadley. He tried to concentrate on the food, rather than how good Hadley smelled.

"No burgers, brats and beer for Lynn Chapin." His whispered comment brought a smile to Hadley's face.

Skewers of spicy shrimp, grilled corn with basil butter and bread salad with broccoli rabe and summer squash filled the tabletop.

Hadley turned toward him, and her mouth was so close, David would have to shift only an inch or two to kiss her. Desire punched like a fist in his gut.

"It looks wonderful." But she wasn't looking at the food. Her gaze was on his mouth.

David saw his own desire reflected in the blue depths of her eyes. It would be so easy to put his lips on hers, to—

Sarah Rose shrieked and lunged forward, nearly clipping David's chin. He jerked back.

"What the—"

"She loves oranges." Across the table, Ami's green eyes danced.

David blinked.

Ami pointed to the salad in front of him, generously mixed with mandarins.

"Oh." David shifted his gaze back to Hadley and the little girl in her arms, who seemed determined to grab everything, not just oranges, from the selections.

Once they reached the end of the table, Ami handed her plate to Beck and lifted Sarah Rose from Hadley's arms.

Hadley waited, plate in hand.

"Let's sit over there." Brynn pointed to a table under a large oak tree. Wind chimes dangled from one branch, filling the air with a soft, soothing melody.

David didn't know whether to be relieved or irritated when Greer and Clay joined them. The first fifteen minutes were filled with talk of the weather before veering to the upcoming Founder's Day celebration.

"Hadley helped me with my family history project," Brynn announced proudly.

"Oh?" Greer lifted a well-shaped brow. Curiosity danced in her gray eyes.

Brynn popped a grape into her mouth. "We made pizza. It was fun. That was before she moved in."

Greer's curious gaze shifted from Hadley to David. When neither said anything, she refocused on her niece.

Brynn leaned forward, resting her elbows on the table. "Did you know Hadley's middle name is Elizabeth, just like mine?"

"I didn't know that." Greer appeared suitably impressed.

"It's a common name," Hadley clarified.

"It came from my birth mother," Brynn announced, stabbing a piece of orange.

David smiled. Both he and Whitney had spoken freely of Brynn's adoption, not only with her, but with family and friends.

The conversation shifted to exploits of the Chapin siblings growing up. David slanted several surreptitious glances at Hadley during the meal, then stopped when he realized he was acting like a lovestruck schoolboy.

"I assume my brother gave you a tour of the old homeplace." Clay paused in his assault on a piece of cherry cobbler the size of Texas to focus on Hadley. "I'm curious what you thought of the medal room."

Hadley smiled apologetically. "I haven't taken a tour."

"After you finish eating, you need to take a trip upstairs to David's bedroom." Clay shot his brother a teasing glance. "If he wouldn't have left for college, Mom would have been forced to take out the bed to make room for the hardware."

David chuckled. "While we're up there, I'll show you Clay's room. We call it the Harry Potter shrine."

Clay pointed a fork at his brother. "Some of those posters are worth hundreds."

Hadley grinned at the brotherly teasing. "I'd love a tour of both rooms, after I help with the cleanup."

"Thanks, but not necessary." Lynn, who'd just walked up, offered a reassuring smile. "I have staff to take care of that chore."

Only then did Hadley notice the two young women in black pants and white shirts already silently clearing the tables.

"Okay, then." Hadley smiled at Brynn. "Are you joining us?"

The child glanced across the yard at the twins, who were attempting to climb one of the many trees dotting the yard. "I'm going to play with Callum and Connor."

"Be careful," David urged, but Brynn had already taken off, headed straight for the twins. He turned back to Hadley. "Looks like it's you and me and a bedroom full of medals."

And that, David decided, was perfectly fine with him.

~

Hadley had paid little attention to the kitchen on her way outside. This time, she paused. The shiny cherrywood floor was a startling contrast to the white kitchen cabinets. She turned to David. "This is striking. Classic and traditional, yet warm and welcoming. Still—"

He lifted a brow.

Hadley shrugged. "I like our-ah, yours, better."

She could tell the comment pleased him. "I'll show you the rest of the house."

Once they were alone in the hall, she touched his arm. "Since we're alone, I want you to know I've enjoyed today…"

"But," he prompted.

"I don't want you feeling like you have to invite me to family events."

A slow, easy smile was his only response.

She couldn't help smiling back. He took her elbow, and they entered an area where two rooms were connected by an elaborately carved colonnade. A floral sofa and chairs had been grouped for conversation near a fireplace. "I hope you consider me your friend."

Hadley's heart performed a series of flutters as she crossed the room and ran a hand along the smooth white surface of the fireplace mantel. "This is lovely."

"It was designed by Robert Adam. Known for his neoclassical style, he trained under his father, William, a well-regarded Scottish architect." David stepped up behind her, standing so close she could feel the heat from his body. "The fluted Ionic columns and classical urns and ewers show his influence."

Hadley turned to face him and found him. Right. There. "I enjoy learning new things."

"The capacity to learn is a gift; the ability to learn is a skill; the willingness to learn is a choice."

At her arched brow, he smiled. "Brian Herbert."

Oh-so-casually, his hands moved to rest on her shoulders.

She'd lifted her face for the kiss they both knew was coming when he suddenly stepped back.

Hadley frowned, then realized the reason. A young woman, dark hair pulled back in a jaunty tail, had entered the room and was loading half-empty glasses on a tray. Though her gaze remained carefully averted, Hadley wondered how much she'd seen.

"Let me show you the upstairs."

The promise in David's eyes had Hadley's mouth going dry. Neither spoke during the short flight up the stairs.

They'd passed several closed doors when David stopped her with a light touch on her arm. He reached around her to push a door open. "This was mine."

Clay had been right. Baseball, football and track trophies filled an entire wall.

Moving to a track trophy, Hadley hefted a statue of a silver runner poised to sprint on top of a bright blue pillar. After reading the inscribed base, her lips curved as she turned to David. "I also ran the eight hundred meters."

He lifted the trophy from her hands, returned it to its spot, then stepped close. They were playing with fire. They could get burned. Heck, who was she kidding? *She* could get burned. Badly.

Hadley shoved the fear aside. They were adults. Friends. What was a few kisses between friends? The secret that stood between them, the one he didn't even know existed, would keep her from letting down her guard and getting too close.

In a month, she'd move out of his home. Life for both of them would go back to normal.

"You're thinking too hard."

Her breath caught as he lifted his hand and slid his fingers through her hair.

"You're incredibly beautiful." His soft voice reached deep, touching a raw, tender place.

"You're the one who's beautiful." She breathed the words. "Gorgeous eyes the color of smoke. Dark hair like highly polished, fine wood. And a body—"

Hadley stopped herself just in time. No need to go down that road and put ideas that would never come to fruition—*couldn't* come to fruition—in his head. Though, the desire shimmering in the air told her he probably shared a few of her lusty thoughts.

Afraid of what he might see in her eyes, Hadley wrapped her arms around his neck and held him. Just held him close, liking the feel of her curves molding against his muscles. Where she was soft, he was hard. So very hard.

"Ah, Hadley." He tipped her head back and gazed into her eyes. "I want you so much."

He lowered his head. His lips were warm and sweet, and Hadley let her eyelids close, savoring the moment.

A smoldering heat began to build inside her as his tongue circled and danced with hers. She did the same to him, each touch, each tingle reinforcing the possibilities.

He tasted like the most delicious candy Hadley had ever eaten, and she couldn't help wanting more. When his hands slipped underneath her shirt, she didn't think of stopping those fingers as they slowly slid upward. With one flick, he had her bra open. Her nipples tingled, anticipating his touch.

The door flew open with a bang. "What do you think of—"

The look of shock on Clay's face might have been laughable at any other time. His voice trailed off with, "The medals?"

David's hands dropped to his sides as he turned.

Hadley thought she heard him mutter a curse, but couldn't be sure as her hammering heart made hearing difficult.

She resisted the urge to straighten her shirt, thankful David hadn't yet pushed it up, or off. Hadley cleared her throat. "David was showing me his medals."

"Is that what they call it now?" Clay chuckled, then shifted toward his brother. "Sorry to interrupt you and the girlfriend. Carry on."

Before either of them had a chance to respond, Clay had pulled the door shut behind him.

"He's got it all wrong." Hadley's voice took on an urgency. "You have to tell him I'm not your girlfriend."

David was silent for a long time.

"I'm Brynn's nanny."

"Temporary nanny." His sharp gray eyes never left her face. "Are you interested in dating me, Hadley?"

"Dating?"

With one hand, David pushed her hair back from her face and cupped her cheek. The tender gesture had her eyes widening. "You know, that thing men and women do when they like each other."

Just say no, she told herself. She couldn't *date* him. Unless he was talking about simply having fun together. Two friends enjoying each other's company.

"You're thinking too hard again." His smile was lopsided, his fingers not quite steady as they trailed along the side of her jaw. "Just tell me what you want."

CHAPTER TEN

"A little birdie told me I'll be seeing you at the Cherry Fun Run." Ami rested her back against the center cabinet in her ruthlessly organized kitchen.

Hadley inclined her head. "What little birdie gave you that bit of news?"

After hours of Friday morning baking, she and Ami finally had time to chat about inconsequential things, such as Hadley agreeing to participate in the upcoming two-mile run. Karin, on delivery duty this week, had just left with boxes of pastries and desserts.

Only a large order of cookies and pies, now boxed and ready, remained. Hadley would drop these off at the Good Hope Living Center on her way home. Or rather, on her way back to David's home.

"Fin gave me all the deets. She said David called and asked ever-so-charmingly if there was any way she could get you added, even though the race has been full for weeks." Ami gave a little laugh. "Of course my sister made it happen."

"That was nice of Fin."

"I'm so excited that you and David Chapin are together." Happiness ran through Ami's words like a pretty ribbon. She was a romantic to the core. "I saw the connection at Lynn's house on Sunday. Beck saw it, too."

David, Hadley thought, should have taken her suggestion to heart. On their way downstairs to rejoin the others, she'd told him it'd be okay with her if they didn't mention they were dating. David had simply stared for a moment. Then he'd told her he wasn't a fan of secrets.

Just remembering made her stomach clench.

Ami put several cookies on a china plate. "Let's sit for fifteen and you can catch me up."

"Now that we're through baking, don't you need to pick up Sarah Rose?"

Instead of separating out the baking duties today, Ami had asked Hadley if they could work on several large orders together. Beck had left with Sarah Rose shortly after Hadley's arrival.

"There's no rush. Beck will bring her home in time for her nap."

After pouring two cups of coffee, Hadley followed Ami into the dining room. Once seated, she immediately took a fortifying gulp of the hot liquid.

While the robust chicory blend Ami and Beck preferred wasn't a favorite, Hadley relished the feel of the hot bitter blend warming her throat.

Stick to the truth, Hadley told herself. The last thing she wanted was additional lies between her and Ami.

Ami wrapped her fingers around a pretty china cup decorated with a ring of pink roses and studied her.

Keeping her expression carefully neutral, Hadley picked up a cookie and tried not to squirm under the assessing gleam in her friend's green eyes. Absently, she took a bite, then widened her eyes as her taste buds registered the hint of bitter.

Lavender cookies with rosewater icing were a Bloom family tradition. They were also an acquired taste. Hadley had grown to like the unique flavor. Which was fortunate, as the Bloom sisters marked each momentous occasion with these particular cookies.

Hadley lifted a brow. "What's the occasion?"

Ami's lips curved.

Hadley set the cookie down. "Gladys nailed it. You're pregnant."

When Gladys had told Ami she was having a baby boy, Ami had insisted she wasn't pregnant.

"We'd been trying, but not having a lot of luck. I did the test last night, and it came back positive." Ami grinned. "Of course, it's too soon to know boy or girl. We'll have to wait a couple of months to find out if Gladys is right."

"She's rarely wrong."

"As long as the baby is healthy, Beck and I will be happy."

"Congratulations." Hadley reached over and grasped Ami's hands. "I'm so happy for you."

"We're pretty thrilled."

"Was it difficult to tell Marigold?"

The brightness in Ami's eyes dimmed. The youngest Bloom sister and her husband had been trying to get pregnant since they married last year.

"I called her last night. She and Cade are very happy for us."

"Marigold is young. She has lots of time." Hadley remembered thinking when her own pregnancy test had turned positive how unfair it was so many couples tried to get pregnant and couldn't, while she had the opposite issue.

"Since they've been trying for nearly a year, they made an appointment with a doctor in Milwaukee to make sure there aren't issues needing to be addressed." Though Ami's voice remained confident, her brows furrowed. "It will work out. Giving birth isn't the only way to become a parent. Look at David."

"He's a wonderful father," Hadley agreed, having observed firsthand that David's love for his daughter ran deep.

"Is that all he is to you, a good father?" Ami's probing question broke through her thoughts.

Actually, Hadley had been surprised at how quickly she'd grown to admire and like David. She gave an absent smile. "That's all he can be."

Ami broke off a piece of cookie, her eyes never leaving Hadley. She arched a questioning brow. "You're both available."

As it was common knowledge David's divorce was final, Hadley figured that question was directed at her.

"Yes." Hadley nodded.

Her friend exhaled a breath and took a long sip of coffee.

"You're attracted to him." Ami's tone, low and soothing, invited confidences. "What's holding you back?"

"It's complicated." Hadley wanted to add a smile, but couldn't get her lips to move properly.

It was a response Hadley often used when anyone pressed too hard or asked for details about her past. Not that Ami was pushing hard. She was simply being a good friend.

"I know what keeping secrets is like." Ami's eyes took on a faraway look. "It can be a very lonely place."

Hadley thought back to the bash Ami and her sisters had thrown for their dad when Steve had reached a milestone with the school district. Such a fun, happy time. Until Eliza had opened her mouth and spewed her venom. "Eliza said horrible things at your father's party."

Ami lifted the cup, but didn't drink. "She tossed the secret I'd kept all those years down like a gauntlet."

"It almost broke up you and Beck." Hadley pursed her lips. "I admit Eliza has changed since she met Kyle. But I still don't understand how you can call her your friend. Not after what she did."

"It hurt Eliza deeply when Lindsay was seriously injured in

the accident. She blamed me for driving after drinking." Ami cleared her throat. "I blamed myself."

Hadley sipped her coffee, not sure how to respond. She wasn't even certain Ami expected a response.

"In a weird kind of way, she did me a favor." Ami broke the silence with her quiet words. "The truth needed to come out."

"Why did it need to come out?" Hadley lifted her hands and fought to keep her voice even. "What happened was past history. All that happened way back when you were in high school."

"If it hadn't come out, what actually happened that night would have been a wedge between me and Beck. I planned to tell him. Eliza just pushed forward my timetable." Ami's gaze searched hers. "Is there something you need to tell David?"

Hadley kept her expression impassive.

"David and my relationship—if you want to call it that— isn't anything like yours and Beck's." Hadley fought off a pang of envy. What she wouldn't give to have David love her the way Beck loved Ami. "There's no need for us to bare our souls. We're just casual."

"I hate to break it to you, but the way you two look at each other could scorch earth." Ami's eyes sparkled as she broke off a piece of cookie and popped it into her mouth.

"He's a handsome guy." Hadley's lips curved, despite her best efforts. "With those gorgeous gray eyes and all that thick, dark hair."

It helped that David was the complete opposite of Justin, who'd been her height and as blond as she was.

Ami's gaze turned shrewd over the rim of her cup. "I can't believe how long it took me to see it. Looking back, it was obvious even at the ice cream social you two have the hots for each other."

Actually, that day Hadley had been more concerned about Gladys's odd "reading" than jumping David's bones.

Of course, she had no doubt the man had very nice bones. Just recalling the hardness of his body when they'd kissed in the bedroom had her face heating.

Ami's laugh reminded Hadley of the tinkling of a bell. "Beck says I'm a born matchmaker. I do so wish I'd been the one to fix you two up."

"David and I are just friends."

"Friends who are exploring possibilities." Ami's green eyes danced.

"I kissed him." Hadley heard her voice soften as the confession spilled from her lips.

Leaning forward, Ami rested her arms on the table, pushing aside the plate. "How was it?"

Hadley crumbled her cookie between suddenly restless fingers. "Which time?"

Ami squealed. "This news surpasses my wildest expectations. Is he a good kisser?"

"Amazing." Hadley lifted her hands. "Before you ask, no, I haven't slept with him and I don't plan to."

"Trust me. Plans have a way of changing." Before Hadley could protest, Ami continued. "I'm just happy you're dating and getting more involved in the community. I was worried about you."

"Really?" Hadley forced a laugh past the sudden tightness in her throat. "Why would you worry about me?"

Without warning, Ami reached across the table. She took Hadley's hand and gave it a squeeze. "When you came to Good Hope, I knew you were running from something, or someone."

"My life is complicated." The well-practiced statement rolled from her lips.

"You know I'm here for you." Ami's gaze remained solemn. "If you ever want to talk, please know that whatever you say to me will be held in strict confidence, even from Beck."

As far as Hadley knew, Ami and her husband didn't have any secrets. Doubt must have shown on her face, because Ami placed a reassuring hand on her arm and repeated, "Even from Beck."

"You're a good friend." Because tears had begun to press against the backs of Hadley's eyes, she took a bite of bitter cookie and chased it with a gulp of the chicory blend. "If I could tell anyone, it'd be you. But sometimes, it's best to leave the past where it belongs and not let it sully the now."

"Sometimes you can't truly move forward without dealing with the past." A shadow traveled across Ami's face, then disappeared. "I'll be here for you, Hadley. Wherever, whenever you need me."

"Thanks." Hadley sat back, determined to get the conversation back on solid ground. "I'm looking forward to the street dance on Friday."

Bopping in the Square was one of many weekly events leading up to the big Founder's Day bash.

Ami's lips curved. "That isn't why you're excited."

Hadley cocked her head.

"At least be honest with yourself." Ami rolled her eyes, an almost indulgent smile on her lips. "You're excited because you'll be going with your good *friend* David."

David knocked on his brother's office door. Hearing a grunt of assent, he pushed the door open and stepped inside. "Am I interrupting?"

Clay motioned him inside with one hand. "I'm alone and I've got no medals to show, so it's safe to come in."

David shot his brother a sardonic look that had Clay grinning like a loon.

His brother had on his principal look. Blond hair carefully combed, dress pants and a cotton shirt with tie.

"Why so formal?" David took a seat in a leather chair facing the desk. "School doesn't start for another month."

"Our biology teacher is moving. Her husband got a job out of state. I have three interviews this afternoon." Clay leaned back in his chair and studied his brother. "Enough about me. How's the sexy nanny?"

David ignored the glint of mischief in Clay's eyes. "Hadley is at Ami's house this morning. They're doing some kind of marathon baking session."

"Does Brynn enjoy baking?"

David shrugged. "No idea."

"I think it'd be boring for Brynn to watch Hadley and Ami bake."

"Brynn stayed home with me." David paused, then qualified. "That is, until twenty minutes ago when I dropped her off at Muddy Boots. She, Mom and Greer are having a girls' lunch."

A speculative look settled on Clay's face. "Isn't watching Brynn and taking her places part of a nanny's duties?"

"Hadley and I talked about our week and figured out how to make everything work." Because David didn't want his brother thinking that Hadley wasn't pulling her weight, he added, "She loves to cook, so in addition to watching Brynn, she'll be making dinner in the evening."

Everyone around the table, enjoying a meal and sharing news, had been something David had taken for granted growing up. That had changed when he married. Whitney hadn't been big on sitting down for family meals, even when it had been just the two of them.

"You'll like that."

"I will." David smiled, thinking of his paltry attempts at cooking. Though he had to admit Brynn never complained. "She's also taking over the laundry, which is something I hate."

"Let me get this straight." Clay steepled his fingers beneath his chin. "In exchange for her cooking and doing the laundry, you babysit Brynn."

David frowned. "Brynn is my daughter. You don't babysit your own child."

Clay studied him so intently, David wondered if there was something more behind his brother's call this morning than simply wanting to give him a baseball uniform.

"Your arrangement doesn't sound like employer-employee. It sounds more like a marriage."

David laughed. "Where do you get your crazy ideas?"

"Think about it." Clay abruptly leaned forward, resting his arms on the desk. "Talking about your week, deciding who does what, working together to see that everything gets done."

"That's called a good working relationship."

"You also have some serious chemistry, if what I witnessed in your bedroom is any indication." Clay straightened. "Have you slept with her yet?"

"Give it up, Clay. Hadley is my employee."

"Camille was your employee." Clay's smile turned to a smirk. "I bet you never kissed Camille. Or had your hand up her shirt—"

"Enough." David's voice snapped like a whip in the quiet of the office. "You didn't see anything. Understand?"

The smirk disappeared. Clay's eyes, the same smoky color as his brother's, held a knowing glint. "You like her."

David thought about telling his brother his feelings for Hadley were not open for discussion. But despite Clay's needling, he knew his brother could be counted on to keep his mouth shut. "I do. She's amazing."

"Hadley is better suited for you than Whitney."

"Whitney and I were together for ten years," David reminded him.

"Sort of, but not really." When David opened his mouth, Clay held up a hand. "I'm betting Hadley will be at the baseball game on Sunday."

"She'll be in town."

"Whitney could have been in town and still not been there." Clay's expression softened as he pushed back his chair and stood. "Life is about choices, bro. If you think you and Hadley might have something, don't back off just because you got burned before."

Clay must not have expected a response, because he turned toward the closet and retrieved a vintage baseball uniform, complete with white stockings that would cover David's legs from knees to feet. "We're the same size, so this should fit you."

Several years earlier, Good Hope had started including a vintage baseball game as part of its Fourth of July celebration. It had proved so popular that the community had decided to include a game as part of the Founder's Day festivities.

"Thanks." David took the uniform from his brother and met his gaze head on. "I'm not taking advantage of Hadley."

"Hadley knows her own mind. I don't think she'd have any trouble telling you to back off." Clay grinned. "For the record, that wasn't the impression I got in your bedroom."

"I have to be careful," David said, more as a reminder to himself, "because of Brynn."

"Be as careful as you think necessary." Clay clapped him on the shoulder when they reached the door. "Just don't overthink and second-guess your own instincts."

On the way to the car, David heard the ding of a new text. It was from Whitney's friend Kim. She was concerned that Whitney seemed unusually depressed and irritable.

David texted back, asking her to keep a close eye on Whitney and let him know if she noticed any involuntary movements—no matter how small—or any changes with Whitney's coordination.

The depression and irritability could simply be Whitney, well, being Whitney. But Kim knew her friend's medical history, and he appreciated her concern. Just because he and Whitney were no longer married didn't mean David didn't care what happened to her.

He parked the car in front of the café. From where he sat, he could see Brynn with her grandmother and aunt at the table by the window.

Being a father came easy for him. His own dad had set a good example. His parents had been a team, guided by their love for each other and for their children.

It hurt to admit that he and Whitney had never been a team.

On the way home, he listened to Brynn chatter about the next step in her Founder's Day project. When she stopped to take a breath, David forced a casualness into his tone at odds with the churning in his gut.

"This evening is the street dance." David tossed the words out there and waited. "I thought we'd go."

Brynn lifted her gaze. When those blue eyes locked on his, for some reason he was reminded of Hadley. "Will Gram be there?"

David chuckled. "I'd say yes. Nearly everyone in Good Hope will attend. This is the official First Friday kickoff leading up to Founder's Day at the end of the month."

Taking the next exit off Highway 42, David turned south onto the road that would take them home. "It won't be just dancing. The town square will be filled with all sorts of booths."

Brynn's expression brightened. "I bet my friends will be there."

Before he could respond, her expression grew somber. "Mindy loved games. She was really good at them. At the school carnivals, she always won something. Last year, she won two cakes and gave one to me. Remember, Daddy?"

David's heart ached at the pain in her eyes. Brynn had suffered so much loss in her young life. "I remember. She let you pick the one you wanted."

"I picked the coconut." A slight smile lifted the corners of Brynn's lips. "Mindy didn't like coconut."

"You were a good friend."

Brynn's lips trembled and her hand shook as she brushed back a strand of hair. She picked up a to-go cup filled with water and took a sip.

"I have a surprise about tonight."

"Surprise?" She turned, and the tears in her pretty blue eyes were replaced by curiosity. "What kind of surprise?"

"Hadley is coming with us."

CHAPTER ELEVEN

"Then he said, 'Hadley is coming with us.'" Brynn giggled. "I almost spit out my water."

The child's eyes danced as she giggled again.

A warmth traveled through Hadley's veins. It appeared she'd worried needlessly about being the third wheel tonight.

The congestion on the sidewalks reminded her of mornings in a big city when everyone rushed to work. But instead of stepping lively, no one seemed in much of a hurry.

Hadley understood. The fact that the day had turned sunny and there was a light breeze off the water practically demanded one linger to soak in the ambience.

Flags and banners advertising Founder's Day hung from the ornate light poles that edged the street. Off in the distance, the high school band's brass section blared a rousing rendition of a tune Hadley couldn't quite identify. Still, the beat was infectious and had her tapping her foot.

Eventually, the budding musicians would vacate their seats and be replaced by a popular band out of Milwaukee who would rock the stage for the street dance.

Right now, the attention was on the vendors.

Hadley nearly groaned when Brynn glanced at a massive grill holding brats and burgers. This evening, she was in the mood for something different. Perhaps because tonight felt different, almost like an adventure.

Brynn glanced questioningly at her father.

David smiled. "You have to tell me, Sweet Pea. I can't read your mind."

"Do you like..." Instead of addressing her dad, Brynn shifted her gaze to Hadley. Her teeth bit her lower lip.

"I like almost everything," Hadley told her. "Except anchovies. And sardines."

Brynn cocked her head. "Do you like whitefish?"

Hadley nodded. "Very much."

Seconds later, they reached a red-and-white-striped tent. A banner proclaiming *Whitefish Forever* hung across the front, while a chalkboard gave options and prices.

As the dinner rush hadn't fully hit, it didn't take long to get their order—six fish tacos, plus a bowl of chowder for Hadley. She tried to pay for her own, but David waved away the money she tried to press in his hand.

They settled into seats at a picnic table under the leafy branches of a large oak.

Hadley lowered her spoon and kept a smile on her face when she saw Eliza Shaw, er, Eliza Kendrick and her husband, Kyle, approach.

"Mind if we share the table?" Eliza asked.

"We'd love to have you join us." David spoke before Hadley could respond. The table was large, and at events such as these, everyone shared space.

Eliza slipped into the spot next to Hadley, while her husband sat opposite her, next to David.

Though Hadley had dressed carefully in a blue-and-white-striped dress and wedge sandals, she felt dowdy next to Eliza.

Eliza was known for her sense of style. At one time, the executive director of the Cherries had favored black. There had been a subtle, but noticeable, change when she began dating Kyle. Color, sometimes bright and bold, found its way into her wardrobe.

Like today. While the bodice and waistband of her sleeveless dress might be edged in black, it was the bright red polka dots that drew the eye. When coupled with Eliza's stunning face, accentuated perfectly by sleek, jet-black hair and gray eyes, it was a striking picture.

Her husband certainly appeared mesmerized. Even as he visited with David, Kyle's eyes kept drifting toward Eliza. When they exchanged a smile, a yearning rose inside Hadley.

Just once, she wanted a man to look at her that way, to smile at her that way, to love her that much.

There was no obsession in the smile Kyle gave his wife, no threat of violence, only love and tenderness.

"The fish tacos are superb." The way Hadley figured, when in doubt, talk about weather or food. "I love the creamy avocado sauce."

Eliza took a dainty bite, considered. "Very tasty."

Then the woman surprised her by shifting her gaze to Brynn. "Do you like them?"

The girl blossomed under the warmth of Eliza's smile.

"I don't like the sauce." Brynn scrunched up her nose. "I scraped it off."

Eliza nodded. "How old are you now, Brynn?"

"Nine."

"My brother has a friend with a daughter your age."

"Is Ethan still living in Illinois?" David asked.

"He is. He shares a large house with several friends, both male and female. They're like family to him."

"Ethan is a partner in a construction company." Kyle took a sip of beer. "I want him to help me build a company here in Good

Hope. Unfortunately, we haven't been able to convince him to move back."

Eliza smiled. "Not yet, anyway."

"I wish his friend with the daughter would move here." Brynn set down her taco. "We might become best friends. Since Mindy died, I don't have a best friend."

The pain in Brynn's voice tugged at Hadley's heart. She slung an arm around the girl's shoulders and gave her a squeeze.

"I'm sure Olivia would love to be your friend," Eliza told Brynn before her assessing gaze landed on Hadley. "Ami mentioned you and David are dating. I approve."

Hadley nearly choked on a bite of fish.

Kyle chuckled. "Consider this fair warning. Since we married, my wife is determined to help as many friends as possible take that trip down the aisle."

Eliza reached for her husband's hand. "What's wrong with wanting everyone to be as happy as we are?"

"Nothing wrong with that." Kyle flipped their hands and laced his fingers with hers.

The fish taco formed a leaden weight in the pit of Hadley's stomach, but she forced a smile. "I'm in the mood to play some games. Are there any you'd recommend?"

David stood back and watched Hadley and Brynn "fish" for prizes in a baby pool filled with toys.

"It's more difficult than it appears." His mother, who'd wandered up several minutes earlier, slipped her hand through David's arm. "Even if the magnet on the end of the pole connects with the one on the prize, the connection often isn't strong enough to reel it in."

"A number of fish have already broken free." David gestured with his head. "Yet look at them. They're having fun. It's all good."

Actually, David was having fun, too. After eating, they'd made the circuit. He'd given most of the games a shot, but had drawn a line at the face painting.

Hadley and Brynn had chosen the "do-it-yourself" booth. They now sported slightly wavy identical rainbows on their left cheeks.

"I feel so foolish. I didn't realize you were interested in Hadley in that way." Lynn gave a little laugh. "Clay tells me you're a couple."

"Hadley is a beautiful, intelligent woman. We enjoy each other's company."

"She appears to enjoy spending time with Brynn." Lynn's lips curved when Brynn and Hadley exchanged high fives after Brynn successfully pulled in a fish.

"You'll get one, too, Hadley." Brynn's words drifted on the breeze. "Be patient and don't pull too fast."

"I always wished Whitney would enjoy spending time with Brynn." Lynn sighed. "Have you spoken with her lately?"

"Not a peep." David thought of the text he'd received from Kim. "We haven't been in contact since she was here over the Fourth."

His mother's lips pressed together. "I suppose Whitney loves her daughter in her own way. But even when she was here last month, she spent more time texting with her friends than having fun with Brynn."

The promise David had made to Whitney, that he would keep her secret—even from his family—weighed heavy on his heart. Though they were now divorced, it still didn't seem his truth to tell. "Whitney has a lot of issues."

Lynn made a dismissive sound.

"Brynn is such a lovely child." His mother shifted her gaze to the fishing "pond." "I'm happy Hadley appreciates her wonderful qualities, even if her own mother doesn't."

Hadley watched Brynn skip off, her hand nestled securely in her grandmother's. Her heart gave a ping.

David gave her shoulder a squeeze. "My mother wasn't about to take no for an answer. She wanted to spend time with her granddaughter."

"Where is Steve tonight?"

"Mom said he fell victim to the stomach bug that's been going around Good Hope." David smiled. "Which left her with her evening open."

"Brynn was excited to go with her."

"I'm excited to spend the rest of the evening with you."

As he studied her, a shiver traveled up Hadley's spine. Just the two of them tonight. Smiling, she looped her arm through his. "We might as well make the best of it."

He laughed.

They made their way through the crowd, pausing at the curb. The beat of the bass and the twang of a steel guitar pulsated in the air. The band was good.

Eons ago, Hadley had loved to dance. She remembered the outdoor concerts at the county fair in Williston the summer after high school. She'd swayed to the music, clapped loudly and fallen a little bit in love with Justin Mapes.

The handsome boy who'd completed his first year of college had been attentive and fun.

At first.

"What's the matter?"

Hadley blinked away memories and gazed into David's assessing eyes. "Nothing."

"Something brought that look in your eye."

There was a brief second of fear. What had David seen? Nothing, she reassured herself. Over the years, she'd become adept at hiding her emotions.

Hadley gestured to the street filled with gyrating bodies. "It's been a long time since I've danced."

David's smile turned wry. "This is more like moving to the beat than dancing."

Studying the crowd, Hadley realized he was right.

"There's Ami and Beck." David took her arm. "Let's say hello."

Ami's face lit up when they drew close. After hearing Steve was ill, Hadley hadn't expected to see her friend at the dance. She wondered who was watching Sarah Rose this evening.

Stop thinking of children, Hadley told herself.

Ami clasped Hadley's hand. She had to yell to be heard above the music. "I'm glad you're here."

Dressed in cropped white pants and a red-and-white shirt sporting a sailboat along the bottom hem, Ami looked summery fresh.

Hadley let the music seep into her bones as she and David began to move in time to the music. One fast song turned into two. Then Hadley lost count. She shimmied, shook her hips and gave in to the infectious beat.

It was a perfect night for dancing. A light breeze kept bugs at bay, and the moon cast a golden net over the square.

While Beck and Ami continually touched each other while dancing, David kept his hands to himself. Something Hadley found mildly irritating.

Hadley had just suggested they stop and get something to drink when the music slowed.

When they turned to go, Ami's hand clamped on her arm. "You can't leave now."

"We're not leaving," Hadley explained. "We're grabbing something to drink. Can we bring you and Beck anything?"

"Stay." Ami's green eyes turned pleading. "If everyone leaves when the slow songs play, the band will keep playing fast ones."

As food and beverage vendors appeared to be currently facing an onslaught of customers, Hadley glanced at David.

"Your choice."

"Let's dance." She looped her arms around David's neck. Though he was taller, her wedged sandals gave her extra height and brought them face-to-face. Hadley hadn't noticed before how good he smelled, a citrusy scent as enticing as it was subtle.

They swayed to the romantic ballad, and she relaxed against him. Just like they had in his childhood bedroom, they fit together perfectly.

His hands rested lightly on her hips. Hadley swore she could feel the heat of his touch through the dress's thin fabric to the skin beneath.

The band must have decided to do a slow set, because when that song ended, they launched into another ballad. The haunting melody stirred long-buried emotions.

When tears stung her eyes, she rested her head against David's cheek and closed them. Slow, regular breaths had helped in the past, so she focused on her breathing.

David must have sensed something was wrong, because his hold tightened on her. Not constraining and possessive like Justin's had been, but strong and comfortable. Letting her know, without words, that if she needed someone to lean on, she could lean on him.

For several moments, Hadley let herself drift, absorbing the words of the song and the feel of a man's arms around her in a type of embrace. When she was finally steady again, she let her eyes flutter open.

Ami, ensconced in her husband's arms, gave Hadley a thumbs-up.

Hadley simply closed her eyes again. This time, she relaxed fully. She wasn't certain how long they danced. Not until the leader of the band announced they were taking a fifteen-minute break did she drop her arms.

It was like stepping out of a dream, she thought. A very pleasant dream.

"They have frozen watermelon-and-strawberry lemonade this year at the Juice Stop stand." Ami leaned close. "I hear it's really yummy."

Before Hadley could reply, Fin and Jeremy appeared.

"What do you think of the band?" Jeremy asked the four of them.

"They're good," Ami told her brother-in-law. "Much better than the one last year."

"They cost considerably more." Fin gazed speculatively at Hadley and David. "But they're certainly a draw. Attendance is up."

In addition to being tasked with bringing film projects to Good Hope, Fin had added overseeing the implementation of certain community events to her job duties. While there was no admission charge for this evening's street dance, the increased foot traffic benefited local merchants.

Fin inclined her head toward Hadley. "I'm surprised you're not working the bakery booth."

Ami answered before Hadley could respond. "I told you Karin and her friend were on duty tonight."

Fin's gaze shifted to David then back to Hadley. "I must have forgotten."

"I better skip the lemonade." Hadley offered Ami an apologetic smile. "Since I'll be up early baking, I'm going to need to cut the evening short."

"I don't want you to have to do that." A look of distress clouded Ami's face. "You and David came to enjoy the festival."

"Sacrifices must be made." With a melodramatic flare, Hadley placed her wrist against her forehead, then dropped the act and winked. "Just remember my dedication when it's time to give out raises."

~

As she and David picked their way through the crowd on their way to the parking lot, the band started up again, returning to the rock 'n' roll hits that appeared to be crowd favorites. For as far as David could see, dancing revelers filled the streets and sidewalks.

David leaned close to make sure Hadley could hear him. "I don't recognize a third of these people."

She smiled. "Ami says strangers are just friends you haven't met yet."

The words had barely left her lips when a man holding a red Solo cup high in the air pushed her aside with his bulk. The motion had beer sloshing over the rim and down the front of her dress. The burly man kept going without sparing her a glance.

Hadley's gaze dropped to her wet chest. She sighed, then rolled her eyes.

If she'd been Whitney, everyone within a ten-mile radius would have heard her curses.

David watched the guy bounce from person to person like a ball in a pinball machine. "He must be one of those new friends Ami was talking about."

Hadley laughed. "Good one, Chapin."

"Looks like you aren't the only new friend he's making this evening."

She followed the direction of David's gaze and saw one of Cade's deputies having a serious conversation with the man. "What goes around."

"Good sport." David looped an arm around Hadley's shoulders. It had been a long time since he'd held a woman in public. Whitney hadn't been into what she deemed public displays of affection.

Personally, he thought his ex-wife's hands-off directive had more to do with him messing up her hair or affecting her ability to mingle easily than PDA concerns.

The crowd thinned as they drew closer to the church lot

where they'd parked. *Thinned* didn't mean clear sailing, only that they could actually make it a few feet without running into a wall of people.

"This is nice." Hadley glanced up at him.

"What is?"

"Walking with you on a late summer evening." She smiled. "I feel safe with you."

Pleased by the sentiment, David tightened his hold on her. "I don't think you have anything to worry about in Good Hope."

"There are bad people everywhere." Her expression remained serious. "Even in small towns."

David thought of Clint Gourley and his crime spree. Granted, Clint hadn't hurt anyone, but people had been afraid. "It's always smart to be cautious."

They walked another block in silence, and his mind kept circling her comment. He'd been wrong to brush aside her concern. "This happened years ago, but I've never forgotten it."

She glanced up at him.

"One of the women I knew from my architecture classes was attacked after a study session at the library. Like most of us, she lived in off-campus housing. We knew she walked home alone. Even though it was late when we broke that night, I never thought to offer to walk with her."

Hadley didn't ask for specifics, merely closed her eyes briefly. When they opened, he saw the sympathy. "I'm sorry for what happened to your friend."

David dropped his arm from her shoulders and took her hand, finding it cold despite the warmth of the evening. "I wouldn't want anything to happen to you."

A curious tension filled the air as their gazes locked.

She touched her top lip with the tip of her tongue. "Because, if anything happened to me, it would be hard on Brynn."

"You don't just matter to Brynn." He cupped her cheek. "You matter to me."

Her throat moved convulsively, but it was her lips that capti-vated and drew him closer. Plump and red, like ripened cherries. He remembered how sweet they'd tasted.

Tugging her close, David pressed his mouth to hers.

CHAPTER TWELVE

The heat of the unexpected kiss scorched a path all the way to the tips of Hadley's toes. She could end the kiss, probably *should* end the kiss. They were standing in a church parking lot, for goodness's sake. But the melding of lips had heat percolating low in her belly, and she forgot everything in the pleasure of the contact.

Hadley wound her arms around his neck, yearning for more.

Then, as quickly as the kiss began, it ended. David stepped back, his eyes dark and unreadable in the dim light.

"We'll pick up Brynn on our way home." A small muscle twitched at the corner of David's jaw.

Hadley nodded, understanding his frustration. She didn't want to stop with a kiss or two. She wanted more. More kissing. More touching. More…him.

Though David's hand remained on the passenger-side handle, he didn't open the door. Concern blanketed his face. "I didn't plan on kissing you."

"Plans change." Hadley reached around him and opened the door. "In case you didn't notice, I kissed you back."

He shoved his hands into his pockets. "Things between us are moving fast."

"It was a kiss, Chapin." She gave the air a casual brush with her hand. "We didn't have sex on the concrete."

She shot him a wink, pulled the door shut and buckled her seat belt.

While he rounded the front of the vehicle, she touched her fingers to her tingling lips. Kissing David—again—might not have been the smartest thing she'd ever done, but then again, it was only kissing.

David didn't need to worry.

She didn't need to worry.

Because that was as far as it would ever go.

David's deepening feelings for Hadley were on his mind when he dropped Brynn off at her rock-climbing class Monday morning. Instead of heading straight home, he decided to grab a cup of coffee and do some thinking.

"You're out early." Behind the counter of the Daily Grind, Ryder lifted a hand in greeting. "I didn't expect to see you this morning."

"Brynn has a class at the Y." David glanced at the nearly empty bake case and pointed. "What kind is that?"

"Pumpkin and cream cheese with pecan streusel." Ryder shook his head. "I'm surprised we have any left."

"I'll take it." David reached for his wallet. "And a coffee, black."

Ryder opened the bake case, looked up. "When you see Hadley, be sure and mention how much I appreciated her helping Cassie at the ice cream social."

David pulled a bill from his wallet and placed it on the counter. "Will do."

"To stay or go?"

"Stay." David took the muffin and coffee around the corner to where a wall of windows overlooked a pretty park-like area.

Pastor Dan glanced up and smiled a greeting.

"You look hard at work this morning." David gestured with his head to the pile of papers on Dan's table.

"Just putting the final touches on tomorrow's sermon." Dan pushed the notes aside. "I'm at a point where I need a break. I'd appreciate company."

David set the coffee and the muffin on the table. Only when he was seated did he notice the lines of fatigue edging the minister's eyes.

"How are things?" David figured the general question was one the pastor could take any way he wanted.

"It isn't easy having someone you love walk away." Dan's hands cupped the red mug sitting before him. "You know how that feels."

David wished he'd gotten the coffee and muffin to go. He had enough on his mind without bringing his ex into the mix. "Whitney and I stopped loving each other long before she left."

The words surprised David, though he realized it was true.

"I've done a lot of thinking since Lindsay broke off our engagement." Dan's eyes took on a faraway look. "One of the questions I've been asking myself is, did I ever really love her? Or was I in love with the person I wanted her to be?"

David took a long drink of coffee. If he was going to get into a philosophical discussion with a minister, he needed to bolster his brain with caffeine. "Come to any conclusions on that?"

The grateful look in Dan's eyes took David by surprise. He realized the man who was there for everyone in the congregation didn't have anyone to confide in. Well, if he needed to talk, David would listen.

"Lindsay told me she broke it off because she couldn't see herself as a minister's wife." Dan's lips lifted in a wry smile. "Which was odd, because I could easily see her in that role."

David brought the cup of steaming coffee back to his lips, but didn't take a sip. He thought of Whitney. She had it in her to be a good mother. David had seen the loving, caring, compassionate side of her on more than one occasion. In the end, the demands of motherhood hadn't been what she wanted. "I guess the more pertinent question is, did she *want* to be the first lady of the congregation?"

"Good point." Dan gave a humorless chuckle. "I don't really know the answer. Lindsay and I haven't talked since she told me it was over. I'm grateful she was honest with me."

David ate a piece of muffin and chased it with coffee. The rich Colombian blend offset the sweetness of the streusel. He pointed his fork at the minister. "When you get burned, it's difficult to trust your judgment."

"It's true." The tips of Dan's ears reddened. "Not that I'm ready to start dating. But when I do, I don't want to make the same mistake again."

Before David could respond, the minister hurriedly added, "Not that Lindsay was a mistake."

David told himself to simply let the comment pass. But his growing feelings for Hadley had him feeling edgy. He set down his cup, leaned forward.

"Your engagement was a mistake." David watched shock widen Dan's eyes. "For some reason, you were unable to see what she was really like, what she wanted. You saw her as you wanted her to be."

Because the minister looked as though he'd just punched him in the face, David tried to smooth the waters. "I did the same with Whitney. Only, I married the woman. Looking back, I can see warning signs I ignored."

Understanding dawned in Dan's eyes. The minister slowly nodded.

"Lindsay had no interest in my sermons." Dan's laugh had little humor. "I thought—hoped—she'd enjoy talking with me about them, but from the beginning, she was hands-off."

David nodded. "When Whitney and I began dating, we were

in college, so our social life was robust. There were nights I would have preferred to watch a movie at my apartment, but that bored her. I thought that would change once we married, as we got older."

"It didn't."

"Life in Good Hope was too slow-paced for her." David glanced down at his coffee. "But even when we were in Chicago, she wasn't happy unless she was on the go."

"I'm sorry your marriage ended."

"Desperately holding on to something that no longer works isn't the answer." David held up his hand when Dan opened his mouth, probably to talk about the sanctity of marriage and vows made. "Whitney's constant disappearing act was hard on our daughter. Brynn didn't understand why her mother was never around and, when she was, why she didn't want to spend time with her."

"Divorce is more difficult when there is a child involved."

"Sometimes, keeping a family together is the answer." David expelled a harsh breath. "Sometimes, it's best to let go. Whitney and I are better apart."

The bells on the door jingled as it opened. From where he sat, David couldn't see the entrance. But he recognized the voice that called out a greeting. *Hadley.*

"You didn't have to bring them over." Ryder's smile held a warmth that had been missing when he'd greeted David. "I could have sent someone for them."

"Delivery is part of the contract."

"Your boyfriend is around the corner."

Hadley appeared a second later, wearing a pink T-shirt emblazoned with "Baking Up Some Love," a pair of cropped jeans and the blue floral Chucks on her feet.

David smiled. Earlier this morning, she'd been baking up a storm in yoga pants and a faded Brewers T-shirt.

Her lips curved as she closed the distance to the table. "What a nice surprise. Two of my favorite men."

"The streusel muffins are fabulous." Before David realized what he was doing, he stood and brushed a kiss across her cheek.

Her cheeks pinked as she shifted her gaze to the minister. "Good morning, Pastor."

"Hello, Hadley." There was an unmistakable twinkle in Dan's eyes.

"I dropped Brynn off at the Y." David lifted the cup to his lips. "I decided to stop in for a muffin and coffee. Dan is working on his sermon notes."

"Everyone raves about your sermons," Hadley told the minister. "Biblically based, yet the lessons are easy to put to use in one's daily life."

"That's kind of you to say." Dan appeared sincerely touched by the compliment.

Hadley returned her attention to David. "I take it Brynn is still at her climbing class."

David glanced at his watch. "The class will be over shortly. Why don't you ride to the Y with me? We may be able to catch a few minutes of the class, and you can see for yourself how she's doing."

"Sure." Hadley spoke equally casually. "I'd love to cheer her on."

"You two have fun." Dan glanced down at his stack of papers.

Hadley wiggled her fingers and shot the minister a warm glance. "Good luck with the sermon."

She wrapped her fingers around David's bicep as they strolled out of the shop. It struck David that he hadn't gotten any thinking time. But when Hadley smiled up at him, he wondered what there was to think about.

∾

Children were exiting the Y when Hadley and David arrived. David headed in to find Brynn while Hadley waited outside.

Though she didn't tell David why she preferred to stay on the sidewalk, Hadley found pleasure in imagining Brynn's response when she walked out the door and saw her standing there. Besides, the sun was warm against her face, and she wanted to enjoy the late summer weather as long as possible.

"Don't you look pretty."

Hadley froze and slowly turned.

Clive stood on the sidewalk, dressed for a workout, the straps of his gym bag across his body. The younger Gourley brother wasn't unattractive. His features were regular, and his body fit and toned. But his pale blue eyes had her shivering in the sunshine.

If eyes really were windows into the soul, it seemed that Clive had lost his soul years ago.

"Hello, Clive." Hadley inclined her head, spoke coolly.

"You and me, we didn't get to finish our conversation the other night." His gaze dropped and settled on her breasts.

It took everything in Hadley not to cross her arms across her chest or take a step back. Only the knowledge that men like Clive thrived on intimidation had her holding her ground.

Justin had been just like this guy, only a younger, smoother, more handsome version. But at the core, the same.

"I didn't have anything to say to you then." With great effort, Hadley kept her tone level, but there was no mistaking the chill. "And I don't have anything to say to you now."

"Uppity bitch," she heard him mutter as she turned, dismissing him.

When Clive grabbed her arm, she inhaled sharply. Then reacted. She whirled and stomped hard on Clive's instep. While he howled, she brought her foot up and kicked him in the groin.

He was on the ground, moaning, when David appeared at her side, Brynn hot on her father's heels.

"Are you okay?" Brynn's voice came out in short puffs.

David frowned. "I told you to wait by the building."

"I wanted to help Hadley, too." Brynn gazed down at the man writhing on the concrete and grinned. "Looks like you didn't need our help."

David studied Hadley. "Do you want me to call Cade?"

Hadley shook her head, barely resisting the urge to kick Clive in the side for good measure. "Naw. He won't bother me again."

"He better not." David crouched down, grabbed Clive by the shirtfront. "Understand? You stay away from me and mine."

"Yeah, whatever." Barely audible, the response wheezed out.

Still, it appeared to satisfy David, who rose. His gaze searched Hadley's face, and the concern she saw there touched her. "Are you okay?"

"I'm fine." Hadley was even better when Brynn's hand slipped into hers.

"I'm fine, too." Brynn smiled broadly when both adults looked at her. "Anissa said I have good problem-solving skills."

For a second, David looked blank at the abrupt change in topic.

"Her climbing instructor." One Hadley knew wasn't easy to impress. "That's high praise from Anissa."

Brynn swung their joined hands. "I think we should celebrate my climb and Hadley's fight with ice cream."

"It wasn't really a fight. It—" Hadley stopped at Brynn's look. "Okay, it was a fight."

"Let's go to IwannaCone." Brynn suggested the popular shop.

"It's barely ten," David protested.

"If you've never had ice cream in the morning, I'd say now is the time to start." Hadley's tone turned teasing. "C'mon, Chapin, it's time to live a little."

CHAPTER THIRTEEN

Live a little.

Hadley's words from earlier in the week struck him as appropriate on this Friday morning.

David stood in the kitchen doorway and simply stared. The table boasted blue fabric place mats with sunflowers as big as a plate. A bouquet of flowers he recognized from the garden sat in the center. Orange juice filled glasses on the table. The rich, enticing aroma of freshly brewed coffee mixed with the scent of spicy sausage.

This, he realized, *was living*. He tried to figure out what was special about today. Nothing that he could recall. As far as he knew, this was just another Friday morning. "What's up?"

The question had Hadley and Brynn, dressed in matching white aprons, whirling.

Brynn grinned. "Perfect timing."

Hadley gestured to the table. "Have a seat."

David hesitated, noting the sparkle in Hadley's eyes and Brynn's broad smile. "I didn't expect this today."

"Sometimes"—Hadley moved to the coffeepot and poured

him a cup, setting it beside the juice glass—"the best things in life are the unexpected."

He took a few steps to the table, reluctant to sit down while they buzzed around the kitchen. "Is there something I can do to help?"

"Nope." Brynn slanted a glance at Hadley. "We've got this covered."

David pulled out the chair and lifted the mug of steaming coffee. He didn't drink, but watched them over the rim.

Hadley put on oven mitts. "Because the pan is large, I'll lift it out of the oven. Do you have the trivet ready?"

"I'll get it." Brynn hurriedly pulled out a drawer to the right of the sink. Once she'd positioned the trivet on the counter, she turned to him. "Hadley and I made a breakfast casserole. She's teaching me how to cook."

"Your daughter is an excellent pupil." Hadley lifted the glass dish from the oven and set it on the trivet in a well-practiced move. "She shows real talent."

Brynn fairly glowed under the praise. "It was fun."

Taking off the mitts, Hadley laid a hand on Brynn's shoulder. "Now, we get to eat your creation. Do you want to serve?"

"Yes." Brynn grabbed plates already on the counter and moved to the dish. "I can do that."

"Remember, it's hot, so don't touch the sides with your fingers."

Brynn nodded, her face set in serious lines. "I'll be careful."

Whitney never allowed Brynn near the oven. But then, neither had he, David realized. He'd usually been in such a hurry to toss something together for them to eat, he hadn't given a thought to having Brynn help. Or to teaching her anything.

Now, here was Hadley, only days into her temporary assignment, already making a difference.

While Brynn dished out the casserole, Hadley filled a mug for herself and got a glass of milk for Brynn. She turned to David.

"There are hash browns in the casserole. I didn't make toast, but if you'd like some, I—"

"I don't need any, but thanks for offering." He met her gaze and gestured with his head toward where Brynn concentrated on putting a neat square of casserole on the second plate. "Thanks for this."

David willed her to see he wasn't talking about the offer of a couple slices of bread.

She inclined her head, and he saw she understood. "Actually, Brynn did most of the work. I just supervised."

With measured steps, Brynn set the plate before him, then put one in Hadley's place at the table before returning to the counter for her own.

He glanced down. The casserole smelled heavenly and looked just as good, with hash browns peeking out the sides and pieces of eggs and sausage covered in cheese. "This looks amazing."

"My grandmother taught me how to make it." Hadley shifted her gaze to Brynn. "Hopefully, you'll remember me when you make it for your family one day."

Brynn nodded solemnly. "I will."

Appearing surprisingly moved by the promise, Hadley blinked rapidly. She cleared her throat and picked up her fork. "Let's see how it tastes."

They ate, drank and talked over the casserole, which David swore was the best he'd ever had. The shadows that had been in Brynn's eyes for so long they'd seemed a permanent part of her had disappeared.

David got a step-by-step replay of how to make a casserole. Hadley smiled indulgently while Brynn took the lead.

What she had done this morning, taking time to give his daughter this new experience, was even more impressive considering she'd been up before dawn baking.

"What made you two decide to cook this morning?" David stabbed the last bite of casserole on his plate.

Hadley and Brynn exchanged glances.

"We want you to pitch really good today," Brynn told him, her eyes large and serious.

Hadley smiled, took a sip of coffee. "We thought you might do better after a hearty breakfast."

David had nearly forgotten the vintage baseball game. As the starting pitcher for Good Hope, his performance would have a lot to do with getting a win against Egg Harbor. Though the game was supposed to be just for fun, every player on his team had a competitive streak. "This was so thoughtful."

Brynn flushed with pleasure. "Hadley and me, we'll be cheering for you. Really loud. Isn't that right?"

His daughter turned to Hadley, who'd risen to gather the dishes.

"Absolutely right." Hadley tousled Brynn's hair as she passed, though her gaze shifted to David. "We're your superfans."

"Hadley. Brynn." Ami waved her arms wildly. "Over here."

When she'd had to park on the grass because the ballfield's parking lot was full, Hadley expected she and Brynn would have to climb to the top of the bleachers to find a seat.

She hadn't considered her friends might save them a seat.

All four of the Bloom sisters moved down on the metal bleachers, squeezing out just enough space for her and Brynn on the end.

"Thank you." Hadley settled into her seat. "I didn't expect you to—"

"We're friends." Ami gave her arm a squeeze as Sarah Rose climbed into Hadley's lap. "Of course we saved you a spot."

Brynn waved wildly. "Hi, Gram."

Only then did Hadley notice that Steve and Lynn were seated on the other side of Fin.

Lynn returned the greeting. Though she acknowledged Hadley, there was an assessing look in her eyes that had Hadley shifting uneasily in her seat.

Hadley reminded herself she was just here as Brynn's nanny. Hadn't Camille taken Brynn to dozens of these events over the years? But she didn't feel like a nanny, surrounded as she was by friends and with a toddler in her lap.

Brynn kept Sarah Rose's interest by playing a game of "spider." Each time the toddler would brush away Brynn's creeping fingers, both girls would dissolve in laughter.

Ami shook her head, her smile indulgent. "Kids."

The sun shone bright in the blue sky, and the smell of popcorn and peanuts filled the air. After their big breakfast, Hadley and Brynn had enjoyed a snack of hummus and crackers before coming to the ballfield.

She would have made something more substantial prior to the noon game, but David had promised Brynn hot dogs after the game.

"There he is." Brynn's excited voice broke through her thoughts, accompanied by a roar from the crowd.

Hadley handed Sarah Rose back to Ami and rose as the players returned to the field for introductions.

"On the mound for Good Hope...David Chapin."

Hadley brought two fingers to her lips and whistled, then clapped and yelled. Next to her, Brynn jumped up and down and cheered.

In Hadley's mind, there was little to no chance David could hear her and Brynn, but when his gaze searched the stands and stopped, she gave him a wave. His lips lifted in a slow, easy smile, and she went warm all over.

At the direction of the announcer, everyone resumed their seats. A few rows down, Gladys rose to her feet, a ball in her hand.

Hadley shifted her attention to Ami. "What's going on?"

Ami shook her head. "No idea."

Prim leaned forward. "Gladys is throwing out the first pitch."

"They've never done that before," Marigold called out from Prim's other side.

"It was a tradition started in the early 1890s by Governor William McKinley of Ohio," Prim, a rabid baseball fan since childhood, announced. "Back then, the dignitary tossed the ball to the starting pitcher from the stands. Though the teams will still be playing by 1860s rules, Max said the committee thought this would be a nice touch."

Hadley watched David move in, his gaze focused on the older woman, his hands bare. Though it still looked strange, Hadley had learned at the first vintage game she'd attended that gloves weren't worn by players in the 1860s.

Gladys drew herself up to her full height and didn't rush. An actress through and through, the woman clearly knew how to play a crowd. The assembled throng inhaled when she pretended to fumble the ball.

But from her position three rows up and to the woman's right, Hadley saw Gladys's lips curve. At precisely the right moment, she lifted her arm, and the ball flew in a perfect arc.

The crowd roared as David caught the ball, then he gestured to Gladys, who took a bow.

"I didn't know she could throw like that," Brynn told Hadley, clearly impressed.

"Gladys is good at everything she does." Hadley remembered what Ruby had said about the woman's "fortune-telling" talent, and a shiver traveled up her spine.

She stared curiously when Brynn pulled out her flip phone. "Who are you calling?"

"I'm texting Mom. I'm telling her we're watching Dad pitch." Brynn's fingers moved slowly. Though texting on such a phone was difficult, it was possible. And this was the child's only option since David refused to consider a smartphone for the nine-year-old.

"Does she text you back?" The second the question left Hadley's mouth, she wished she could pull it back. Brynn's relationship with her mother fell under MYOB.

Brynn pushed Send, then sat back, her eyes looking old for a child. "Sometimes, she'll write me back, but she's pretty busy."

"I imagine she is." Hadley slung an arm around the girl. "Look. Your dad is ready to throw out the first pitch."

Hadley found the game much more enjoyable when you had someone to root for. Even when he was off the field, Hadley couldn't keep her eyes off of David. She knew this infatuation wasn't wise.

Not something to worry about, she told herself. She was simply enjoying the moment. It would be over all too soon, and she would be alone with only memories to sustain her.

For now, she would enjoy this sunny, summer day and let herself fall just a little in love with the handsome pitcher.

Though David's mother and Steve had to leave, the Bloom sisters and their families stayed to enjoy a picnic at the park near the stadium. The twins were in their element in the bounce house, while Brynn played with a friend on the playground.

David slanted a glance at Hadley, who was animatedly speaking with Ami. For once, Hadley didn't have Sarah Rose in her arms. Instead, the toddler and her cousin Adelyn were being pushed on the baby swings by Fin and Prim.

Today, David had played the best ball of his life. He hadn't been hot, he'd been on fire. Good Hope shut out Egg Harbor, a fact that gave everyone on the team a great deal of satisfaction after having lost the Fourth of July game to their rivals.

With every pitch he'd thrown, David had been conscious of

Hadley and Brynn in the stands cheering him on. His girls. Cheering for him.

"Hey, David, I have something to ask you."

David smiled. Marigold's directness was only one of the things he admired about the youngest Bloom sister. He took a sip of cola, shifted on the bench to face her. "Ask away."

"Well, you know Cade and I have been trying to have a baby."

With that comment, Marigold captured everyone's attention at the table, including that of Hadley, who stiffened beside him.

David glanced her way, then realized Marigold expected a response. "I think I may have heard something about that."

"Just for the record, we're having a lot of fun trying." The sheriff slung an arm around his wife's shoulders, then brushed a kiss across her cheek.

"True." Marigold's wide mouth curved up in a feline-like smile before her expression turned serious. "The doctor we saw in Milwaukee is going to give me some medication to help me ovulate. That may take care of the problem."

David shifted uncomfortably. *TMI*, he thought. He really didn't need—or want—to know any of this. "Ah, that's good."

"Yes, well, we have also been looking at other options for starting a family."

Wishing the hair stylist would simply get to the point, David took a gulp of cola and nodded.

"Cade and I were talking, and we realized we've never asked you about your experience with adoption." Marigold's voice remained calm, but her hands fluttered. "I don't even know if you did an agency adoption or a private one. If you prefer not to discuss it, just tell me to mind my own business."

David offered Marigold a reassuring smile. "It's not a secret, and I'm happy to answer any questions. Keep in mind, the adoption was over nine years ago and took place in Illinois. State laws on adoption can vary."

"Did you go through an agency?" Marigold prompted.

"We went through an attorney. It was a private adoption."

"Why did you choose that avenue?"

David nearly smiled again. It was as if the hair stylist had a set of questions in her head and was ticking them off one by one. "We thought it would be faster."

"Was it?"

"It was, although an agency may have been just as quick." Already anticipating her next question, he added, "From the time we filled out the paperwork, it was about six months until the attorney called and we learned our baby girl was due any day."

"Wow. Not much notice." Marigold blinked, clearly startled. "Was adoption a last-second decision on the birth mother's part?"

"I would expect it's usually a difficult decision." David couldn't even imagine the angst, the second-guessing. "The attorney only said the birth mother was determined her child go to a good home. The fact that Whitney planned to be a stay-at-home mom and I was close to my family weighed heavily in our favor."

For a second, no one at the table spoke. David wondered if their thoughts were going down the same road as his. Whitney had hardly ended up being a stellar mother. But he could have done better by his child, too, and he would do better going forward.

"What made you decide on adoption?" Marigold asked.

How to explain this, David wondered, without saying too much? "There's a serious genetic condition that runs in Whitney's family. She didn't want to take the chance of the child inheriting that condition."

"Is Whitney at risk of developing the condition?" This time, it wasn't Marigold who asked the question, but Hadley.

David shifted in his seat. "It's possible."

He started to turn back to Marigold when Hadley spoke again, her voice strung as tight as a piano wire. "I assume this condition, if inherited, is serious enough to cause major health issues. It seems odd that a birth mother would have chosen to place her child with a family in which the mother could become seriously ill."

David hadn't known until after they'd gotten Brynn that Whitney had lied on the application. She hadn't mentioned the genetic condition. And since she'd kept her family history from even her primary-care doctor, her health record was clean.

He shrugged. "I guess we were lucky."

Hadley's eyes were dark, her expression solemn. "I guess you were." A sudden chill filled the air.

"Actually, when I learned that Whitney had kept the truth from me, I was conflicted." David blew out a breath. "I was horrified she'd deceive the birth mother to get a child, but I loved Brynn so much, and the adoption had already been finalized. What would have been the point in revealing the truth then?"

"No point." Marigold filled the silence when Hadley said nothing.

"I convinced myself that Whitney did it only because she wanted Brynn as much as I did, but later I realized she often lied just for the heck of it."

When it was time to gather the children and head home, David considered taking Hadley's hand as they walked with the others to the playground. The back-off signal she was transmitting had him keeping his hands to himself.

She slowed her steps so they would be out of earshot of the group. "Brynn was texting her mother during the game. I didn't say anything because I didn't know if that was okay with you or not."

David wasn't sure what had erected the wall between them, but at least she was talking. "Brynn texts her mother all the time. She likes Whitney to know what's going on, sees it as a way for them to stay close."

"She says her mother rarely texts back."

"I spoke with Whitney about that." He pressed his lips together. "So far, no change."

Hadley only nodded.

He took her arm, stopping her. "Did I do or say something to offend you?"

Surprise flickered in her blue eyes. "Why do you ask?"

He simply cocked his head. For a second, David thought she might deny it or play dumb, but continue to freeze him out. That had been Whitney's MO.

Hadley paused, exhaled a breath. Her fingers raked through her hair. "Hearing the care Brynn's birth mother went through to find her a good home, only to have Whitney...well, it makes me angry."

"I understand. Brynn's birth mother entrusted a precious gift to us, and we failed her." His gaze shifted to the playground where Brynn pushed Sarah Rose in the swing. "Sometimes, even with the best intentions, situations don't turn out as planned."

"You're right." She blew out a breath and appeared to steady. "All we can do is move forward and learn from our mistakes."

"Brynn in my life isn't a mistake." David took Hadley's hand and met her gaze. "I believe she was meant to be my daughter."

After a long moment, Hadley nodded. "I believe that, too. Let's go home."

CHAPTER FOURTEEN

The knock on her door Sunday morning had Hadley burying her face in her pillow. "Go away."

The words came out like a croak.

The pounding continued. Maybe it was in her head. She'd awakened during the night and taken a couple of Advil for the headache that had settled behind her eyes. Almost immediately, she regretted getting up as her stomach rolled.

Stumbling back to bed, she cursed herself for having that second hot dog at the baseball game. That had to be why she felt like puking.

The knock sounded again. Closer this time. On her bedroom door?

"Hadley?" It was David's voice. Deep and filled with concern. "We need to leave for the Cherry Fun Run in fifteen. Are you still coming?"

The Cherry Fun Run. Hadley groaned. She'd forgotten that was today.

Get up, she told herself. You'll feel better if you just get up.

"Just a minute." Hadley pushed herself up to a sitting position, placing her hands on the mattress when the room began to spin. Once it righted itself, she stood, swayed. "I need to—"

The next thing she knew, she was on the floor with David kneeling beside her. His gray eyes searched her face.

"I don't feel so good." She tried for a smile, but couldn't find the energy.

"Did you hurt yourself when you fell?" Even as he asked, his hands were on her, checking her arms and legs and head. "You've got a bump on your head, but it's not bleeding. You didn't lose consciousness."

"My head hurts."

Those beautiful eyes sharpened.

"Not from the fall." She swallowed against the bile rising in her throat. "I woke up with a headache."

Hadley swallowed again. "And lots of nausea."

"You caught what's going around." Through aching eyes, she watched the tension leave his shoulders. "Those are the same symptoms Steve Bloom reported. Vanessa Eden and Izzy Deshler came down with it, too."

"Is she going to be okay?" Brynn's plaintive voice sounded from the doorway.

"She'll be fine," David answered without turning around. "Hadley has that stomach bug that's been making the rounds. We won't be going to the run today."

"You can go." Hadley tried to wave them away. "I don't want to ruin your day. I'll be fine. I'll just…lay here."

"We're not leaving you." David turned to his daughter. "Brynn, she's running a fever. Could you get a washcloth, run some cold water over it, then bring it to me?"

"I'll get it."

"Be sure and wring it out good," he called to her retreating back.

"I'm sorry." Hadley's lips trembled.

He brushed a gentle hand across her forehead. "What do you have to be sorry for?"

Hadley thought of all the lies between them, thought how he was going to feel when he learned she'd been keeping secrets. He would hate her. If she were him, she'd hate her. She couldn't bear it if David hated her. Tears slipped down her cheeks.

"So much," she said. "There's so much."

"It's okay." His voice soothed as much as his hand. "I'm here."

She clutched his hand as if it was a life preserver that could keep her from going under. Though she knew there was no saving her. Not after what she'd done. "Don't leave me."

Hadley told herself to buck up, not to be such a baby. It was what her father the police detective had said to her when she was sick. He'd been a man's man, uncomfortable with tears and emotions. She knew he'd loved her, thought he had, but he never told her.

Justin had known all the right words. He'd quoted poetry, told her she was the most beautiful girl he'd ever seen. He'd been a Prince Charming come to life. *Her* Prince Charming. At first.

"I don't need anyone." Hadley put her hands against David's chest and pushed. "I don't need you."

The lie of it made her want to cry some more. She was tired of all the lies. So very tired. Her throbbing head made her weepy.

"Relax." David gently brushed her hair back from her face.

"Here it is, Daddy." Brynn handed her father the washcloth and knelt beside him. The eyes that searched Hadley's face seemed too large. "Are you going to be okay?"

Hadley mustered a smile. "Absolutely."

David wiped her face with gentle hands, removing the tears and perspiration, cooling the heat.

"It feels so good." The cooling cloth, his strong arms around her gently supporting her. David didn't shower her with pretty words, but he cared. He was showing her he cared.

Every day, by his consideration and kindness, he showed her he cared. "You're a good man."

"I'm glad you think so." His gaze searched her face. "Do you want to go back to bed? This floor can be pretty hard."

"I'd like to sit in a chair." The thought of lying down had her stomach churning.

"Your wish is my command." Getting to his feet, he bent over and scooped her into his arms.

Instead of setting her down in the chair in her sitting area, he strode into the hall. "Where are we going?"

"Somewhere I can keep an eye on you." David didn't stop until they'd reached the living room. He had Brynn move aside a cotton throw, then deposited Hadley into an overstuffed chair, lifting her feet up on the ottoman.

Cool air had her skin turning to gooseflesh. Only then did Hadley realize she wore only a cotton sleep shirt that stopped at midthigh. If David noticed all the bare skin, he gave no indication.

He tucked the throw around her, then stepped back, his gaze sharp and assessing. "How are you feeling?"

Behind him, Brynn looked like a pale, lost ghost.

"Better. Thanks." Hadley summoned a smile. Her gaze settled on Brynn. "That cool washcloth really made a difference."

Hadley was rewarded with a quick smile.

David stepped back. "Now that you're settled, what can we get you?"

"I took four Advil during the night, so I can't have any more of that for a while." Hadley leaned her head against the back of the chair. "I'm fine for now."

"Brynn, there are bowls in the lower cupboard to the left of the dishwasher." David turned to his daughter. "Get the biggest one you can find and bring it, please."

Confusion furrowed Brynn's brow. "Why?"

"Your dad is afraid I might get sick all over his nice furniture."

David shook his head. "Your stomach is upset. You're unsteady on your feet. If you feel like you're going to be sick, I don't want you to try to get up."

Shame washed over Hadley. "I'm sorry."

"We're going to take care of you." His hand on her shoulder was as comforting as a caress. His gaze shifted to his daughter.

"Right away." Brynn hurried from the room.

"I'm going to whip up some breakfast for Brynn."

Hadley lifted a hand before he could ask. "Nothing for me."

He nodded. "Later, maybe, some toast or a banana."

Eventually, Hadley supposed, but right now the thought of eating had bile rising in her throat. "Maybe."

"Here you go, Daddy." Brynn handed him a large Pyrex bowl.

"Perfect size." David placed it beside Hadley on the table next to the chair. "If you need it, it's there."

"Thank you." Her lips began to tremble, then she realized it wasn't just her lips, it was her whole body. She gave a violent shudder. "All of a sudden, I'm freezing."

Brynn grabbed another throw and brought it to her, tucking it around Hadley with awkward movements.

The child's gaze locked with hers. "I don't want you to be sick."

"Me, either. But I heal quickly. Just wait and see."

David smiled at his daughter. "Why don't you get a book? You can sit here and watch over Hadley while I make us breakfast."

"I could read to her?" Brynn's voice turned eager. "That would—"

David had started to shake his head, but Hadley answered before he could.

"I'd like that. As long as you don't mind if I shut my eyes while you read?"

"You can even sleep if you want," Brynn told her. "I don't mind."

Hadley fell asleep to the sound of Brynn reading *The Secret Garden*, a childhood favorite of hers.

When she awoke hours later, the fever was gone and her headache had gone from hurricane force to a minor rainstorm. Even her stomach seemed...stable.

"You're awake."

Very slowly, Hadley turned her head.

David was on the sofa, computer open on his lap.

"Where's Brynn?"

Setting the laptop aside, he searched her face with his sharp-eyed gaze. "First, how are you feeling?"

"Better. I think the fever broke."

He stood then and moved to her side, resting the back of his hand against her forehead. "I believe you're right. How's the stomach?"

The loud growl that answered him had even Ruckus lifting his head to stare.

"That's better, too. In fact, I think I could try some toast." She glanced around. "Where's Brynn?" she asked again.

"She's in her room making you a present."

Hadley's lips lifted in a slow smile. "What kind of present?"

"A secret one. She wouldn't even tell me what it is. But she's been working on it for nearly an hour, so...who knows."

Hadley found she could return his smile without effort. "What were you doing?"

His gaze followed hers to the laptop. "You fell asleep while Brynn was reading. She and I had breakfast, then I settled down to work."

Her heart became a heavy mass in her chest. "And to watch over me."

"And to watch over you," he conceded.

Tears filled her eyes and spilled over.

"Hey." He crouched beside her chair and wiped them away with the pads of his thumbs. "There's no need to cry."

"What's wrong?" Brynn stood in the doorway, a bunch of papers in one hand, a stricken look on her face. "Is she worse?"

"No." Hadley took a breath and brought her emotions under control. "In fact, I feel so good, your father was just about to make me some toast."

Brynn's suspicious gaze shifted to her dad.

"It's true." David gave Hadley's shoulder a squeeze, then straightened. "Her fever is gone, and her stomach growled so loud it woke Ruckus."

Brynn's giggle had everything in Hadley relaxing.

"Would you mind keeping her company while I make the toast?" David started toward the kitchen as if he already knew his daughter's answer.

"I can show her my book." The words spilled from Brynn's lips. "It's my present."

"You wrote a book for me?" Hadley asked Brynn as she dropped down on the arm of the chair.

"It's a book about us." Brynn thrust the papers that had been carefully stapled together into Hadley's hands. "It's called *The Adventures of Hadley and Brynn, Forever Friends.*"

The tears wanted to come again, but Hadley blinked them back and smiled at Brynn. "I can't wait to read it."

Hadley's illness derailed plans to visit the beach on Monday. But Tuesday afternoon found the three of them soaking in the vitamin D. Too late, Hadley realized the only bathing suit she'd packed when she left her apartment was her bikini. The momentary thought of stopping by construction zone central to retrieve her one-piece struck her as ridiculous.

Before the towels were even on the sand, Brynn had shed the clothes she'd worn over her suit and turned toward the water.

"Wait." Hadley reached into the brightly striped beach bag and pulled out the sunscreen. "You need to put this on first."

After casting a longing glance at the water, where her friend Lia splashed, Brynn took the tube from Hadley's hand and slathered on the lotion.

"I'm coming," Brynn called to Lia.

"One more second." Hadley took the sunscreen and applied it to Brynn's back, then gave the child a friendly shove. "Have fun."

Long legs kicking up sand on the way, Brynn joined her friend in the water.

Hadley's heart gave a ping. "She looks so grown-up."

"She's still a child." David gestured to the beach toys. "She insisted I bring these with us."

Hadley lifted a bright orange plastic shovel from the mesh bag. "I like digging in the sand. I especially like building castles."

"I do, too." David gave her a lopsided grin. "I thought that was the architect in me."

"No." Hadley kept her voice matter-of-fact and her gaze averted as she casually peeled off her shirt and stepped out of her shorts. "That's the boy in you."

Her skin heated beneath his assessing gaze. Brynn wasn't the only one yearning for cold water. "I think I'll join Brynn and Lia."

"Not so fast."

The touch of his hand on her arm had her turning.

At her questioning glance, he held up the tube she'd dropped on one of the towels. "Sunscreen?"

She'd made such a big deal with Brynn, she could hardly tell him it wasn't necessary.

"Almost forgot." Hadley shot him a sunny smile, trying not to stare at his broad chest covered with a light dusting of dark hair. The sunscreen went on in record time, and she shifted to head toward the water.

"Not so fast." David stepped close. "Can't forget your back."

Hadley's breath caught as his skilled fingers skimmed across the skin of her upper back before moving lower. She tried to concentrate on the white sand, on the other families who'd come out on this weekday afternoon to enjoy the unusually warm August day.

But the feel of David's fingers on her flesh had her desperately wanting to turn around, wrap her hands around his neck and give him a ferocious kiss.

"All done."

His husky voice reminded her of how he'd sounded the last time she'd been in his arms. When had that been? Too long. Way too long.

When he pressed the tube into her hand and turned, Hadley realized the sweet torture hadn't ended. This time, it was her turn to touch him.

~

"I must be weaker than I think." Hadley's glance drifted toward shore. "Or more out of shape."

"From what I can see, you're in excellent shape." David grinned and continued to tread water.

He and Hadley had spent time playing in the water with Lia and Brynn before swimming farther out. The sun was warm, okay, hot, but the cold water offset the rays.

This was the first time this summer he'd taken Brynn to the beach. What had been so doggone important that he'd denied both of them this simple pleasure until now? Of course, it wouldn't have been nearly so fun without Hadley.

"Let's swim back. Build a sand castle. Chill for a while."

Seeing the fatigue on her face, David cursed himself for his insensitivity.

"Come closer. I'll hold you and you can rest for a few minutes. Then we'll swim back." This was meant to be a kind offer, not a self-serving one. They were, after all, far from shore.

But when Hadley obligingly wrapped her arms and legs around him while he continued to tread water, David was unprepared for the jolt of lust. For the first time, he wished the water was ten degrees colder.

Though his hands were busy with the water, her mouth was incredibly close. He forced his attention to her eyes. Her beautiful blue eyes held flecks of gold, just like Brynn's.

Despite David's resolve, his gaze refused to linger there, dropping instead to her full mouth. He knew how good it felt, how right it felt, to press his lips to hers...

"Thanks for the break." Hadley unfastened her hands and legs and pushed back from him. Color rode high in her cheeks from the sun. "Race you back to shore."

David caught up with her and grabbed her foot just as she reached the sand. Hadley gave a little scream and collapsed as if she could make it no farther. With her lower legs and feet still in the water, she rolled over, her body covered in sand.

Leaning over, David bracketed her upper body between his arms. "I've got you now."

She laughed up at him, blue eyes dancing. "Now that you've got me, what are you going to do with me?"

He knew what he wanted to do, what he'd longed to do since they were interrupted before, but before he could kiss her, Brynn and Lia pounced, laughing like hyenas.

"Play shark with us, too, Daddy. Please?"

Hadley raised a brow. "Shark?"

David grinned when the girls continued to plead. "Duty calls."

With an overly dramatic growl, he dove underwater and went after his prey.

CHAPTER FIFTEEN

"For an architect, you make a pretty good shark." Hadley leaned against the front porch rail.

David blew on his nails, pretended to polish them against his shirtfront. "It's a special talent, honed over numerous trips to the beach."

"The girls sure loved it." While Hadley relaxed in the sun, she'd watched the "shark" go under the water time and time again to grab Brynn's and Lia's legs. "Between that and the sand castle, they had a perfectly lovely afternoon."

"I can't recall the last time I heard Brynn laugh so much." A soft look filled David's eyes. "Seeing her happy means the world to me. With everything she's been through..."

Hadley placed a hand on his arm. "She's resilient. Brynn will be just fine."

His gaze met hers. "Your being here has helped."

Just hearing that, having him say it, had tears pushing against the backs of her lids. Blinking rapidly, she turned away, sliding her hand along the railing. "Do you think if I'd promised her a Monopoly marathon, Brynn would have come home with us?"

"Not a chance."

Hadley whirled. "But she loves board games."

"The puppet theater Lia got for her birthday is set up now. Brynn was dying to see it." David lifted his hands, let them drop. "She likes playing with her friends."

Expelling a resigned breath, Hadley climbed the steps. When she reached the porch, instead of heading directly inside, Hadley turned and rested her back against the rail. "You probably think I'm being ridiculous."

"Not at all." Understanding filled David's eyes. "You're simply going through what I did a couple of years ago. Being home with me and Camille had always been enough for Brynn. All of a sudden, she wanted friends over. Or, like what happened today, those friends' parents invited her over."

"Darn Lia's mother," Hadley muttered, only half joking.

"When I complained, my mother told me to remember it's good for Brynn to play with kids outside of school." David joined her at the rail. "Being reminded these socializing activities are good for her made her absence easier to accept."

"I know you're right." Hadley sighed. "Children learn and grow by being with other kids. As an only child, I spent most of my time with the kids in the neighborhood."

"Me, too."

Her surprise must have shown.

"While I wasn't an only child like you, my sister and brother were a number of years younger, and we didn't have much in common. Of course, that's changed now that we're adults."

"Okay." Hadley expelled a melodramatic sigh. "You've convinced me. I'm not going to ruin what has been a wonderful day by whining."

The smile he shot her sent a flood of warmth rushing through her veins.

"Andrea and Jim are good parents," he assured her. "We can trust them."

We.

It was the first time David had ever referred to the two of them as a unit, at least as far as Brynn was concerned. Though pleasure surged, Hadley told herself it likely was a simple slip of the tongue.

She glanced at the darkening sky. "Is rain in the forecast today?"

"Last I knew it was a twenty percent chance." He stood beside her and studied the clouds. "Weatherman David Chapin says it appears closer to one hundred percent."

Big fat drops splatted on the walkway and the steps to the porch. The rising wind carried the rain to where David and Hadley stood.

"Time to head inside." She backed away from the rail.

"Agreed." David had the door unlocked and open in seconds.

"Just in time." Hadley tried not to shiver as a gust of wind rattled the windows.

They stood for several seconds, watching as the wind did its best to bend the trees. The droplets now fell in sheets.

"How 'bout I rustle us up some food?"

Those intense gray eyes boring into her made rational thought difficult. But he wasn't asking her to strip naked, Hadley reminded herself. He was just offering food and, perhaps, conversation. "Sounds good."

The smile he flashed had her feeling even more off-balance. "I'll start dinner."

They actually started with showers—taken separately—to wash off the sand, then met up in the kitchen.

They made the meal together. Nothing fancy, just thick beer bread and homemade vegetable soup his mother had dropped off yesterday.

At the beach, summer had reigned supreme. Now the rain and drop in temperature made it feel like fall was knocking at the door.

Once they'd finished eating, they moved into the living room with glasses of wine. Hadley dropped down onto the overstuffed sofa facing the cold fireplace.

To her surprise, instead of choosing one of the chairs, David sat on the sofa. Not right beside her. A couple of bodies could have easily fit between them. But something about sharing the piece of furniture felt...intimate. Dismissing the feeling as ridiculous, Hadley angled to face him when he spoke.

"Camille called just as I got out of the shower." David took a long drink of wine.

Inclining her head, Hadley studied him. "What did she want?"

"She feels badly about leaving Brynn so abruptly. She wants to stop over sometime this week and say a proper good-bye."

Hadley gazed at him over the rim of her glass. "What did you say?"

"I told her I'll look at the schedule, call her back tomorrow." He shrugged. "I'll see what we can work out."

"How do you think Brynn will react to her visit?" Hadley's heartbeat quickened. "Camille has been like a mother to her."

David's brows pulled together, and he slowly shook his head. "Brynn is fond of Camille. But saying she's been like a mother is a stretch. Whitney made sure she and Brynn never got too close."

"Was Whitney jealous?"

Hadley took his careless shrug to mean she should draw her own conclusions. They weren't difficult to draw.

Even though Whitney had often been absent, she hadn't wanted her daughter to form a bond with anyone else. Hadley was glad the woman lived out of state, fiercely glad she was no longer a big part of Brynn's life.

"How could she do that to her child?" Condemnation rang heavy in Hadley's voice. "She didn't want Brynn, but she didn't want her to love anyone else."

"It's easy to judge Whitney harshly." David's eyes were hooded now, giving no secrets away. "Things are rarely as black-and-white as they appear. Whitney never objected to my mother and

Greer being a part of Brynn's life. But Camille wasn't family and could leave at any time. Which she did."

How could he be so gracious, Hadley wondered. Or did he still have a thing for his ex? The thought brought a swift stab of pain.

"I suppose." It was the best Hadley could come up with at the moment.

She must not have sounded very convincing, because David's lips twitched.

"Why don't you tell me how you really feel?"

"I don't know what you mean."

The twitch became a full-out grin. "You have a mama bear look in your eyes."

"I don't want to see Brynn hurt." Hadley expelled a ragged breath. "Not more than she already has been."

She started when she felt David's hand cover hers.

"Believe me, I understand. I feel the same."

Hadley met his gaze, and something fluttered in her belly. She remembered the kiss and the desire that had filled her. Getting involved sexually with David would be foolish.

Worse, her actions could end up hurting Brynn.

That was something she was determined not to do.

David saw Hadley's guard go up, even before she slipped her hand away. As disappointment surged, he told himself she was being smart.

He was playing with fire. "With Brynn at Lia's, this is our opportunity to become better acquainted."

Though he and Hadley had spent numerous hours together, much of that time had been in the company of other people. He'd seen how Hadley related to others and his daughter, but there was still so much about her he didn't know.

"I suppose you're right." She gazed up at him, her expression unreadable. "Do you want to talk?"

"Talking is good." David's gaze fell on the deck of cards Kyle had shoved at him the last time he'd seen him. Eliza's new husband had instructed that once he and Hadley used them, David should pass them along to another couple. *Relationship cards* was what Kyle had called them. "These are cards with questions. We could answer a few."

A dimple he hadn't known she possessed flashed in Hadley's left cheek. "I've heard about those cards."

Puzzled, he tilted his head. "What have you heard?"

"They're lethal."

"They're just cards." He flipped the deck over in his hands. "With questions on them."

A blond brow arched. "Have you read any of the questions?"

"Forget the cards. It was just a thought." David started to place the deck back on the end table.

Her hand on his arm stopped him. "From what I understand, you have to answer at least three of the questions before you can pass on the deck."

"Seriously?" He scoffed at the idea of being required to do anything related to a game. "Who says we have to follow the rules?"

"Good point." Hadley's teeth caught her lower lip for a moment before she gave a dismissive wave. "I've been listening too much to Ami's sisters."

"I got these from Kyle," he pointed out.

"One of them must have passed the deck on to him. Or to Eliza."

David sat back in his seat, considered. "If they played along, maybe we should, too."

His gaze settled on Hadley as he left the final decision up to her. "What do you think?"

"Lethal."

"Is that a no?"

Her lips curved. "I've never been one to shy away from a challenge."

There it was again, that tell-it-like-it-is spirit he admired. With Hadley, what you saw was what you got. There would be no surprises.

"How bad could answering three questions be?"

Her blue eyes twinkled. "Exactly."

David found himself looking forward to the game. "If these are as lethal as you say, we'll need another glass of wine."

"We might need a bottle."

As David headed to the kitchen, his steps were light. He didn't care what the Bloom sisters had told Hadley.

This was going to be fun.

Hadley took a sip of her second glass of pinot while David shuffled the cards. He had big hands. Not the kind that would hurt a woman or child, but ones made to soothe. To caress.

God, she hoped these questions didn't deal with sex. She was already having difficulty keeping her mind off of David's mouth. She kept imagining the pleasure his lips could give. Not only when melded against hers, but when pressed against other parts of her body.

Heat traveled up her neck.

"Cut?"

She blinked. "What?"

He grinned and held out the cards. "Do you want to cut the deck?"

Not trusting her voice, she gave her head a shake.

"How do you want to play this?"

She cleared her throat. "What do you mean?"

"Should we each answer the same question? Or only answer

the one we draw?"

There was no right or wrong answer. "It seems to me we should answer the same questions."

"We'll draw three."

"And we'll take turns going first," Hadley added.

He cocked his head, frowned. "That means one of us will go first twice."

"With an odd number of questions, there's no way around it," she pointed out.

"We could do four."

"Let's see how we feel after we get through three." She studied him for a moment, then smiled. "We'll do rock, paper, scissors. The loser goes first twice."

David hesitated. "Doesn't it seem rather juvenile to decide the rotation based on that?"

"Maybe I'm a kid at heart." Her teasing had a smile blossoming on his lips. "We need to make this fun."

She had the feeling it was past time David had fun.

Hadley won the rock, paper, scissors challenge. It was obvious David didn't play that game often. Rookie male players usually went with rock. That's why she'd chosen paper.

"Appears I'm on the hot seat." A smile hovered at the corners of David's lips. "But your turn is coming."

Hadley simply smiled, filing away the knowledge that David wasn't a sore loser.

He surprised her by taking a card from the top of the deck, instead of delving into the center. He flipped the card over, read it, scowled. "This is unfair."

Puzzled, Hadley leaned over, bringing her dangerously close to him. She didn't recognize his cologne. Whatever it was, she liked it. The fresh citrus scent did strange things to her insides.

She forced herself to read the question. When you were growing up, did you have any favorite family traditions? Do you have any now?

Hadley met his gaze. "What's wrong? The questions seem

fairly straightforward."

David pointed to the card. "What's wrong is there are two of them."

"You picked it." She leaned back. If she didn't put distance between them, she might kiss him. God, he smelled good. "I'm sure your family has plenty of traditions."

As if realizing this was a battle he couldn't hope to win, David took a contemplative sip of wine.

It should have been a simple matter for him to pop off an answer. Easy, because she'd meant what she said about his family having lots of traditions. Instead, he took his time and considered his choices.

So methodical. So cautious.

"Probably my favorite tradition, and you're right about there being many in the Chapin household, occurred on Christmas morning." His lips curved, and the warmth of remembrance filled his eyes. "Long after we quit believing in Santa Claus, we'd hurry downstairs to open gifts. Hot chocolate with whipped cream and slivers of candy canes would be waiting. A ring of kringle, fresh from the oven, filled the air with the scent of cinnamon, vanilla and yeast."

After recently visiting his family home, Hadley had little difficulty seeing it. The scene he described sounded like something straight out of a Hallmark movie. A flood of longing gripped her.

She cleared her throat. "Please tell me you've kept up that tradition for Brynn."

That type of heartwarming holiday scene was something Hadley had always wanted for herself, something she'd wanted for her children.

David hesitated. "The cocoa comes out of the microwave, and the kringle comes from Ami's shop rather than fresh from the oven, but yes, I've kept those traditions for Brynn."

"I bake kringle for Blooms Bake Shop." Hadley couldn't keep the wonder from her voice.

"You've been a part of Brynn's Christmas and you didn't even know it." He touched her arm. "Your turn."

She blinked.

He flashed a smile. "Your turn to answer."

Hadley shifted. Instead of letting herself get caught up in *his* traditions, she should have been searching for one of her own.

"My father usually worked holidays." She kept her tone matter-of-fact. "Extra money was always needed."

David didn't bother to hide his surprise. Or his disapproval. "Even Christmas?"

She lifted one shoulder and let it drop. "The year my mom left, it was shortly before the holidays. The November through New Year's Day time period was difficult for him."

Opening his mouth as if to argue the point, David shut it without speaking.

"If we're talking traditions, I'll go with the first day of school." Hadley smiled. "My dad would stay up—he worked nights—and we'd go to a diner close to our apartment and have breakfast. Then he'd drop me off at school."

"Any special things you'd eat?" David prompted.

She shook her head. "Not for me, anyway. It was just nice to sit at a table with him and talk."

"Didn't you do that every night?"

Hadley gave a little laugh. "We mostly ate at the counter or in front of the television."

Though David kept his face impassive, disapproval radiated off him in waves.

"It might not have been ideal, but Dad did his best." She lifted her chin. "But I think that's why I enjoy making a meal and sitting down to eat it."

"It's a two-part question."

"Kringle. For years, I've baked it on Christmas morning." Hadley saw no reason to add that she enjoyed that particular tradition alone. "Next."

Once again, David picked the top card.

"You know you don't always have to pick from the top. There are a bunch of other ones in the middle."

Her teasing tone didn't appear to faze him. He flipped over the card, then exhaled a heavy breath.

Hadley smiled at his pained expression. "C'mon, it can't be that bad."

When he didn't respond, she lifted the card from his fingers. *Do you blame yourself when a relationship fails?*

She glanced up at David, her eyes meeting his. "This is pretty heavy. We can skip it. Just draw another."

"No." He gulped down the rest of the wine in his glass. "I drew it. I'll answer it."

Which meant he likely wouldn't be handing out passes when it was her turn to answer.

"First, I need to clarify that I haven't been involved in many 'relationships.' I dated in high school, but no one seriously. That was true for my first couple years in college. Then I met Whitney. She was my first serious relationship." His eyes grew shuttered. "A relationship that led to marriage, then ended in divorce."

Why did it seem worse, Hadley wondered, that Whitney had obviously been his first love? Out of all the girls in high school and women in college he'd date, Whitney had been the one he'd fallen in love with and married.

Hadley remained silent.

After what seemed an eternity, David continued. "Do I blame myself for our marriage failing? I take responsibility for bringing Whitney to Good Hope. I brought her here, even though deep down I wondered if small-town life would be a good fit."

"Did you force her to move here?" The question seemed to come from far away, even though Hadley knew it had originated from her own lips.

"Of course not. I'd never do that." David set down his empty wineglass and raked a hand through his hair. "Whitney was excited about building a new house. But—"

"But..." she pressed when he didn't continue.

"She quickly lost interest." Though David tried to hide the emotion, hurt deepened his dove-gray eyes to slate. "I tried to involve her in the house plans. I wanted her involved, but she told me she trusted my decisions. That should have been a red flag. She didn't care enough to provide input."

He pushed to his feet and strode to the window. "Perhaps if we'd stayed in Chicago, we might still be married."

"At what cost?"

He whirled, his gaze piercing.

Hadley slowly got to her feet. "At what cost to you and Brynn? I don't presume to be an expert on your marriage. From the little I observed, Whitney didn't want to be married and she certainly wasn't interested in Brynn."

"You don't know—"

"I saw enough." Hadley refused to let him play the martyr. "She checked out of your marriage long before she left you."

"These cards are a lot of fun."

His dry tone had her nearly smiling, until he gestured with his head toward the question on the card.

Only then did Hadley realize he was telling her he'd answered and it was now her turn.

"Do *you* blame yourself when a relationship fails?" His assessing gaze never left her face.

"Yes." Hadley spoke without thinking, which was never a good thing. "But not in the way you think."

He returned to the sofa, and she dropped down beside him.

"I blame myself for getting into a bad situation in the first place. For failing to see what was right in front of me." A bitterness filled her tone that she couldn't suppress. "I pride myself on being a smart, savvy woman, yet I make huge errors in judgment."

David's expression sharpened, those gray eyes like finely honed swords. Instead of speaking, he simply nodded and waited for her to continue.

Hadley clasped her hands together in her lap and did her best to focus on the question. "I won't take the blame when the other party is clearly a screw-up, but I will take responsibility for not heeding warning signs flashing in yellow neon."

"Someone hurt you." The softly spoken words and concerned expression were bad enough. When David reached over and covered her hands with his, Hadley wanted to weep.

Calling on her inner strength, she managed a shrug.

"You loved him."

"What?" Hadley shook her head. "No. No. No. I never loved him."

The vehemence in her tone had David's eyes widening.

With great effort, Hadley brought herself under control. If she didn't, this discussion could lead to revelations she wasn't prepared to make. "Let's leave it that I take the blame for not seeing what was right in front of my eyes."

"What did—?"

"My turn to draw." Hadley cut him off, ready to move on. More than ready to push all thoughts of Justin Mapes from her mind.

David held the cards she attempted to grab. "Technically, I've only drawn two cards." He tried to hide an emerging grin. "Who knew you were so eager to answer?"

"Yes, but as you pointed out, the first card had two questions. Give me those cards." Her brusque order only caused his smile to widen. After a second, he handed her the deck.

She shuffled.

He declined to cut.

Hadley picked a card from deep in the deck and read the question.

"Is it another twofer?" David studied her with an intensity

that had her squirming.

"Nope." She kept her voice offhand. "Just one. An easy question."

"That doesn't seem fair."

"Who ever said life was fair?" She'd meant the words to be teasing, lighthearted even. She was halfway through uttering them when an image of Justin flashed before her.

"Hadley?"

Something in the way David said her name, something about the way it rolled off his tongue, had her relaxing.

She held the card high and read aloud, a freshly filled glass of wine in the other hand. "Are you into public displays of affection?"

"That's the question? That one doesn't even require any thought."

"Don't blame me for drawing an easy one." She waved an airy hand. "You're the one who kept picking the top card instead of going for the middle."

"Since you consider it easy, you must have an answer."

"I don't mind displays of affection as long as they're tasteful. Holding hands, an arm around the shoulders, even a kiss now and then, those are okay with me." Hadley remembered how good it felt when David touched her. Then she thought of Justin, and her blood went to ice. "When it's someone you like."

His gaze searched hers. "Are you saying you don't mind when I take your hand?"

"I'm saying I like it when you touch me."

The bold declaration surprised them both. Heat flashed like a lightning bolt in David's smoky gray depths. "That goes for me, too."

Hadley resisted the urge to fan herself. "It appears mutual attraction has been confirmed."

David took her hand and brought her fingers to his lips. "The question now is, what are we going to do about it?"

CHAPTER SIXTEEN

Hadley gazed into David's soft, gray eyes and realized she couldn't let this go any further without being honest with him. When she'd moved into his house, she hadn't expected to fall in love with him. But, she realized now, that's what had happened.

She took a second to let the wonder of it sink in. After Justin, she'd worried she'd never be able to fully trust any man. She trusted David. Though she didn't know how he would react to her news, it wouldn't be with violence.

"Before we move forward on this, ah, attraction..." Hadley swallowed in an attempt to bring moisture to her suddenly parched throat. "There is something I need to tell you."

Puzzlement filled his eyes. "You look so serious."

"It's difficult to say." She removed her hand from his and reached down to stroke the top of Ruckus's head. Her next words might squash David's budding attraction, but she had to be honest with him. Hadley steeled her resolve. "I'm not even sure where to start."

Something in her eyes must have put him on alert. He straightened, his gaze searching her face for the answer. "It's usually best to start at the beginning."

Where was the beginning? Was it rooted in childhood? In a father who showed love by actions, rather than pretty words? Or did it go back even further? Back to when her mother left and a little girl worried she hadn't tried hard enough to make her mother happy?

Hadley reined in her thoughts. There was no point in going back that far. This news was like a Band-Aid that needed to be ripped off in one pull. "I'm Brynn's birth mother."

Startled shock, followed by disbelief, widened his eyes. "What did you say?"

Hadley repeated the words, stumbling a little over them this time.

"You can't be." Even as he said it, David knew it was possible. The attorney hadn't given them the name of the woman who'd given birth to Brynn, but the age was right.

Still, she could be lying. He didn't possess the information needed to corroborate Hadley's claims. He and Whitney had received only the basics—age, personal and family medical history and education. Though open adoptions were common, Brynn's birth mother—she'd barely reached the age of majority at eighteen—had preferred a closed adoption. That had suited them, as Whitney had been concerned about the demands the birth mother might place on them, worried the woman might one day show up and want her baby back.

A bolt of ice shot down David's spine. "Start at the beginning."

Hadley flinched at his sharp tone, her fingers tightening around the hair at Ruckus's neck. When the animal looked up at her with pleading brown eyes, she released her hold.

David listened as she recounted the name of the Chicago attorney they'd dealt with and the particulars of Brynn's birth at Rush-Presbyterian. "Tell me about the father."

This was the part that had initially concerned David. According to the attorney, the birth mother insisted she'd gotten pregnant as the result of a one-night stand with a man whose name she didn't know and had no way to contact.

As birth fathers had rights, it had been a loose thread, but one, according to the attorney, impossible to immediately tie off. They'd taken Brynn home from the hospital, and once thirty days had passed, the attorney had checked the Illinois Putative Father Registry. As the birth father hadn't registered, his parental rights were terminated. The night they got the news, he and Whitney had opened a bottle of champagne.

Hadley tilted her head, hesitated for only a second. "I don't...I don't know who he was. It was a one-night thing. I never even got his name."

Her voice may have gone up a full octave, but her gaze remained steady on his face. "I was young and stupid. Very stupid."

Hadley covered her mouth with her hand, let out a shaky breath, then repeated, "I don't know his name."

She was lying. She definitely knew more than she was telling. But did he really want to go down that path? Though he'd always believed Brynn deserved information about her birth parents, this was a sticky area.

What if Hadley was in contact with Brynn's birth father? Could that be the reason she'd decided to make this claim now?

David lifted a brow, forced casual into his tone. "Surely, he gave you his first name."

Her gaze darted to one side then back to him. For a second, David thought she was going to tell him. Instead, she shook her head. "I think it was a fake name."

"What made you believe it was fake?"

Irritation skittered across her pretty face. "It was a long time ago. What does it matter now?"

"He could come back." His tone was flat and hard. "He could want to get to know his child."

Hadley bit her lip. "You don't have to worry about him."

"How can you be so certain?"

"He never knew I was pregnant." This time, she looked him straight in the eyes. "He doesn't know Brynn exists."

There was a certainty in the statement that he found both reassuring and puzzling. But pushing on this particular issue wasn't going to get him anywhere. And he had much more pressing questions. "You came to Good Hope because of my daughter."

David wasn't certain what he expected her to say. Perhaps lie and say it was a fluke.

"I did."

She rose. Ruckus lifted his head from his paws and, like David, watched her move to the mantel.

"Why now?"

The question hung in the air for several heartbeats. There were many others pushing against David's lips, but with great effort, he held them back. His patience was razor thin by the time she finally spoke, her voice so soft he had to strain to hear.

"My father died. I-I felt alone in the world. I started to worry about my chi—" Hadley stopped herself, took a breath, then continued. "About Brynn. It was probably part of the grieving process, but I needed to know she was okay."

David never took his eyes off her. "You could have asked the attorney for a status update."

She brought a fist to her chest, her tone fierce. "I needed to see for myself."

"How did you find us?" If Jerome had given her information, David would have the attorney's license.

"I used my father's life insurance money to pay a private detective." Her fingers clasped and unclasped. "It took him a long time. I'm not certain everything he did was legal but he got results. Even after I had the information, I didn't immediately act on it."

"Why not?" The blood rushing through his veins burned like acid.

"I made a promise when I signed the adoption papers."

The lost look in her blue eyes tugged at his heartstrings, but he shut off the emotion. David thought back to when Hadley first arrived. "A week, maybe two, was all it should have taken for you to determine Brynn is in a loving home. Why did you stay?"

"I want my daughter to have a mother and father who love her." Hadley's gaze turned to the window, where rain splashed against the glass. "My mother left when I was young. My dad did his best, but I missed not having a mom. I wanted more for my child."

There it was again, David thought, that quick pinch of guilt when he thought of the pain the divorce had brought to Brynn's life. "When you moved here, Whitney and I were still together."

Abruptly, Hadley returned to the sofa and sat. "You and Whitney might have lived under the same roof, but you weren't together. She'd already checked out of the marriage."

David started to deny it, but couldn't. "I've done everything I can to give Brynn a happy, secure childhood. I will always be here for her."

"I believe you."

Frankly, he didn't care what she believed. It was her on the hot seat, not him. Unable to sit, even for one second longer, David sprang up and began to pace.

"I-I told myself seeing her from a distance would be enough." Hadley's gaze dropped to the tightly clenched fingers in her lap before rising back to his face. "I remember the first time you came into the bakery. I was able to talk with her. That was more than I ever dreamed. That should have been enough."

"Obviously, it wasn't." Despite the fear, David managed to keep his tone even.

"When Whitney left, it tore a hole in Brynn's heart. I saw it.

Though they occasionally communicate via text, your ex-wife is as lost to Brynn as my mother was to me." When Hadley pinned cool blue eyes on him, David felt the slap of her disapproval. "And if Whitney gets sick from this 'genetic condition' and dies, Brynn will grieve her loss all over again. Why? Because you and Whitney lied."

"I told you I didn't realize Whitney had—"

"But she did lie. You found out about it and did nothing, which makes you complicit." Hadley was as fierce and protective as a mother bear. "That's the past. Let's talk about now. Brynn needs a mother to be there for her during all the ups and downs she'll face as she grows. She needs me in her life."

"I didn't realize Whitney had omitted part of her family's medical history from the application until the adoption was a done deal. For that, I apologize." David's tone remained cool. "But Brynn is my daughter. If what you say is true, you gave up your rights to her when you signed the adoption papers. Why now?"

She blinked. "I-I don't understand the question."

"Why are you telling me all this now?"

She swallowed convulsively, then cleared her throat. "Unless I misread the signs, we were on the verge of making love. I couldn't allow our relationship to go any further without telling you the truth."

"A relationship that has a web of lies as its foundation is no relationship at all." Bile climbed up his throat, burning with each step. "You used me to get close to her."

She shook her head vigorously, and her hands rose, palms out.

"I didn't use you, David. You came to me, asked me if I wanted a job. Our relationship felt real, *was* real. I genuinely care for you. In fact, I've fallen in love with you."

He waved the admission away. Right now, he wasn't sure where the truth ended and fiction began.

"You've laid a lot on me." He chose his words carefully, feeling as if he was negotiating a minefield while the world spun around him. "I need to think about what you've said, what you want, and decide where we go from here."

Hadley gave a jerky nod. "Okay. Fine."

"You'll give me a DNA sample. You won't say anything about this to Brynn. Not yet." His gaze searched her face. "If, when, we do tell her, it will be after careful thought."

"I'll be happy to provide a DNA sample, but why would I lie about a fact that can be so easily proven?"

A valid point, David acknowledged as he rose and gestured to the door, signaling the conversation was over. Then he remembered she lived here.

Damn it all to hell.

"If you prefer, I can get a room at the motel in town"—Hadley pushed to her feet—"while you consider how you want to handle this."

David raked a hand through his hair. All he knew was he wanted her gone. Out the door. Out of his sight. But what would Brynn think when she came home in the morning and Hadley wasn't here?

Still, he needed to strategize, and he couldn't think with those blue eyes watching him. "I believe that would be bes—"

The unexpected ringing of his cell had him jerking. He pulled it from his pocket, prepared to silence it when he saw it was Lia's dad.

Taking a steadying breath, he answered. "Hey, Jim. Everything okay with the girls?"

"Brynn is complaining her stomach hurts. Andrea took her temperature, and it's 100.7. Not high, but—"

"I'll be right there."

"That's probably best. When you don't feel well, there's nothing like your own bed."

"I'm leaving now." David disconnected the call and met Hadley's worried gaze. "Brynn isn't feeling well. It sounds like she caught what you had. I'm picking her up, bringing her home."

Grabbing his keys from the side table, he headed for the door without another word. He hoped Hadley would be gone when he returned.

He'd worry later about what to tell Brynn.

∼

David thought he'd made it very clear that Hadley should be gone when he returned. But twenty minutes later, she opened the door when he approached with Brynn in his arms.

Once they were inside, she stepped close, smelling of vanilla and sweetness.

"I've got your bed ready." Hadley brushed a tendril of hair back from Brynn's pale face. "Unless you'd prefer to sit up in the chair for a little bit?"

"I don't want to go to bed. I want to be here with you and Daddy."

For the first time since he'd returned with Brynn, Hadley looked directly at him. She gestured with one hand toward the overstuffed chair that had been her resting spot when she'd been ill.

With great care, David set his daughter down and kept a tight leash on his emotions.

He'd expected Hadley to be gone. Packed up and moved out. Okay, not entirely accurate. Because he knew the depth of her feelings for Brynn, he'd worried she'd still be here.

"Daddy said you might be gone when we got home. That you might be visiting a friend." Brynn's bottom lip trembled, and her eyes swam with tears. "I wanted him to call you to tell you to come home because I needed you."

"Oh, baby," Hadley kissed Brynn's cheek, slanted him a glance. "I'm right here. Don't you worry, I'm not going anywhere."

∼

David slammed the box of chicken noodle soup—Brynn's favorite—into the cart. Though his daughter had insisted she didn't want anything to eat but soda crackers, Hadley had mentioned that perhaps later she might want some soup.

When Brynn agreed, he decided a quick trip to the grocery store was in order.

He was letting Hadley stay for Brynn's sake, he told himself. Just for a few days, until his daughter was better. Brynn had sobbed on the drive home when he'd mentioned Hadley might not be there. He couldn't ask Hadley to leave now.

On the way to the store, David had left a message for the attorney who'd handled the adoption. Before he discussed anything with Hadley, he needed a clear understanding of his rights. It seemed to him she wouldn't have any legal claim to Brynn, but this was too important not to be one hundred percent certain.

That was also why he'd ordered a DNA test kit before he stepped out of his car.

A sense of betrayal hung like a sodden coat around his shoulders. He liked Hadley. She was smart and funny and kind. She'd said she was falling in love with him, but how could he believe anything she said now?

He glanced at the list she'd given him. Papayas. The bananas, David could understand. His mother swore by them. *Mother.*

David whipped the cart around the corner with vicious speed, and metal struck metal.

"Whoa, cowboy." Dan's smile widened when he saw it was David on the other side of the cart. "I'd say you were definitely driving over the limit."

"Sorry 'bout that." David forced a smile. "Brynn's not feeling well, and Hadley sent me to the store—"

He stopped himself. Hadley hadn't sent him anywhere. He'd chosen to come to the grocery store and pick up a few essentials.

She didn't tell him what to do. He was the one with the power, and she best not forget it.

"I'm sorry to hear Brynn is ill." Dan moved his cart to the side, though David wasn't sure why. Other than a couple clerks at the registers, he swore he and Dan were the only ones in the store. "Is it the stomach virus?"

David nodded.

"I'll keep her in my prayers."

"Thank you." Now that they'd exhausted the small talk, David was eager to move on and be alone with his thoughts.

"I didn't realize rain was in the forecast for today."

The weather. His world had imploded and the minister wanted to discuss barometric pressure fluctuations?

David tamped down the irritation. How he was feeling had nothing to do with the pastor. Besides, it wasn't as if he wanted to discuss the bombshell Hadley had laid on him today. "I like rain."

"When I'm inside and dry, I like it just fine, too." Dan studied him. "I do some of my best thinking when it's storming outside."

That was the difference between him and Dan. Right now, David couldn't seem to marshal his thoughts into a logical pattern. At least he'd had enough sense to call the attorney. Order the DNA kit.

"Is that what you were doing when I rammed my cart into yours?" David kept his tone light. "Thinking?"

Dan waved aside the question. "I can see something is troubling you. Is there anything I can do to help?"

The minister had asked him the same question last year when Whitney had told him she wanted a divorce. David had been stunned by his wife's request, though he shouldn't have been surprised.

Their last year together, Whitney had been gone more than she'd been home. The demons driving her wouldn't let her rest.

Not for long. He'd mistakenly assumed that was all that her frequent trips meant.

"It's something I have to work out for myself." Once the words left his mouth, David realized it was nearly word for word the response he'd given last year.

Just like then, Dan smiled, though concern clouded his eyes. "If you need to talk, I'm here for you. Day or night."

Rumor was the day-or-night availability had been what had pulled Dan and his fiancée apart. Lindsay hadn't been able to handle that a minister's time wasn't his own.

David assumed there had been more going on behind the scenes. It had been that way with Whitney. Most people in town believed her to be a spoiled, selfish woman interested only in her own pleasures. Though David no longer loved her, he cared about her. More important, he understood what drove her.

The silence lengthened.

"I appreciate the offer." David pulled his cart back and to the side, giving Dan room to pass. "And the prayers for Brynn."

Dan studied him for a long moment. "Speak with someone you trust about what's on your mind. Often, when thoughts get jumbled in our head, all it takes to achieve clarity is voicing them to a friend."

CHAPTER SEVENTEEN

David strolled into the YMCA the next morning. He wasn't here to have some heart-to-heart with his brother. No matter what the preacher said, that wasn't how he and Clay rolled. He simply needed to work off the stress of having Hadley still under his roof.

That was where she was right now, baking in his kitchen while his daughter slept. Regardless of how he felt about Hadley, he could count on her to take good care of Brynn.

With quick, efficient movements, David changed into the workout clothes he kept in his locker, then joined Clay and several other men he recognized as teachers on the court.

He caught his brother staring a couple of times when he drove in hard for a lay-up, or stole the ball from someone who wasn't paying close enough attention.

By the time the pickup game ended, he had to wipe the perspiration from his face with a towel. The rapid beat of his heart began to slow as they left the court and headed for the showers.

David felt more like himself. Calm and in control. He still didn't know what to do about Hadley, but eventually he'd make a logical, rational decision based on what would be best for his daughter.

Their daughter. *If*, and that was a mighty big *if*, what Hadley had told him was the truth. He'd know about that soon enough. The DNA kits should arrive later today.

Lost in his thoughts, David showered and dressed, leaving the sweat-soaked clothes in the private locker where they would be freshly laundered by staff.

Out of the corner of his eye, he saw Clay walk up, hair damp and sticking up on one side. His brother dropped his gym bag on the floor. "You were on fire, bro. I believe that was a record number of three-pointers."

David shrugged. "Sometimes you're hot."

"And lucky."

David's smile vanished as he thought of Hadley. "I don't feel lucky."

"Where are the girls?"

After pulling his keys from his pocket, David inclined his head.

"Hadley and Brynn. You know, daughter and girlfriend."

"Hadley isn't my girlfriend." David tried for casual, but the words came out stiff and unyielding.

"Ah." A smile lifted Clay's lips, and a knowing glint filled his eyes. "You had your first fight. It was inevitable. What did you do to piss her off?"

"I wasn't the one who lied." David spat the words. "She isn't who I thought she was."

The comment garnered his brother's full attention.

David cursed. With a couple of thoughtless comments, he'd piqued Clay's insatiable curiosity. The last thing he wanted to talk about was his issues with Hadley.

Which was why it made no sense to walk out of the building with his brother to the parking lot. Or why, instead of continuing on to his car, he paused by Clay's Land Rover. "Thanks for letting me join the game."

Clay put a hand on the side of his vehicle. "Tell me what's going on with you and Hadley."

David had opened his mouth, not certain of the exact words he would use to put his brother off, when his cell rang. Ready to let it go to voice mail, he remembered Brynn. Sick. At home.

He held up a finger and jerked the phone from his pocket. His breath caught at the name on the display.

Clay was listening, of course he was listening, but right now David didn't care. "Jerome, appreciate you getting back to me so quickly."

His fingers tightened around his phone as Jerome reassured him Brynn's adoption records remained sealed. "I need to know if Hadley Newhouse is the birth mother. You met with her. You arranged all this. Just tell me yes or no."

David huffed out a frustrated breath as the attorney went into a spiel about confidentiality. He listened until he couldn't take it anymore. "I already ordered a blasted DNA kit. Is that my only option?"

More legalese.

"One last question, and I'll let you go. Does she have any legal right to my daughter?" Everything in David relaxed at the assurance that the birth mother—Jerome carefully avoided using her name—had given up all rights to Brynn when she'd signed the adoption papers nine years ago. "Thanks. If I come up with more questions, I'll be in touch."

David clicked off, shoved the phone back into his pocket and faced his brother.

The expression on Clay's face had changed from one of curiosity to watchful waiting.

"Now you know. Hadley is claiming to be Brynn's birth mother."

"You're talking to your attorney about all sorts of legal stuff, yet she's the one watching Brynn while you're here."

Though said as a statement, a question lurked beneath the surface.

"Brynn is sick. She came down with the same stomach bug that had Hadley down for the count this past weekend."

"Even more interesting." Clay's eyes remained focused on David. "You left your sick child with her."

"She would never hurt Brynn." Of that, David was one hundred percent certain. "She loves her."

Not *likes*, David realized. *Loves*. He'd told himself he was lucky to have a nanny who liked Brynn, who cared about Brynn. *Like* and *care* were too weak to describe the emotion that swirled in Hadley's eyes whenever she looked at his daughter.

Loved. Hadley loved Brynn. And if he wasn't mistaken, Brynn loved her back.

Which made for a helluva mess.

David closed his eyes for a second as emotion surged.

His brother's hand settled on his shoulder. "Are you afraid she'll try to take Brynn away from you?"

"No. But she wants to be a part of her life."

"Would that be so bad?"

At David's incredulous look, Clay shrugged. "I mean, it's not like Whitney would care. It's obvious Brynn likes Hadley."

"She lied to me, Clay."

"Let me get this straight. The fact she's Brynn's mother doesn't bother you, it's that she lied to you?"

David scrubbed his hands over his face, as if that would somehow clear his muddled brain. "I don't know. At this point, I just don't know."

"If it were me, I'd be happy."

Whatever David had expected his brother to say, it wasn't this. "Are you crazy?"

"Think about it." Clay rested his back against the side of his vehicle, ignoring the wet sheen on the glossy black paint. "You had to be wondering if you'd ever find a woman who could love not only you, but your daughter. Hey, you've found her."

"She lied to me," David repeated, with less surety.

"How did you find out?"

"What?"

"How did you find out she's Brynn's birth mother?"

"I don't know that for certain," David began, but Clay waved that argument aside with an impatient slice of the hand. "Okay. She told me."

"Why now?"

Had his brother asked, or had the question simply been circling so long in David's head it had had to come out?

"Things between us were heating up." David pulled his brows together. "She said she didn't want things to go any further without—"

"Coming clean."

David slowly nodded.

Clay clapped him on the shoulder as huge rain droplets splatted at their feet. "An admirable thing to do, but that's my opinion. I'd vote for giving her a chance. What do you have to lose?"

Sliding into his car, Clay shut the door and drove away as thunder boomed and rain began to fall in earnest.

"My heart," David muttered to himself as he hurried across the parking lot to his vehicle. "That's what I have to lose."

Hadley glanced at the clock on Ami's kitchen wall. Now that Brynn was back to her perky self, Hadley had decided to do her baking at Ami's house. While David had yet to order her out of his home, things had been strained between them the past couple of days.

Brynn hadn't appeared to notice—yet—and Hadley didn't want her to worry. Giving David space seemed wise. As had agreeing to do a DNA test. Her sample, and she assumed one from Brynn, were already on their way to a lab for expedited processing.

He was only being cautious, she told herself. Though she had to admit his lack of trust stung just a little. Which was ridiculous, considering she'd lied to him about her identity for years.

Sighing, she started wiping down Ami's kitchen counters, her last task before heading home. Karin had picked up the last of the bakery boxes only minutes earlier.

The doorbell rang, then rang again.

Only then did Hadley remember she was alone in the house. She hurried to the door.

Flashing a bright smile, Prim stepped into the foyer. Hadley waited for the twins to race each other through the door. But today, there were no redheaded boys and no pounding footsteps, only Prim and her baby.

Hadley liked Prim. She admired her strength. When her first husband had died, leaving her a widow at twenty-six with twin toddlers, Prim didn't buckle. She stayed strong and made a new life for her and her sons, eventually moving back to Good Hope.

"I'm afraid Ami and Beck aren't here." Hadley lowered her voice in deference to the infant with wisps of strawberry-blond hair sleeping peacefully against Prim's chest.

"You don't need to whisper. Addie is used to her brothers' loud voices. This girl can sleep through anything." With gentle fingers, Prim brushed the top of her daughter's head.

A text tone from the depths of Prim's massive bag had the baby's eyes springing open.

Hadley lifted a brow. *"Who Let the Dogs Out?"*

"A brief error in judgment. I let the boys pick it." Prim gave her daughter's back a few soothing strokes and murmured something. Whatever she said must have worked, because Addie's eyes closed.

Slipping her hand into the bag, Prim rummaged around for an extra chorus before pulling out the phone. She glanced at the screen.

"Everything okay?"

"Max and the boys are putting up the rock-climbing wall in the town square." Prim dropped the phone back into the bag. "He'll text me again when they're ready for lunch. Apparently, the food trucks are set up and ready to go."

Since Ami's house was located near the business district, Hadley had noticed the fully equipped vehicles encircling the town square. There were hot dog trucks and ones specializing in grilled-cheese sandwiches. There was even a vegetarian truck serving a particular favorite: rosemary fries.

"Your sister left an hour ago for the café." Hadley hesitated as Prim shifted the baby in her arms. "I don't expect her back."

"That's okay." Prim waved a dismissive hand. "I just need a quiet and cool place to sit for a few minutes."

"Well, you've come to the right place. I'll be out of your way in five minutes."

A startled look of surprise skittered across Prim's freckled face. Then she smiled. "I didn't mean you. Actually, I'd love some adult conversation."

The warmth of Prim's words wrapped around Hadley like a favorite sweater. When she'd arrived in Good Hope, Hadley had tried to keep from forming any attachments.

Ami would have none of it. At the time, none of the other Bloom sisters lived in Good Hope, and Hadley had become a surrogate sister. Then, one by one, the others had returned. Instead of having one good friend, Hadley found herself with four.

While chatting with Prim, Hadley fixed a pot of herbal tea and carried it to the living room. Moments later, she returned with two pretty china cups and a plate of cherry shortbread cookies.

Prim took a bite of cookie and shut her eyes. "These are absolutely fabulous."

"They're a relatively new offering and very popular." Hadley didn't say the recipe was hers, or that she was the one who'd suggested Ami give them a try.

Prim gestured with one hand toward the floral plate. "You have to help me eat these."

Hadley reached for a cookie, but couldn't stop her gaze from drifting in Adelyn's direction. "You're lucky. You have a loving husband, three wonderful kids and a flexible career you enjoy."

Like her husband, Prim was an accountant who did much of her work from home.

Prim studied her for a long moment. "There was a time, after Rory died, I thought I'd never be happy again. I certainly never expected to marry or have more children."

"Then you met Max."

The woman's hazel eyes softened, and her lips curved. "I'd known Max my whole life. But we reconnected when I moved back to Good Hope."

"Meant to be," Hadley murmured and crunched on the shortbread.

"I think so, but"—Prim's gaze turned thoughtful—"we came so close to letting it all slip away."

"You did?" Hadley remembered when Prim and Max had started dating. They'd been neighbors and co-chairs of the Independence Day parade. "From the outside, it looked like smooth sailing."

Prim's gaze settled on Hadley. "Most of us bring some sort of baggage into a relationship. Being honest about your fears, not only with yourself, but with your partner, can be difficult."

Prim stared expectantly, and a chill traveled down Hadley's

spine. She shifted uneasily in her seat. Hadley had agreed to cookies and tea. She hadn't agreed to bare her soul.

When the silence lengthened, Prim cocked her head. "How's it going with David?"

Hadley waved an airy hand. "It's not serious."

"Do you want it to be?"

Hadley could see why Prim was such an effective parent. When her firm gaze landed on you, you couldn't lie.

Not to her. Not to yourself.

Hadley had done a lot of soul-searching the past couple of days. She'd looked hard at her feelings for David. The fact that he was a good father added to her admiration. But she didn't love him because he was Brynn's father, she loved him for who he was as a man.

The kind of man who hadn't kicked her out of his house when he found out she'd lied, because that would have traumatized his daughter. The kind of man who didn't scream or call her names or hit. The kind of man who remained civil and courteous under extreme duress.

This was the man she'd fallen in love with, and she wanted, oh, she wanted so very much, to be a part of his life.

"Hadley?" Prim prompted. "Are you in love with David Chapin?"

"Yes." Hadley met her gaze. "But I don't think he feels the same."

Not anymore.

CHAPTER EIGHTEEN

"A Frito-dog?" David read the list of ingredients and frowned. "They come with onions and jalapeños. You don't like either of those."

A pleading look blanketed Brynn's face. "They can leave them off. I'm sure they would, if you ask nicely."

David rocked back on his heels. Hot dogs weren't the most nutritious of foods. Wasn't part of a father's job making sure his child ate well?

The trouble was, other than the vegetarian truck—which Brynn had turned up her nose at—most carried items with no better nutritional value than the Frito-dog.

"It's only once a year."

David turned. Prim, Max and their two boys stood behind them in line. "Is that your subtle way of telling me I should let her have the Frito-dog?"

Max grinned.

"We're having one," Connor, one of the twins, announced.

"Maybe two." His brother, Callum, cast a speculative look in his mother's direction.

"One is enough." Prim offered David a warm smile before shifting her attention to his daughter. "Hello, Brynn."

For the first time, David noticed the baby clasped to Prim's chest in some kind of wrap. He started to ask about it when he realized he'd lost her attention.

Seconds later, her gaze returned to him. "Where's Hadley?"

David had known someone would ask. It was inevitable. These Friday events leading up to Founder's Day were big deals in Good Hope. A man would be expected to bring the woman he was dating.

"Hadley is baking," Brynn piped up, and her smile faded. "That's why she's not with us."

David had been glad for an excuse he could give his daughter.

"I stopped by Ami's house earlier, and Hadley was there. The house smelled wonderful." Prim smiled at Brynn. "She and I enjoyed some of the cookies she baked this morning. They were—"

"What kind of cookies?" Callum stepped close, crowding his mother, an accusing look in his eyes. "We didn't get any cookies."

The boy glanced at his twin, who confirmed the oversight with a head shake.

"Why didn't you bring—?"

His father's hand on the boy's shoulder stopped Callum midsentence. "We've spoken about this before. You don't interrupt adults when they're having a conversation. And you never speak to your mother in that tone."

Connor gave his brother a *you're so busted* smirk.

"What do you say to your mother?"

Apparently familiar with the drill, the child didn't hesitate. "I'm sorry, Mommy."

Prim tousled his hair, then turned back to Brynn. "I'm sure Hadley would be here if she could."

David and Brynn ate at a picnic table with the Brody family. For all their high jinks, Brynn appeared to genuinely enjoy being around the boys. When Adelyn woke up, Brynn sang silly songs to the baby, who watched her intently.

The boys were more interested in trying to shove each other off the bench than in their sister. After the third time of reprimanding them, Max announced they would be skipping dessert and the climbing wall.

"Not listening and acting up is a sign you need some quiet time at home." He silenced the boys' pleading with one glance before his gaze shifted to David. "Are you coming to Jeremy's on Sunday?"

David lifted his hands. "I'm not sure a croquet tournament is my thing."

"Fin wants us there. As many people as we can manage to round up." Prim shot a pointed glance at her husband, clearly wanting him to give a little push.

"Fin is considering having Good Hope host a vintage croquet tournament around the May Day festivities next year. Sort of like what we do with the baseball game around the Fourth." Max's tone turned persuasive. "It should be fun. Who doesn't like hitting a ball with a mallet?"

The desire to decline brought an excuse quickly to David's lips, but he swallowed the refusal. Keeping busy might be a good thing. "What about Brynn?"

"Kids are welcome." Prim smiled at Brynn. "Fin has hired Dakota and a couple other college girls to entertain the younger ones."

Prim's gaze shifted to her sons, who stood kicking the ground with the tips of their sneakers. "Rumor is the climbing wall will be moving to Rakes Farm after tonight."

Like hunting dogs that had caught a scent, the boys froze at attention. "Will we get to climb the wall?"

Prim's gaze softened. "Probably."

"It sounds like fun." Brynn tugged on David's hand. "I bet a lot of my friends will be there."

David nodded to Max and Prim. "We'll be there."

Once the Brody family disappeared from sight, Brynn wanted to check out the climbing wall. They were standing in line when Brynn squeezed his hand. "You know what will make Sunday absolutely, positively perfect?"

"No rain?"

Brynn chuckled and rolled her eyes. "Hadley being there. She loves climbing as much as I do."

Hadley didn't accompany them to the party on Sunday. She'd still been baking when they left. Without a single glance in David's direction, she'd promised Brynn she'd stop by Rakes Farm if she got the chance.

She never showed.

All afternoon, Brynn kept asking if he'd seen Hadley. After the third no, she quit asking. The pinched look on his daughter's face reminded him of the way she'd often looked when Whitney hadn't shown up for an event.

Though David felt bad for Brynn, it had been easier not having Hadley at the party. There was an uncomfortable tension between them. Until the DNA test results came back tomorrow, he didn't have anything of substance to say to her.

Part of him trusted her. She was the woman he'd fallen for, the one who brought light into his life and made him believe in second chances. But the logical, rational part of his brain told him not to discuss anything of substance with her until the test results were in and he could be certain she was indeed Brynn's birth mother.

He didn't know why she would lie when the fact was so easily proven, but he had to know for certain.

David pulled into the driveway and just sat there for several long seconds. Hopefully by this time tomorrow night, he'd have some answers. After unlocking the front door, David stepped inside after Brynn.

Ruckus greeted them with enthusiastic barks, then went back to lie on the rug near the hearth.

"Hadley." Brynn called out her name, but David wasn't surprised when she didn't answer. The house had an empty feel.

Surely, she wouldn't have left without saying good-bye to Brynn. Unless she was worried what the results of the DNA tests would show...

A muscle jerked in his jaw.

Brynn's brows pulled together in worry. "Where is she?"

"Probably out running a few errands."

Hadley appeared in the doorway leading to the kitchen, and Ruckus offered a welcoming woof.

"Actually, I was on the back porch watering the plants." Hadley's gaze shifted from David to Brynn. "Did you have fun?"

Brynn lifted a shoulder, let it drop.

"They had the climbing wall up." David filled the awkward silence. "Brynn made it all the way to the top. Twice."

"Wow. Congrats." Hadley moved to Brynn's side, raised a hand for a fist bump, but lowered it when the girl only looked away.

When he stepped back, he noticed that the book Brynn had made for Hadley lay open on the coffee table. Without thinking, David scooped it up and began to read.

"We like to climb walls." The childish penmanship made him smile, as did the picture of two blondes, one tiny, one tall, climbing and waving at each other from the top of a rock wall.

He flipped the page.

"We teach our dog tricks." There was Ruckus sitting up while the small blond-haired girl handed him a dog cookie and the woman smiled.

"We defend ourselves against bad people." This picture showed Hadley with her booted foot on Clive Gourley's chest.

The other pages were more of the same. Hadley and Brynn reading to each other, cooking together, building sand castles...

"This is nice." He smiled at Brynn.

"Nice and stupid." Brynn snatched it from him. "I don't even know why I made it."

While Hadley watched in horror, Brynn tore up the book, tossing the bits of paper to the floor.

"Hey"—Hadley stepped forward—"that was mine, not yours."

"You didn't want it anyway. Just like you didn't want to come to the party today. Or climb the rock wall with me." Brynn's blue eyes flashed. "You'd rather stay home and text your friends or play on the computer."

Visibly startled by the vehemence in the girl's tone, Hadley took a step back.

"I bet if you were my mom, you'd be too busy to help with my family-tree project, too."

"Is that why your mom texted you this afternoon?" David gentled his tone. "To tell you she couldn't help?"

"She's too busy." Brynn sneered the words, then shifted her gaze to Hadley. "Just like you. You promised you'd come."

"I said I'd try—"

"You didn't try, though, did you?" Brynn's accusatory gaze pinned Hadley, who'd bent over to pick up the pieces of paper that had once been a book. "You never planned to come."

Hadley's fingers tightened around the paper scraps as she stood. "It didn't work out for me to come today. I wish I could have been there."

"Don't lie to me."

Hadley's face blanched as if she'd been slapped.

"Brynn."

The child whirled on him, her eyes filled with accusation. "You made Mommy leave. Now you're making Hadley leave. I hate you both."

Stunned, David watched his daughter stalk down the hall.

"Brynn Elizabeth." Hadley's voice sliced the air like a knife and had the child stilling. "Come back here. Right now."

With chin jutted high and hands clenched at her sides, the girl returned to the room.

David could only stare. Never had he seen this behavior from his daughter.

"Do you think speaking to your father in such a manner is acceptable?" Hadley's tone remained firm. "Is that how we speak to someone we love?"

Brynn shook her head, but her mouth remained sullen.

"What do you want to say to him?"

"I know she didn't—" David began, but the look Hadley shot him had the rest of whatever he'd been about to say dying in his throat.

"I'm sorry, Daddy. I don't hate you." The quiver remained in the child's voice when she turned to Hadley. "I'm sorry I tore up your book. I don't want you to leave."

"I'm not leaving." Hadley dropped into a nearby chair. She gestured with one hand. "See? Not going anywhere."

"My daddy is mad at you."

Hadley's expression gave nothing away. "Is that what he told you?"

Brynn shook her head. "I can just tell. He's mad and you're sad."

David's first instinct was to deny it. After all, he wasn't really angry at Hadley. But before he could speak, Hadley responded.

"I am sad. I've really enjoyed our time together, and soon I'll be back at the bakery and you'll be in school all day. I'm going to miss you lots."

"But I'll still get to see you, won't I?"

Hadley hesitated for a barely perceptible second. "Do you know where Blooms Bake Shop is?"

Brynn giggled, and the sound eased the tension in the room.

"Well, then you know where to find me." Hadley's tone softened. "Brynn, someone once told me that often, when we raise our voice and lash out, it isn't really about the other person, it's about something going on inside us."

Tugging on Brynn's hand, Hadley pulled the child onto her lap. "Will you tell me what's troubling you?"

Brynn rested her head against Hadley's, their blond strands a perfect match. "Mommy said she can't help me with my Founder's Day project. She says she's too busy, but she isn't. She just doesn't want to help me."

"We don't know that, Sweet Pea." David chose his words carefully. "Your mother hasn't been feeling well lately. That might be why she can't help."

"Is she okay?" Brynn's eyes went wide.

"Far as I know. And I'm happy to help you with the project." David glanced at Hadley. "I know Hadley will do what she can to help you, too."

Brynn turned eager eyes to Hadley. "You'll help me?"

"Absolutely." Hadley brushed Brynn's hair back from her face with a gentle hand. "There is nothing I wouldn't do for you. Nothing."

His daughter flung her arms around Hadley and buried her face in her neck. "I love you."

Over Brynn's head, Hadley's eyes met his.

In that moment, David realized Hadley was more of a mother to Brynn than Whitney had ever been.

It was clear his daughter loved Hadley. And Hadley loved Brynn.

Brynn had nailed it. He *had* been "mad" at Hadley, but the anger had been mixed with a large dose of hurt. She'd betrayed his trust. His knee-jerk assumption had been that she'd used him to get close to Brynn. On closer examination, that theory didn't hold water, as he was the one who'd approached her about being Brynn's temporary live-in nanny.

The problem was, he'd started to dream of a future with her

and now felt like a fool. Today, listening to Max and Beck talk about family had made him think of the dreams he'd once shared with Whitney.

While there was no denying his wife hadn't put one hundred percent effort into the relationship, neither had he. Not in the last few years, that was for sure. It had been easier to simply not say anything whenever she planned another trip with her friends.

Another trip without him.

Without Brynn.

He'd told himself he'd remained silent because of Brynn. He hadn't wanted his daughter caught in the middle of her parents' turmoil. Now he could see that all he'd accomplished was letting his marriage slip away.

There had been little emotional intimacy between them. Other than early on when she'd told him about her father's tragic death from Huntington's, she'd rarely shared her thoughts or fears.

Each time he'd attempted to bring it up, she'd shut down the discussion. By the time they split, he hadn't had a clue what was going on in her head.

He'd let her push him away.

Now, he was pushing Hadley away.

Just until he got the test results, David told himself. Once he had those in hand, he and Hadley could work on rebuilding their relationship.

As long as it wasn't too late.

CHAPTER NINETEEN

Hadley tucked Brynn into bed, gave the child a kiss, then left the room. David had already pulled a favorite book from the shelf. Though Hadley longed to stay and listen, she knew father and daughter needed this time together to smooth out the recent bump in their relationship.

While David was upstairs, Hadley commandeered the kitchen and assembled ingredients on the spacious granite countertop. She tried to banish all thoughts from her brain of the book Brynn had demolished. *The Adventures of Brynn and Hadley* had meant so much to her. She hoped that one day Brynn would make her another book, this one filled with even more adventures the two of them had shared.

Opening the oven door, Hadley slid in the tray containing dollops of cookie dough arranged in neat rows, then set the timer. When she didn't hear any footsteps coming her way, she briefly considered making another batch.

Instead, she cleaned. By the time the oven timer dinged, the kitchen gleamed.

"Something sure smells good." David leaned against the doorjamb. He sniffed the air, his casual tone at odds with the tense set of his jaw.

Recalling their prior ease with each other, Hadley experienced a pang of regret.

"Chocolate chip cookies with walnuts." After donning an oven mitt, Hadley lifted the baking sheet from the oven and placed it on a cooling rack. "Would you like one?"

"Chocolate chip cookies? Hot from the oven?" He shot her an amused glance. "Actually, I don't think one will do it. I'd like several. And I'd like you to join me."

Hadley hid her surprise. This was as close to a normal conversation as they'd had in days.

"I'll put the cookies on a plate." She kept her tone light. "You get the milk."

"It's a beautiful evening." David opened the refrigerator, speaking over his shoulder. "Let's go wild and crazy and eat on the porch."

He'd extended an olive branch. Not a big one, but a branch nonetheless. She supposed she could reject it and demand to know what had changed since earlier today when he could barely be bothered to speak two words to her.

"Sounds good."

The air was warm, and a light breeze kept the bugs away. Hadley sipped her milk and nibbled on a cookie. "You must have read more than a chapter. You were in her room a long time."

"We read three." David's lips tipped up. "I believe I enjoy the reading aloud as much as she does."

"Is she asleep?"

"Out for the count." David lifted his glass, but didn't drink. "It was a busy, somewhat difficult day for her."

"I should have gone to the party."

David lowered the glass. "Why didn't you?"

"I know you're angry with me. I didn't know if I could spend several hours pretending it's all good between us."

He inclined his head and took a drink of milk.

"I didn't think of Brynn, didn't even consider she might be looking forward to seeing me, to climbing the wall together. I thought only of myself. It was a mistake, and hurting her is on me." Hadley regretted missing the precious time with Brynn. "From now until the end of the month, I'm going to savor all the moments with her I can. Going back to my apartment, to simply being that nice lady at the bake shop, is going to kill me."

"If the DNA results show you're Brynn's birth mother—"

"I *am* her birth mother." Hadley spoke in a fierce whisper, even though they were alone on the porch. Alone, that was, except for Ruckus, snoozing at her feet.

"I've been thinking." David slanted a glance at her. "Once the results are back, we should tell everyone."

Hadley's heart flip-flopped. She'd wondered about the next step, but hadn't expected this. "Are you saying we'd tell everyone I'm her birth mother?"

She couldn't imagine what else he could be talking about revealing, but wanted to be sure.

"Yes. After we tell Brynn." His gaze searched hers. "I don't see a reason to keep her connection to you a secret. Unless you have some objection."

Excitement threatened to engulf her. She tamped it down. "What will everyone think?"

Those smoky gray eyes turned sharp and assessing. "Do you care?"

"I care that they'll feel betrayed." Hadley looked him in the eyes. "Just like you feel betrayed."

"They'll get over it."

"Are you over it?" A hard ball formed in the pit of her stomach when he didn't immediately respond.

"I'm getting there. The cookies help." The quick smile he shot her had the knot dissolving.

"The results should arrive in my in-box tomorrow." He lifted a brow at her sharp inhale.

"This will be the start of a new life for me," Hadley explained.

"The start of a new life for us." A muscle in his jaw jumped. "One with no secrets."

Hadley ignored the second comment.

"I'm champing at the bit to get started," Hadley said, almost to herself, "but I'm also terrified."

Without warning, David did something she hadn't expected. He reached over and took her hand.

"No worries." The look in his eyes was as steady as the clasp of his hand. "You. Brynn. Me. We'll get through this…together."

"I'm sure you're wondering why I asked to meet with you." Hadley glanced at the four women gathered around Ami's dining room table.

Her conversation with David last night on the porch had her realizing she needed to be proactive. There was no reason to wait for the DNA results to hit David's in-box. Hadley already knew they'd confirm her story.

Rounding up all four Bloom sisters on a busy Monday morning hadn't been easy, but Ami made it happen. When Hadley had said there was something of vital importance she needed to tell her and her sisters, Ami had asked if it could wait until evening.

That might have been too late. At the moment, David planned to tell his family at the dinner party his mother was throwing tomorrow night, an intimate affair that would include the Bloom family. But plans could change, and David might get a wild hair to tell his mother sooner. Perhaps the second he received the results.

If that happened, Lynn would tell Steve, and soon everyone in the two families would know. Hadley owed her friends better. They needed to hear the news from her. First.

The Bloom sisters had welcomed her into their family, introduced her to their friends and helped her become a part of the community. How had she repaid their kindness? By lying to them. Not overtly, though each time she'd pretended to have no connection to David or Brynn, she'd deceived them.

Fin glanced at her phone. "I don't want to be rude, but will this take long? Next weekend is Founder's Day, and I have a zillion things on my plate."

"We know the big celebration is next week, Fin." Marigold rolled her eyes and reached for one of the chocolates scattered atop the table. "We're all busy. But Ami says this is important."

"I shouldn't eat chocolate." Prim's hand hovered over a truffle, her daughter asleep on her chest.

"Indulge, Primrose." Ami's blessing was all it took for Prim to grab the candy.

"Something tells me this is serious stuff." Marigold studied Hadley as she unwrapped her chocolate.

"I'll get to the point." Hadley took a breath and plunged ahead. "I didn't just happen to come to Good Hope three years ago. I had a purpose, a mission."

Clearly intrigued, Fin quit scrolling and put down her phone. She widened her eyes and spoke in a conspiratorial whisper. "Is this your way of telling us you're a spy?"

"You behave." Ami punched her sister in the arm, then cast Hadley an apologetic look. "Sorry."

Though Ami and Fin might look nearly identical, when Hadley had first met Delphinium, she hadn't liked her much. Ami was soft and nurturing, while Fin seemed to be all sharp edges.

Her feelings had changed when Fin returned to Good Hope last summer and they'd become better acquainted. Hadley had discovered that lurking beneath the woman's somewhat crunchy outer shell was a soft, gooey center.

Not that Hadley witnessed the gooey center all that much. The only time she was guaranteed a glimpse was when Fin looked at her husband...or her sisters. There was no doubt the woman knew how to love and love deeply.

There had also been Fin's kindness to Mindy, a little girl battling terminal cancer. Instead of insisting her wedding to the town's mayor be picture perfect, Fin had allowed the child to live out her dream of wearing a flower girl dress with a princess skirt and feathers.

Thinking of Mindy's death brought tears to Hadley's eyes. What if she lost Brynn? What if David changed his mind and cut off all access to her daughter?

"Hadley." Ami's hand was on her shoulder.

Hadley blinked away the moisture and met Ami's concerned green eyes.

"I don't want to rush you. I can see whatever you have to tell us is difficult. But"—Ami gestured to the women around the circle—"our time is limited."

Heart hammering, Hadley took a breath. "I'm Brynn Chapin's birth mother."

Someone, Marigold maybe, inhaled sharply. Otherwise, for several heartbeats, there was only silence.

"David said it was a closed adoption." Marigold's blond brows pulled together in puzzlement. "Did he contact you?"

"He didn't contact her." Fin's green eyes were cool. "If he had, there would have been no reason for her to lie."

Lie.

The word hung unchallenged in the air.

"Marigold is correct. It was a closed adoption. Five years ago, I hired a private detective to find my daughter." Hadley kept her breathing steady. "He located her in Good Hope."

"Why then?" Fin's eyes turned sharp and assessing. "What changed?"

Keep it simple, Hadley told herself.

"My mother left when I was in grade school. My dad was a police officer. Five years ago, he was killed in the line of duty." The fact that she could recite the facts as if giving a report might come across as cold, but Hadley had to keep a tight control on her emotions or she'd break. "His loss hit me hard. I felt alone in the world. I started worrying, wondering if my child was happy. I used my father's life insurance money to hire a detective."

Ami's brow furrowed in confusion. "You mention being alone in the world, but don't you have relatives in North Dakota?"

A cold chill traveled up Hadley's spine. One slip of a tongue, made years ago, tied her back to North Dakota. "My grandparents are old and frail."

"I'm sorry about your dad." Sympathy filled Ami's eyes. "We know how hard it is to lose a parent."

The other sisters nodded.

"Why didn't you tell me any of this?" Tears filled Ami's eyes, but she hurriedly wiped them away with the pads of her fingers. "Forgive me. I cry at the drop of a hat when I'm pregnant."

"Doesn't change the fact it's a valid question." Fin spoke softly to her eldest sister before pinning Hadley with a take-no-prisoners gaze. "I can understand not telling the rest of us. What's your excuse for lying to Ami?"

Hadley absorbed the impact of the punch and flushed. "It's a small town. I didn't want David to find out."

"You expect us to believe you thought Ami would tell someone?" Fin's voice grew frosty. "Everyone knows she's completely trustworthy."

"Fin, stop." Ami shot her sister a warning glance. "When Hadley arrived, she and I were strangers."

"She's been here three years, Am." Fin's green eyes flashed. "She should have told you."

"Fin is right." Hadley expelled a ragged breath and offered Ami an apologetic look. "I should never have kept such a secret from you."

"It's okay," Ami assured her, though Hadley heard hurt beneath the reassurance.

"We've all kept secrets." Prim's hazel eyes, so like her father's, held none of Fin's reproach. "I believe everyone here can attest that, while bringing truth out into the light is difficult, total honesty is always best."

"David and I plan to tell Brynn tonight." Hadley spread her hands, hoping to get quickly through the rest of it. "Tomorrow, before the dinner party at his mother's house, David will tell his family. I-I think of you as family, so I wanted you to know first."

Hadley felt a stirring of hope when Ami reached over to take her hand.

"How did David take the news when you told him? It had to be a shock." Marigold popped a chocolate into her mouth.

"It was a shock." Hadley licked her dry lips. "And a difficult conversation."

Ami squeezed her hand. "He's a good man."

"David is a wonderful man. I couldn't have picked a better father for Brynn." Hadley froze, immediately realizing her faux pas. Before this meeting, she had been determined to do everything possible to keep from mentioning the word *father*.

All she could hope was her gaffe wasn't enough to jar anyone's curiosity.

The gleam in Fin's eyes told Hadley she wasn't that lucky.

"Speaking of fathers, where is Brynn's baby daddy?" With precise movements, Fin carefully unwrapped a chocolate, but made no move to pop it into her mouth.

"Fin," Ami huffed. "I don't see that's any of our business."

"She opened the door," Fin pointed out. "I'm walking through it."

"It's okay." Hadley spoke through frozen lips. "I don't know where he is. We're not in contact."

"Where do you go from here?" Marigold asked. "I mean, once everyone is told?"

"David has indicated he'll let me be a part of Brynn's life." Hadley spread her hands in front of her, gazed down at her unadorned nails. "That's something I want very much."

"What about Whitney?" If Ami had thought to silence her sister with a few pointed glances, it hadn't worked. Fin pointed a candy at Hadley. "What does she think of this latest development?"

"David has sole custody of Brynn."

Like a dog with a bone, Fin refused to let go. "That doesn't answer my question."

"She *is* Brynn's mother," Marigold interjected, with a note of apology.

Hadley could argue the point, could remind them how Whitney had distanced herself from Brynn, even while living under the same roof. All that aside, Whitney was the only mother Brynn had known. "It's up to David to contact her."

Prim worried her lower lip. "He might want to do it sooner than later. Once word gets out, she'll hear."

"She's in Florida."

Fin shot her a pitying glance. "Two words. Open Door. Once the news makes the e-newsletter's gossip section, everyone will know, including Whitney."

Hadley's breath caught in her throat. Why hadn't she thought of this before? If her name and the fact she had a nine-year-old daughter showed up online, anyone searching the internet could bring up the story.

Justin might connect the dots.

For several seconds, a squeezing pressure filled Hadley's chest, making breathing difficult.

"David wouldn't want Whitney to read it in the newsletter."

Hadley forced a calm she didn't feel. As soon as the family was notified, she would seek out Katie Ruth and beg her not to mention her name in an article. "I'm sure he'll contact her personally."

To stave off more questions, Hadley pushed to her feet. "Thanks for coming. Again, I'm very sorry for not saying anything sooner."

Ami rose and enfolded her in a hug. "We're good."

After releasing Hadley, Ami stepped back to let Marigold and Prim embrace her. Fin remained seated, chair pushed back from the table, one long leg crossed over the other.

Ami glanced curiously at her sister. "I thought you were in a hurry."

"You go ahead. I'll lock up." Fin waved a perfectly manicured hand. "I have a few Founder's Day questions for Hadley. There's no need for you to wait around for that discussion."

Fighting a shiver of unease, Hadley watched the three other sisters leave.

"You had questions about Founder's Day?" Hadley wasn't sure what Fin would need to ask her.

"I need several more volunteers to serve as greeters."

Fin's direct gaze had Hadley shifting from one foot to the other. She tried to make the gesture casual, but Fin missed nothing. "What would be involved?"

"An hour shift on Saturday."

"What would I need to do?"

"Stand in one corner of the square and greet people. Thank them for coming." As if reading minds was another one of her talents, Fin added, "David and Brynn could help."

"Text me the specifics. I'm happy to help."

"Excellent." When Fin leaned over to pick up her bag, Hadley expelled a sigh of relief.

"Oh, and Hadley." Fin rose, slinging the designer purse over her shoulder. "Discovering someone withheld vital information while professing to come clean can be almost worse than keeping the initial secret."

Hadley's smile froze on her lips. Her heart gave one solid knock against her ribs. "I don't understand what you mean."

"I think you do." Fin's eyes softened to a deep bottle green. "I went down that path and nearly lost everything that mattered to me. David Chapin is a good man. Trust him with *all* your secrets. Otherwise, you could lose him forever."

CHAPTER TWENTY

David arrived at Peninsula State Park fifteen minutes early. He'd requested Hadley meet him at the picnic area closest to Eagle Tower at noon, but had given her no other details.

After placing the picnic basket on the bench, he pulled out a cloth and covered the tabletop. His hands shook a little as he lifted out the bottle of champagne and two glasses.

It had been so long since he'd tried to impress a woman that he feared falling miserably short. He'd hated putting Hadley through the past few days, hated keeping her at arm's length until the DNA results came in, but had felt he had no choice.

Brynn's welfare was his priority, and he wouldn't be a good father if he hadn't verified Hadley's story. But he hadn't been surprised when the results showed she was Brynn's mother. In his heart, he'd known it all along. Now, his head knew it, too.

As he emptied the food from the basket, Hadley's words to Brynn kept circling in his head. When she'd said that sometimes when we lash out, it isn't really about the other person, it's about something going on inside us, he'd thought, *Bingo*.

He and Whitney had rarely fought, mainly because she hadn't been around much. When they had argued, it usually had started over something small, like her texting with friends one of the few times they ate dinner as a family.

The texting disagreement hadn't really been about phone usage at dinner as much as it had been about Whitney being gone so much. And the fact that even when she was in town, she was checked out.

Would it have made a difference if he'd phrased his concerns differently? He had his doubts. Whitney was a master at twisting to her advantage anything he said. They hadn't had a heart-to-heart in years.

He didn't want that kind of relationship with Hadley. They had a chance to build something special, a closeness and trust strong enough to endure the ups and downs of the years to come. In order for that to happen, they needed to start out solid.

"Well, this is a nice surprise."

David looked up, and there she was, dressed casually in khaki shorts and a shirt the same color as her cherry-red lipstick. Her hair, hanging in loose waves to her shoulders, fluttered in the breeze. "It's noon. I thought you might be hungry."

"You made lunch." Pleasure rippled through the statement.

"It's not much." He gestured to the table. If he'd had more time, he'd have asked his mother's cook to whip together something, instead of raiding the refrigerator. "Hummus with carrots and celery. And grapes."

"I love hummus." Her gaze shifted to the bottle. "And Cristal. Are we celebrating?"

"I hope so." David made short work of uncorking the bottle, then filled each glass, handing one to her. He lifted his glass.

Her gaze turned watchful.

"To fresh starts and honesty."

She took a cautious sip. "I assume you got the DNA results."

"I did." David gestured to the table. "Let's sit."

Once Hadley had taken a seat, he slid onto the bench across from her and reminded himself this woman wasn't Whitney. She didn't hold a grudge. She didn't stalk off or refuse to speak to him when he'd done something that upset her.

"It hurt you when I asked for the sample."

She opened her mouth, as if to deny it, then nodded. "It felt as if you didn't trust me."

"My heart knew you spoke the truth. And I see so much of you in Brynn." He smiled, then sobered. "But this is my child. I might trust, but for her sake, I had to verify."

"You're a protective dad. That's a good thing." Hadley's lips quirked upward. "I'm sure I'd have done the same thing in your position."

Without his gaze leaving her face, David took her hand and brought her fingers to his lips. "Still, I'm sorry for what I put you through the past few days."

"I wasn't worried." Hadley shrugged. "Besides, I'm the one who turned your life upside down."

"What you've done is bring joy into my life and the life of my daughter."

Hadley picked up a carrot stick, bit into it. "I guess the burning question now is where we go from here."

He lifted his glass. "We celebrate and move forward."

She clinked her glass against his, then surveyed him over the rim. "Any ideas about the moving forward part?"

Oh, David had a lot of ideas, but there was the matter of a confession...

Hadley Newhouse didn't run or shy away from the truth.

He could do no less.

"Being with you made me realize how empty my life was before."

Hadley took a sip of champagne, her warm blue eyes inviting confidences. God, she was beautiful.

"While we eat, I have a story to tell you."

She reached for another carrot stick. "I love stories. Will it have a happy ending?"

He nearly crossed his fingers, something he hadn't done since he'd been a boy. "I hope so."

"Once upon a time," she prompted.

"Once upon a time, a couple and their daughter moved back to Good Hope. The man hoped the change would give the marriage a much-needed boost."

David rose and began to pace. "In Chicago, their social life centered around parties and galas, rarely anything family-related."

Hadley snapped the carrot stick in two, dipped one half in the hummus. "You mentioned the woman wasn't close to her family."

Had he said that? For years, David had steered clear of discussing the potential minefield that was Whitney's family. "Not close at all. But I was referring to the man and his wife doing things with their daughter."

Hadley's fingers tightened around the carrot.

"Once in Good Hope, he looked forward to picnics, barbecues and parties where kids weren't just invited, but welcomed."

"From what I've observed, there are a lot of those activities here." Hadley's comment served as a nudge to continue.

"The couple received an abundance of invitations, especially at first." David raked a hand through his hair. "The woman refused to even consider most of them. Not surprisingly, the invitations dried up after a while."

"What about his family?"

"They didn't give up. Family events became the only ones the woman would occasionally agree to attend. More often than not, he and the child went alone."

Hadley studied him for a long moment, and a softness filled her eyes. "That had to be difficult for him."

"It wasn't the life he envisioned, the kind of life he wanted for himself. Or for his daughter."

Listening to his friends talk about their wives and children had only made David think of the dreams he'd once shared with Whitney and how empty his life had become.

"There was little emotional intimacy between the man and woman. She never shared her thoughts or fears. And he'd quit asking. They separated, divorced."

David dropped back onto the bench.

"I'm sorry." She reached over and gave his hand a squeeze. "I hate to point it out, but so far I'm not hearing a happy ending."

"The story is still being written." David laced his fingers with hers. "The man met another woman. A woman who was his perfect match. There were ups and downs, but the trials allowed them to see what each other was like, down deep."

Hadley pulled back her hand, causing him to look up. Her eyes were dark and serious. "What are you saying, David?"

"I see today as a day of new beginnings." His gaze didn't waver. He was certain of the course he was proposing. "I want you and I to continue to develop a solid relationship. One built on trust and mutual respect. I'd like Brynn to grow up seeing what a healthy relationship between two adults looks like."

Her fingers shook slightly as she reached for another carrot. She cleared her throat. "I'd like that, too."

"I made mistakes in my first marriage." His voice cracked. He paused to clear his throat. "You told me something that could easily have ended the closeness we were building. My request for confirmation could have had the same effect. But we approached the issue like adults and made it through difficult days."

"We did."

"I have another story that I'd like to tell you." When she opened her mouth, he hurried on. "This one involves a promise of secrecy made years ago."

Curiosity flickered in her baby blues, but she didn't push, instead taking another sip of wine and nodding to show she was listening.

"When I proposed, Whitney didn't immediately accept. She

told me she wouldn't be able to give me the children she knew I wanted." David resumed pacing. "I thought it was because of female problems. She said no, it was something more serious. Before she told me, she made me swear never to tell anyone else. I gave her my word. Until now, I've kept that promise."

"Why tell me?"

David didn't hesitate. He'd given this a lot of thought.

"I believe, because of our relationship and yours with Brynn, you need the information." He moved around the table to sit beside her. "I don't want there to be any secrets between us."

"Truly, don't feel like you have to—"

"Have you heard of Huntington's chorea?"

Hadley blinked. "Isn't it a neurological condition?"

"It's a hereditary brain disorder." In the early years, David had read everything he could about HD. "Whitney's father died from it. It's a horrible condition with an ugly death. There is no effective treatment."

Understanding filled her eyes. "That must be the genetic condition you mentioned that runs in Whitney's family. The reason she doesn't want to have children."

He nodded. "If your parent has HD, you have a fifty percent chance of carrying the defective gene."

Hadley cocked her head, and he could see her trying to process the information. "Whitney made you promise not to tell anyone she's a carrier. But why? She can't help being a carrier, and she did what she felt was best for her by not having children."

"If you have the faulty gene, you don't carry the disease, you get it."

Hadley inhaled sharply. "She has the gene?"

"Maybe. Maybe not. She's refused to be tested."

"Living your life under such a dark cloud has to be horrible. I wonder if that's why she holds herself back from forming attachments." For a second, sympathy hovered in Hadley's blue eyes, then they were ice. "While I can sympathize, that information should have been on the adoption application."

"I agree." David blew out a breath. "I thought she'd included it. It wasn't until after the adoption was finalized that she confided she'd deliberately left it off."

Blowing out a breath, Hadley took a long drink of champagne. "Well, we can't go back and change the past. When will she know if she has the disease?"

"Symptoms usually start when the person is between thirty and fifty." David rubbed his jaw. "It will be difficult for Brynn if she gets sick."

A muscle in Hadley's jaw jumped. "Is she showing any signs?"

David hesitated. "I didn't notice anything when she was here over the Fourth. Then again, she wasn't here long, and we weren't around each other much."

Hadley dipped a carrot stick into the hummus, but made no move to eat. "Do you anticipate she'll change her mind and get tested?"

David was struck by how nice it was to have a meaningful conversation that showed no signs of deteriorating into uncontrolled drama.

"Whitney and I haven't spoken of HD in years." David shrugged. "Even when her dad died, she shut me out and refused to discuss what she was feeling."

"Not talking about it doesn't mean it isn't on her mind."

David nodded. "I sometimes wonder if that's part of all the partying with friends. When she's at the clubs, drinking and dancing, she's simply a young, beautiful woman with her whole life ahead of her."

"Being in Good Hope had to be difficult for that reason."

David inclined his head.

"Seeing the happy families could have been a reminder of what might be taken from her." Hadley shook her head, her eyes dark with sympathy. "Watching children playing and wondering whether you'd be around when your child was ten or fifteen, or looking at your husband and worrying you'd shortchanged him."

"Maybe." David's voice came out raspy, as if he hadn't used it in a while. He cleared his throat. "I'm not sure Whitney is as self-aware as you think. Or as unselfish in her thoughts."

Hadley blinked, as if surprised at the coldness seeping into his voice.

"I sympathize, I do. That doesn't make me blind to her faults. Whitney is a selfish, self-absorbed woman." He finished off his champagne, splashed more in his glass. "You should know her friend Kim texted me last week, concerned about Whitney's recent behavior."

"You stay in touch with your ex-wife's friends?" The sharpness of Hadley's tone appeared to surprise her as much as him. "Sorry."

David tightened his fingers around the stem of the glass. "Whitney is Brynn's mother. What happens to her affects Brynn."

"You're right, of course." Two bright spots of pink dotted Hadley's cheeks.

"The problem is, Whitney has a mercurial temperament. That makes it difficult to distinguish between what's normal and what might be signs of the disease." David heaved a sigh. "Kim promised to contact me if things deteriorate."

"It must have been incredibly lonely."

"What do you mean?"

"Keeping the secret. Not being able to share your fears with your family and friends." The compassion in her voice stroked and soothed. "Whitney had you. You had no one."

The concern in her eyes touched him.

"You're a good father," she added.

Coming from her, David knew that was high praise.

"I loved Brynn the second I held her in my arms." He smiled at the memory. "That first month, I was terrified. Every day."

"Bringing an infant home has to be scary."

"It wasn't just that." He waved a hand. "Birth fathers in Illinois have thirty days to stake their claim. Despite being assured by the attorney that you didn't know his name and he didn't know you were pregnant, I worried he'd show up and want her back."

"About that…"

Hadley had gone pale, and David wondered if she was reliving that difficult time in her life.

"It's okay." He attempted to pull her close, but she pushed back.

"No, it isn't okay." She gripped his forearms, her eyes dark with distress. "I've still been lying to you, David. That ends today. It ends now."

"What are you talking about?"

"For nearly ten years, I've kept what happened the summer I got pregnant locked tight inside me. I convinced myself that not telling anyone the whole story was the only way to keep my daughter safe. But like your promise to Whitney, the truth about Brynn's father has eaten at me."

David's heart stopped beating. Simply stopped. He pulled away from her. "What about him?"

"It's true Brynn's birth father never knew I was pregnant." Hadley twisted her hands together, then lifted her gaze to meet his head on. "I do know his name. I know where he is. I can also assure you that, if by some fluke he discovers he fathered a child, you don't need to worry about him showing up on your doorstep."

David raised a hand to his head. The roller coaster was poised for a drop at the top of a hill. "How can you be so sure?"

"Because he's in prison."

CHAPTER TWENTY-ONE

Prison.

Several years earlier David had been hit by a two-by-four on a job site. The impact had stolen his breath. He remembered the feeling. The shock. The pain. He felt the same way now.

Brynn's birth father was in prison. Hadley, despite all her previous assurances to the contrary, not only knew the man's name but that he was incarcerated.

Details, he needed details. David took several seconds to find his breath and steady his emotions. "Tell me everything you know."

Hadley flinched at the no-nonsense tone he'd made no attempt to soften. She lifted her chin. "His name is Justin. My grandparents live in the same small town where he grew up."

This was far worse than David had imagined. This boy, or man, hadn't been a stranger, but someone she'd known well. "You knew him a long time?"

"No," she said, surprising him. "He was several years older. The first time I met him was right after I graduated from high school. I went to North Dakota to spend the summer with my grandparents."

When she hesitated, David made an impatient go-ahead motion with one hand. He couldn't quite wrap his mind around what she was saying.

Despite the heat from the now blazing sun, his skin felt numb. The cold went all the way to his bones.

"Justin was home from college for the summer." Her lips curved briefly. "I was flattered that a handsome college man couldn't take his eyes off me. It wasn't long until we were a couple."

David wondered why the image of Hadley with this man so many years ago bothered him. "Continue."

She flushed at the brusque tone, but nodded as if understanding the effort it took for him to keep a semblance of composure.

"He swept me off my feet." Her laugh held a hard edge. "Corny, but true. Compliments. Flowers. A lot of attention."

Pain filled her eyes, and she glanced away.

The silence lengthened. Finally, David had to say what she'd implied. "You fell in love with him."

A startled look crossed her face. "I never loved him. While I was flattered and attracted to him, he was too intense for me."

"Yet, you slept with him."

"One time, and it…" Her voice trailed off before she cleared her throat. "Just one time."

David pulled his brows together. The haunted look in her eyes had him reaching for her hand. When he located his voice, it was warm and soothing. "Did he force you, Hadley?"

She hesitated, then slowly shook her head. "I honestly don't think he heard me say no. By then, we were so far—"

"The son of a bitch." David wished the man was in front of him now. Though he'd never been a violent man, he wanted to punch him. The guy had no doubt heard her say no. He just hadn't cared to stop. "I'm sorry."

Hadley's fingers trembled in his. "One time was all it took."

Gaining control of his emotions, David kept his tone low and conversational. "What did he say when you told him you were pregnant?"

"I didn't tell him."

"Why not?"

"After that night, he became very possessive. He grabbed me, hard enough to leave a bruise, because he'd heard another guy had been flirting with me at a party." Her face turned ashen. "He took my phone and scrolled through my text messages. When he saw the guy had texted me, he slapped me."

David's fingers tightened on hers. He swore again.

"That's when I ended it."

"He doesn't sound like a guy who'd just walk away."

Her gaze shifted to a tree with a gnarled trunk. "Flowers flooded my grandparents' home, followed by dozens of text messages saying he was sorry, insisting he loved me, begging me to give him another chance."

"Did you give him that chance?" David kept his voice easy, not wanting to upset her further.

"No. There was something wrong with him. He kept it well-controlled, most of the time, but, well, there was something wrong."

"That's why you didn't tell him about the baby."

"I was already back home by the time I discovered I was pregnant."

"What did your parents say?"

"Remember, it was just me and my dad. And no, I didn't tell him." A twisted smile lifted her lips. "Dad had warned me to keep my distance from Justin Mapes. He knew the family."

The apple didn't fall far from the tree.

"You didn't tell your father because you felt guilty for seeing the guy after he told you not to?" David felt as if he was trying to solve a puzzle that was missing a few dozen pieces. Or maybe his anger over what had happened to Hadley wasn't allowing him to think clearly.

"I didn't tell him for several reasons. My dad had a temper, and I wasn't certain how he'd react to the news. Mainly, I kept quiet because I didn't want to take the chance that Justin—or his family —would discover I was pregnant." Hadley cleared her throat. "The Mapes family are big into bloodlines. After what my dad told me about Justin's father and the out-of-control behavior I'd witnessed with Justin, I didn't want them anywhere near my baby."

Brynn. Bile rose in David's throat as he thought about his sweet, loving daughter being subjected to violence. "You made the right decision."

Her eyes widened, his comment clearly not expected.

"Brynn's safety takes precedence over Justin's right to know." He cocked his head. "How did you keep the pregnancy from your father?"

"My father had started dating. Our place was small, and though he insisted otherwise, I was in the way." The light in her eyes dimmed. "My friend had recently moved to Chicago and gotten a job. I told him I wanted to delay college until I had more money saved. He agreed."

"That's why you were in Chicago."

She nodded.

"Did you consider keeping Brynn?"

"I wanted to keep her. I tried to figure out a way to make it work." Her gaze met his. "But, always, thoughts of what would happen if Justin found me—found us—haunted me. Besides, what kind of life could I give her? I grew up in a single-parent household where there was never enough money. I wanted the best for her. Two parents who would love and cherish her. A happily married couple who could give her the kind of life I couldn't."

David didn't know what to say. Despite Hadley's best effort, Brynn lived in a single-parent home with an absentee mother.

The exact fate Hadley had hoped to avoid. "Justin has never found out."

"No."

"Why is he in prison?"

"The violent tendencies I'd glimpsed in North Dakota apparently evolved over the years. Five years ago, he was charged with aggravated criminal sexual assault. He was sentenced to twenty-five years in Joliet."

"How do you know this?"

"I keep tabs on him."

David arched a brow.

"Trust me, it's not because I care." She didn't bother to keep the disgust from her voice.

"Do you have any idea when he'll be eligible for parole?"

"Not for another sixteen years." Her smile was fierce. "In Illinois, that charge requires the criminal serve eighty-five percent of his sentence. By the time he gets out, Brynn will be an adult."

"That's a relief." David searched her face. "Why not tell me this before, Hadley? Did you think I wouldn't understand?"

She moistened her lips with the tip of her tongue. "I've done everything possible to keep Justin from knowing about Brynn. I believed not telling *anyone* was the only way to keep her safe."

"Why tell me now?"

"The same reason you told me about Whitney." Those beautiful blue eyes met his. "I don't want lies between us."

David closed his eyes for a second, fighting for composure. "Thank you for trusting me, for being honest with me and for caring for Brynn."

"I love her."

Simple words could say so much. Explain so much.

"She loves you, too." He tightened his hold on her hand. "You did an unselfish thing, allowing her to be adopted."

"I thought it was best, but..." A haunted look filled her eyes. "What's she going to think when she discovers I gave her up?"

"You didn't *give her up*." David emphasized the phrase used all too commonly in these situations. It was simple semantics, he thought, but words held power. *Giving up* a child implied a lack of value, and David knew how much Hadley valued Brynn. "You went to great lengths to place her in a loving family. You wanted to make sure she was well cared for."

"What if she asks about her birth father?" Hadley asked quietly.

"We tell her the truth."

"No." Hadley shook her head vigorously, panic blanketing her face.

David kept his tone level. "We won't lie to her."

"If she knows, she could tell someone." Fear had Hadley's words coming out in a rush. "I know it seems like a long shot, but think of that six-degree thing. Justin is incarcerated, so he's out of the picture for now, but like I said before, bloodlines matter in his family."

"All good points." David watched the stiffness ease from Hadley's shoulders at his agreement. "But his family has no claim on her. I'm certain there is a way we can answer Brynn's questions honestly without giving information that could bring Justin's family to our doorstep."

Hadley expelled a shaky breath.

"We won't give her his name. We'll tell her she can know his name when she's old enough to make decisions about what to do with the information." David tapped his fingers against his thigh as he considered. "For now, we'll leave it that her birth father was someone you once dated. Period."

"I could say he's not a nice man."

David hesitated, then shook his head. "Wouldn't that spawn more questions? Like, why you'd be with someone who wasn't nice?"

"I didn't think of that." Hadley pulled away, flinging out her hands in frustration. "The problem is, I don't know what is the right thing to say."

"We'll figure out something." He kept his gaze steady on hers. "There's a new child psychologist in town. We could speak with him. If we feel comfortable after visiting with him, you and I will talk with Brynn."

"Are you really okay with telling her who I am?"

"I want her to know what a strong, brave, wonderful woman she has for a mother." Then David did what he'd been wanting to do all afternoon. He kissed her.

Hadley and David met with Dr. Gallagher that afternoon. The psychologist had had a last-minute cancellation and was happy to fit them into his schedule.

Speaking freely about her worries had been a relief. With David's strong, supportive presence beside her, it had been surprisingly easy to share. Hadley wondered if Brynn might benefit from a few sessions with Dr. Gallagher.

It was nearly suppertime when they picked up Brynn from Clay's office and returned home.

"Can I read in the hammock until supper?" Brynn asked as they stepped inside the house. "I've been at school all afternoon."

A smile lifted David's lips.

Hadley's tone remained easy. "Why don't you toss a few balls for Ruckus first? He's been inside most of the day."

"After we play catch, then can I read?"

At Hadley's nod, Brynn was out the back door in a flash, dog at her heels.

As she and David strolled into the kitchen, she saw his laptop on the table, open to some sort of architectural design program. Routine, she thought, everyday life. One day, her life might be back to being simple.

But she would never let it be the way it was before, when she kept her thoughts and feelings to herself, when the wall she'd erected didn't allow anyone to get too close.

Never again, Hadley vowed. No matter how hard, she wouldn't shy away from having the difficult conversations or speaking from the heart.

David stepped up behind her, wrapping his arms around her waist. He nuzzled her hair. "What are you thinking?"

"We should tell her outside." On the drive over, Hadley had given the matter considerable thought, considering and rejecting a variety of possibilities. "Maybe go for a walk. There's something about being active that makes conversation come easier."

David didn't immediately agree, so she added, "Some of the best talks I had with my dad were when we were at the sink doing dishes."

"You're right." He turned her in his arms. "For me, it was when my dad and I were shooting hoops."

"I just want to get this over with."

"Don't worry." He tipped her chin up and kissed her gently on the lips. "You're not alone. We're a team. Remember that."

Hadley nodded, a lump forming in her throat. Then, squaring her shoulders, she headed for the back door.

David was a firm and steady presence as he followed her outside and down the steps to the terrace. Though butterflies fluttered in her belly and the hands at her sides trembled, she found comfort in his nearness, in the strength emanating from him.

The fact she agreed this step was necessary didn't stop Hadley from worrying.

When she spotted her daughter in the hammock, book open, chuckling at something she'd just read, Hadley almost turned and went back inside. Who was she to turn this little girl's world upside down?

David stepped to her side. "This is the right thing."

"I hope so."

As if sensing her unease, he looped an arm around her shoulders, gave them a squeeze. "You'll see."

"Looks like a good book," Hadley called out.

Brynn carefully inserted a lace bookmark to save her place, then scrambled out of the hammock. "It's really funny. Gram got it for me."

"I loved to read when I was your age," Hadley said. "We'll have to talk favorite books sometime."

Brynn's eyes lit up. "I have lots of favorites."

Hadley smiled. "Me, too."

"How about a walk in the woods?" David asked.

"Can Ruckus come, too? Please?"

The dog, who'd been snoozing beside her, was on his feet, his hopeful look matching the one on Brynn's face.

"Sure. No problem." David's voice sounded unnaturally hearty. "The more the merrier."

Brynn appeared puzzled for a second, as if sensing something amiss. Then she smiled.

"Your dad mentioned a walking trail." Hadley slanted a glance at David, received a nod.

"It's really cool." Brynn did a little twirl. "Wait until you see the meadow."

"Meadow?" Hadley arched a brow. "In the middle of the woods?"

"There was this big explosion one night—"

"Lightning hit," David explained. "One tree went down, took out a couple nearby."

"People came and hauled away the wood. For fireplaces," Brynn explained. "They left stumps for us to sit on."

"It's one of our favorite spots." David gave his daughter a wink.

"I can't believe I never heard about it," Hadley mused as Brynn turned and led them into the thick grove of trees.

"We don't talk about it much." Brynn's voice drifted back. "It's a secret."

David coughed to hide his chuckle.

Both Hadley and David kept the conversation easy until they reached the clearing. As promised, there were tree stumps and scraggly strands of grass.

The absence of trees let sunlight fill the area, while a light breeze whispered through the surrounding trees.

Brynn turned in a circle, arms outstretched, her face lifted to the light. "Isn't it wonderful?"

Hadley's heart overflowed with love for this child. Not only was Brynn lovely on the outside, but she had a beautiful heart.

"This is the perfect spot for a story. I have one I'd like to tell you." Hadley patted the flat surface of a stump. "Interested?"

"I love stories." Brynn's eyes sparkled. "Are there fairies in this story? Princesses? Pigs?"

"Pigs?" David looked so startled both Brynn and Hadley giggled.

Hadley shook her head. "No fairies, princesses or pigs, but there's a girl with long blond hair and big blue eyes."

"Like me." Brynn touched the strands pulled back in a high pony.

"And like me." Hadley fingered a lock of her own hair.

"Our hair is the same color." Brynn sounded surprised, as if she'd just noticed.

"Yes, it is." A trickle of sweat rolled down Hadley's spine. Dear God, she hoped telling Brynn was the right decision.

"Tell me the story," Brynn ordered.

"Brynn." David shot her a warning look. "Don't push."

"She said she had a story to tell me," Brynn protested, then smiled at Hadley. "I'll be patient."

It was the smile that did it. Full of innocence and trust, that smile made Hadley realize she didn't want unnecessary lies between her and this sweet child she dearly loved.

Hadley took a deep breath.

David offered her an encouraging smile.

Brynn gazed expectantly.

"When I was a little girl, barely older than you, I would go visit my grandparents every summer. They lived in a small town in a different state."

"I bet that was fun. I always have fun with Gram."

"It was fun. My grandma taught me how to cook, and my grandfather taught me how to bake." So many wonderful memories forever tainted by the events of that summer. Hadley cleared her throat and continued. "I met a boy there. He was older, already in college. When I returned home that fall, I discovered I was going to have a baby."

Brynn's eyes grew wide. Clearly, she hadn't anticipated this twist. "You had a baby?"

Hadley's heart pounded against her ribs. "I did."

"A boy?" Brynn leaned forward, her eyes bright with curiosity. "Or a girl?"

"A girl." Hadley's lips trembled before she regained control. "A beautiful baby girl."

Brynn's brows pulled together. "I've never seen your girl. Where does she live?"

Hadley clasped her hands together. "I wanted the best for my child. Her father and I weren't together. I wanted her to have both a mommy and a daddy. So I chose a family who could give her everything I couldn't."

Brynn nodded sagely. "She was adopted, just like me."

"That's right." Hadley forced the words past the lump in her throat.

Beside her, David expelled a shaky breath.

"Do you know where she is?" Brynn tilted her head. "Have you visited her?"

"I went to where she lives with her family." Hadley spoke carefully as her heart swelled with emotion.

"I bet she was excited to see you." Brynn thought for a moment. "Probably scared, too."

"Scared?" Hadley pushed the word past suddenly frozen lips.

"Wondering if you liked her." A sadness briefly filled Brynn's eyes, then cleared. "She was lucky."

"Why lucky?" David spoke for the first time since Hadley had begun the story.

"Now she has two mommies."

Hadley wanted to retreat, but she couldn't back out now. "You're that little girl."

Confusion blanketed Brynn's face. "What little girl?"

Hadley almost said *my little girl*, but swallowed the impulse. "You're the child I gave birth to all those years ago."

The glance Brynn shot her father was a wordless plea.

David moved to his daughter and crouched before her. Taking her hand, he met Brynn's confused gaze with a steady one of his own. "What Hadley is trying to say is, she's your birth mother."

Brynn shifted her attention to Hadley. Blue eyes met blue eyes. "You're my mommy?"

What did she say to that? Hadley's mind raced. Should she reiterate she was Brynn's *birth mother*? Or simply go with the child's assessment?

Hoping she was doing the right thing, Hadley nodded.

Brynn's quivering lips lifted in a faint smile. "That's why we look alike."

"You think we look alike?"

Brynn thought for a moment, then nodded. "Lia thinks I look like you."

Pleasure flowed through Hadley's veins like warm honey.

"I realize you already have a mommy, but I hoped maybe you'd want me to be a part of your life, too."

"Two mommies." Brynn considered. "Angela at school has two mommies. They're lesbians. That means there's two mommies and no daddy."

"You've got a daddy." She only meant to reinforce David's relationship to Brynn, but the spark that lit in the child's eyes made Hadley wish she'd chosen her words more carefully.

"Do I have two daddies, too?"

Tricky, tricky, Hadley thought as the earth shifted beneath her feet.

"Only one," David answered, his tone warm and reassuring. "Just me."

Brynn studied him for a long moment before her gaze shifted to Hadley. "What about my other daddy? Can I see him?"

"I haven't seen your birth father in years." The psychologist had advised them to stick as close to the truth as possible. Hadley could not, would not, use the word *daddy* in reference to Justin. "I'm very sorry, but I don't know how to get ahold of him."

All true, as Hadley had never attempted to navigate the penal system.

Brynn's gaze narrowed and remained firmly fixed on Hadley's face. "Where does he live?"

Despite the cool breeze rustling the leaves, perspiration slid down Hadley's back. She took a breath to steady her nerves and her voice. "I don't know where he lives."

Again, honest. She didn't know the exact prison cell number where he resided.

Hadley summoned a smile. "If he ever contacts me, I'll tell you."

Brynn appeared to mull over the words, then nodded. "I have another question."

Nodding, Hadley held her breath.

"Since my other mommy doesn't have time, will you answer the questions for my Founder's Day project?"

CHAPTER TWENTY-TWO

That night, after Brynn had gone to bed, David suggested to Hadley they take their own walk, this time down the long, winding lane to the road. Brynn had taken the news about Hadley being her birth mother better than he'd hoped, but the stress of the day had left them both restless.

Hadley glanced at the hall leading to Brynn's bedroom. "Is it okay to leave her alone in the house?"

David pulled out his phone. "There's a monitor in her room. I have an app that will let us know if she calls out."

"In that case"—Hadley pushed to her feet—"I'd like to walk."

A full moon made what would otherwise be a treacherous walk in the dark pleasurable. An owl hooted in the distance, and far off, a coyote howled. The air retained the warmth of the day, and the light breeze chased any bugs away.

"I guess it went well. I thought it did, anyway." David cursed himself for sounding like an unsure schoolboy, though that was exactly how he felt.

When Brynn had asked about her other "daddy," his heart had sunk. David shoved his hands into his pockets. "You did a good job answering her questions."

"Thanks to Dr. Gallagher." Hadley's face looked pale in the moonlight, but there was a peaceful set to her features that hadn't been there hours earlier. "If he hadn't walked through some of the questions she might ask and helped us with answers that were truthful, I'd have been floundering."

David reached over and took her hand. He intended to give it a brief squeeze, but when her fingers linked with his, he didn't let go.

He'd never realized how much comfort could be gained from a simple touch. Without taking time to think, he stopped and pulled her into his arms.

Hadley wrapped her arms around his shoulders and rested her head against his chest. She sighed heavily, and David was seized with a rush of emotion.

Comfort given, he thought, comfort received.

Wasn't that how it was supposed to be in a relationship? Were they in a relationship? At the moment, it sure felt that way. "It was reassuring to have the doctor agree with us that it's best to keep Brynn away from Justin and his family."

"It was nice having a professional opinion." Hadley sighed as he stroked her hair. Her head fit perfectly just under his chin.

"You're part of her life—and mine—now." David kept his voice light. "No getting away from us."

He felt her smile against his shirtfront.

"I don't want to get away." Her voice took on a tremulous quality. "I've never been happier than I am right now."

"Because of Brynn."

"And because of you."

His heart became a heavy mass in his chest. "I never thought I'd trust a woman again."

When Hadley stiffened in his arms, David wanted to curse. Why was it so hard for her to accept a compliment? To realize that, in coming to him and telling him about Brynn's father, she'd shown him, better than any words she could have said, her true character.

"Where do we go from here?"

Had she really voiced the question that was in his heart? The last thing David wanted was to move too fast, to push her for a commitment she wasn't ready to make.

He'd tried to deny his growing feelings, but tonight, when they'd formed a united front and answered Brynn's questions, he'd known there was no going back.

He wasn't falling in love with Hadley.

He was in love with her.

Everything in David's head screamed it was too soon to talk about forever.

One step at a time, he told himself.

Did proper etiquette demand you answer someone's question before kissing them?

Screw etiquette.

Without warning, he lowered his head and closed his mouth over hers. Hadley's lips were soft and welcoming. Her arms rose to encircle his neck.

They kissed and kissed some more. He longed to show her how much she meant to him. Show her in a way that words could never properly convey.

He continued pressing his lips lightly to hers, teasingly, his mouth never pulling away. David forced himself to take it slow. Going slow wasn't easy when she tasted like the most delicious, decadent candy he'd ever eaten. When he wanted nothing more than to gorge himself on the sweet taste of her.

A hot riff of sensation rocketed up his spine. He spread his hands over her buttocks and pressed her against his erection.

When Hadley moaned, he deepened the kiss. Need all but erupted in him. He skimmed his hands up her sides to rest just below her breasts. When he spoke, his voice was shaking and raspy with need. "Let's go back to the house."

220 | CINDY KIRK

"I know what you want, Mr. Chapin." Her voice might be teasing, but he saw desire in the eyes gazing back at him. She leaned close and whispered in his ear, her breast pressing against his arm. "I want it, too."

"You're a beautiful woman." David's fingers lifted Hadley's chin, and he studied her for a long moment. "Inside and out."

Under his intense gaze, Hadley's lips began to tingle. When she moistened them with the tip of her tongue, his eyes went dark and the air between them pulsed with energy.

He kissed her fingers, featherlight.

Her heart began to skip. How could such a simple touch be so arousing?

His gaze met hers. "I'm still figuring all this out."

"I'm not asking for promises."

He brushed a strand of hair back from her face. "You should demand nothing less."

Hadley just smiled and kissed him lightly on the mouth.

A look she couldn't decipher skittered across David's face. "I haven't been with a woman since Whitney."

Her heart gave a solid thud.

"It's…" She swallowed against the emotion rising to clog her throat. "It's been a while for me, too."

Unexpectedly, he muttered a curse.

"I don't have protection." His laugh held no humor. "Like I said, it's been so long…"

Her mind raced.

"I don't have condoms, either." Hadley kept her voice matter-of-fact, although the slight tremor might have told him she wasn't as calm as she appeared. "But I am on the pill, so birth control is covered. And I'm clean."

"I got checked, too. Shortly after Whitney and I split."

It took a second for what he said to register. He'd gotten checked for STDs after his *wife* had left. Which could only mean he thought Whitney had been…

"What I'm trying to say is I'm clean, too," he added.

"Looks like we've both been cleared for active duty." Hadley offered him an impish smile. "If you're okay with not holstering your gun, we're good to go."

He laughed. "You say the darnedest things."

Heat rolled up Hadley's neck in a rush. She attempted to pull her hand from his, but he held on and brought it to his lips.

"I find it an endearing quality." David pressed a kiss in the center of her palm, and when his eyes met hers, they seemed to glitter in the moonlight. She saw her own desire reflected in the smoky gray depths, and a question.

Hadley responded by inclining her head ever-so-slightly and was rewarded with a slow, slightly wicked smile.

Without uttering another word, his mouth closed over hers. There, under the branches of a large oak, the moon casting a golden glow, she kissed him with all the love in her heart.

Her fingers toyed with the buttons on his shirt. His chest was broad beneath her palm, his body as firm and hard as an athlete's. The citrus scent Hadley had come to associate with him teased her nostrils.

Leaning close, Hadley nuzzled his ear, then planted a kiss at the base of his neck, his skin salty beneath her lips. But when she reached for his belt buckle, David's fingers closed over hers.

"Inside."

"It might be fun out here."

"Tempting, but someone driving down the road might decide to turn in."

Laughing, they sprinted down the drive, hand in hand. Hadley had to stifle her laughter as she reached the house, not wanting to wake Brynn. "Which room?"

"Yours. It's the farthest from Brynn's bedroom." Still, when he took her hand, they tiptoed down the hall as if Brynn slept mere feet away.

Ruckus followed behind them, slipping into the room before David closed the door to her suite behind him.

David pointed to the dog, then to the red plaid dog bed. "You. Over there."

Hadley trailed a finger up his arm. "What about me? Where do you want me?"

"You're right where I want you." He pulled her to him. His warm, husky voice reached inside her to a raw, tender place. "Now, we take this slow and enjoy."

Before Hadley could draw a breath, his lips were back on hers, exquisitely gentle and achingly tender.

She wound her arms around his neck and lifted her face, sighing with pleasure as his mouth caressed her lips.

His hair was a jumble of waves, one lock falling rakishly across his forehead. That was her last coherent thought as they tumbled down on the sofa cushions.

David pressed his lips lightly to hers, teasingly, his mouth never pulling away. Hadley kissed him back, forgetting everything in the pleasure of the contact. A smoldering heat flared, a sensation she didn't bother to fight.

"I want you naked." Desperation made her voice husky. Hadley pressed her body against him, moving seductively against his erection.

"What happened to slow?" His voice was a throaty rasp.

"Next time." With fingers that trembled with urgency, she started on buttons. Their shirts hit the floor at the same time. One flick of the closure and her bra joined the shirt at her feet.

She started to unzip her skirt, but then his broad hands closed over her breasts. She squeezed her eyes shut when he cupped them high in his hands, circling the peaks with his fingers. Thumbs teased the tips for several excruciating seconds before his mouth replaced his hands.

She curved her fingers against the back of his head, not wanting the exquisite sensations coursing through her to stop.

Hadley prided herself on her calmness under pressure, but she couldn't wait to run her hands over his body, to feel the coiled strength of skin and muscle sliding under her fingers.

She couldn't wait for him to touch her in the same way, longed to feel the weight of his body on hers. Wanted to feel him inside her.

Hadley pulled his face to hers and gave him a ferocious kiss. The type of kiss that said, *I want you now.*

In seconds, David's pants joined her skirt on the floor.

Trying to calm her unsteady breath, Hadley took a moment to study him in his black boxers. She tapped a finger against her lips. "It's a good look. But I think I'd like you better naked."

"Ditto."

Emboldened by his quick response, Hadley hooked a finger in her lace panties, watched his eyes drop from her breasts to the tiny triangle.

She took a step closer. "You show me what you have, and I'll reciprocate."

His gaze never left hers as he stepped out of his boxers and his erection sprang free.

"You're beautiful," she murmured.

He pointed to her panties. "You're still dressed."

"This"—she eased the tiny triangle of silk down an inch —"hardly counts."

His eyes glittered. "We had a deal."

She gave a little laugh and closed her hand around the length of him.

"Keep doing that," he growled when she began to stroke him, "and this will be over before it begins. I'm ready to self-combust."

Pulling her hand away, he pushed her up against the wall and kissed her with an intensity that had her squirming with pleasure.

"Touch me," she whispered, "like I touched you."

With eyes still on her face, David reached down and gave a

swift jerk on the silky fabric. In tatters, her panties fell to the floor.

He looked up. "Sorry."

"No, you're not. Neither am I." Her lips curved. "They were in the way."

"I could have worked around them, but having them gone makes this much easier." David cupped her, and one long finger slid inside.

Hadley's body clenched around his finger, her breaths now coming in pants. She surged against the pleasure swelling inside her like the tide. Just when she thought she would implode, he pulled back.

Easing her down to the rug, he continued to kiss her while those magical fingers, now on her breasts, sent shock waves of feeling through her body.

His mouth lingered there—licking, sucking, tasting—before beginning a downward journey. She squirmed when his tongue circled her navel, those magic fingers still on her breasts.

Consumed by the pleasure, she let her head fall back. When he asked her to open for him, she didn't hesitate. She wanted him inside her.

Then his mouth dipped lower.

Her heart began to pound. As his tongue circled, her breathing grew shallow. Hadley moved her hips, but not to push him away. No, she didn't want to push him away.

She simply couldn't remain still, not when he was making her feel...

The orgasm slammed into her, and she cried out.

David continued to stoke the fire until the heat dropped to a simmer.

"Ohmigod." She expelled a ragged breath, her skin still tingling. "I never—"

David planted a kiss on her belly. "I'm glad it was good for you."

She propped herself up on her elbows. "You sound as if we're done."

"Aren't we?"

Hadley gazed pointedly at his erection.

Suddenly, his arms were around her again, and the intense pleasure was back, rolling like large waves propelling her to great heights.

She wanted him inside her, needed him inside her. Just when she thought she couldn't go one second longer, David sank his hard length into her.

Hadley's legs swept around his hips, holding him to her. She met him thrust for thrust. Trust—and love—made the joining even sweeter.

It was as if she and David had been transported to a world made up of just the two of them, one filled with warmth and caring and incredible need. Hadley had never experienced anything like the emotions and feelings David stirred in her.

Her pleasure began to build. Hadley told herself to hold on, to make the feelings last, but her passion was so strong she couldn't stop it. She clung to him, riding the waves until she shuddered.

As her body released and muscles contracted, she tightened her hold on him. She never wanted to let him go.

David continued to stroke, to caress, until he'd wrung every last drop of pleasure from her before he took his own release, plunging deep once more and crying out her name.

She was still breathing hard when he rolled off of her. But instead of getting up, he pulled her to him, kissing her neck, her face her lips.

Content and sated, Hadley laid her head on his chest and snuggled against him. Her eyes drifted shut, then popped open when Ruckus growled.

She might have scrambled up if David hadn't placed a restraining hand on her arm.

"It's only the wind." David shot Ruckus a reproving look.

The dog plopped back down on the rug and began to gnaw on his foot.

"Why did he growl?" Hadley linked her fingers with his.

"Apparently, he doesn't like seeing two people having fun."

Hadley laughed and planted a kiss at the base of David's throat. She couldn't recall the last time she'd been this happy.

"This has been the best day." Her arms remained wrapped around his warm flesh, reveling in the feel and scent of him.

"An amazing evening." David's voice rasped, deep and unsteady.

After several minutes of cuddling, Hadley sat up and stretched. "I should clean up."

David pushed to his elbows and admired the long, lean body with curves in all the right places.

With blond hair tousled and lips swollen from his kisses, she couldn't have looked any lovelier.

"Please don't tell me you're getting dressed."

She answered by scooping up her clothes from the floor and flashing him a cheeky smile.

David expelled an audible sigh. What he'd always suspected was true.

All good things *did* come to an end. At least for this evening.

CHAPTER TWENTY-THREE

Silence really could be deafening, David realized.

He sat with his mother and two siblings in the parlor of the family home. David and Clay had each confiscated a chair, while his sister and mother sat on the pretty floral sofa.

David told them the whole story. He expected a barrage of questions. He hadn't expected them to simply stare in disbelief.

His mother cleared her throat. Wearing a silky blue dress with pearls, she appeared overdressed for what was supposed to be a simple family dinner. Her hair, worn for years in the same stylish bob that suited the shape of her face, sported fresh blond highlights.

When she'd greeted him at the door with a broad smile, he'd been hopeful. There was nothing his mother liked more than having her entire family under the same roof. With his revelation, the bright smile wavered, then disappeared.

"Does she plan to fight you for custody?" Lynn's voice held a steel edge.

"What?" Hadn't she listened to anything he'd said? "No. Of course not."

"I don't understand why you sound shocked." His mother's

blue eyes were ice. "She admitted she came here with a specific purpose. Over the past three years, she's wheedled—"

"Stop right there." David didn't care if he sounded harsh. His mother's tendency toward knee-jerk reactions was the primary reason he'd insisted on telling his family without Hadley present. "Hadley did not wheedle her way into anything."

"I think Mom is concerned Hadley may have a hidden agenda." Greer, a younger version of their mother, kept her voice soft and conciliatory. "She loves Brynn. We all do. We don't want to see you—or her—hurt."

"Hadley loves Brynn, too." David leaned forward, resting his forearms on his thighs, searching for a way to convince his family there was absolutely no reason to worry. "She wants to be a part of her daughter's life. I want that, too."

"And your life?" Greer smiled. "I've seen the looks between the two of you. Definitely not PG-rated."

Despite the lightness of his sister's tone, David saw concern in Greer's eyes. He hadn't planned on getting into his plans for the future with Hadley, but right now it didn't feel as if he had a choice.

"I care very much for Hadley," he began. "She's a wonderful—"

"Are you sleeping with her?"

David didn't know who was the most shocked by his mother's question, him or his siblings.

"Mom." Clay shook his head in warning. "I hardly think that's our business."

"It most certainly is our business." Lynn's voice went shrill. "Your brother is a wealthy man. And a lonely one. A smart woman knows how to take advantage of—"

"Enough." David's voice cracked like a whip. "My relationship with Hadley is not open for dissection. You need to accept that, as Brynn's birth mother, she's now part of our family."

Lynn's blue eyes flashed. "Or what, David?"

Only under extreme duress did the normally implacable Lynn

Chapin snap. David had seen it after his father died when she'd lashed out at the funeral director who'd messed up the memorial service. She'd done it another time when Whitney had forgotten to pick up Brynn from kindergarten.

The forgetting part his mother might have forgiven, but not the way Whitney had acted afterward, as if leaving a five-year-old waiting alone for nearly an hour was no big deal.

David had underestimated how the news of Hadley's tie to Brynn would affect his mother. Forgotten how fiercely protective she was of her only grandchild, and yes, of him, too.

Forget the ultimatums.

"Mom." He kept his tone low and fixed his gaze on her face. "Hadley loves Brynn. And Brynn loves Hadley."

David held up his hand when she opened her mouth to protest. "As far as Hadley and me, well, I realize we haven't been together long. While I can't explain it, she and I share a special bond, too."

"I've seen the connection, Mom," Clay admitted.

David was grateful for his brother's support. There were already too many adversaries in the room. David needed an ally.

"Hadley and I are taking this slow." David reached over and took his mother's hand, his gaze never leaving her face. "You have my word that Brynn will remain my number-one focus and her happiness my number-one priority."

"I'm happy you aren't rushing into a commitment." There was a hint of apology in his mother's tone. "I only want the best for you and Brynn."

Greer slipped an arm around her mother's shoulders in support. "David is too sensible to rush into anything permanent."

"It seems my brother has this situation under control." Clay pushed to his feet. "Now, what time are we eating? I'm starved."

"Steve asked me to marry him." Lynn cast a loving look at the lanky man at her side. "I said yes."

Hadley added her own voice to the cheers coming from the family surrounding her. Beside her, Brynn jumped up and down.

Hadley liked Steve Bloom. From everything she'd witnessed in the past three years, the man was a stellar father. According to Ami and her sisters, he'd also been a wonderful husband, caring for his cancer-stricken wife until her death.

Now, he'd been given an opportunity for happiness once again, with Lynn.

David's hand captured Hadley's. He brought it to his lips. The obvious show of affection made her blush, but she didn't pull away. She loved this man and liked it when he touched her. Liked it very much.

On their way to personally congratulate the happy couple, David was waylaid by Cade, who had a couple of questions about the blueprints David had drawn up for him and Marigold. Hadley waited, but after a minute, then two, passed, she reminded herself she and David weren't joined at the hip.

Everyone attending the party this evening now knew she was Brynn's birth mom. Not much had been said, though Hadley had caught Lynn studying her thoughtfully several times during the meal.

Earlier, when dinner had concluded and they'd been feasting on the cherry pies she and Brynn had made, Hadley thought Lynn might say something. But she'd only complimented her and Brynn on their baking skills.

When she reached the smiling couple near the doors to the terrace, Hadley extended her hand. "Congratulations. I know you'll be very happy together."

"Thank you, Hadley." Steve's hazel eyes sparkled behind silver wire-rimmed glasses. He pressed her hand between his and gave it a squeeze. "I was glad to hear you've been reunited with your daughter. I can attest there's nothing like a daughter."

The sincerity in his words brought tears to Hadley's eyes.

"We're both happy you're here," Lynn echoed.

While his fiancée looked cool and chic in blue silk and pearls, Steve was comfortably rumpled in khakis and a madras shirt.

"Speaking of daughters." Hadley glanced around the room. "Have either of you seen Brynn?"

Lynn's brows pulled together. "The last time I saw her, she was headed to the backyard to play with Callum and Connor."

"Hanging with a bunch of grown-ups tends to be tedious for children that age." Steve smiled indulgently.

Connor burst through the French doors with a clatter.

The older man's gaze sharpened.

"Brynn's in the pool." The boy's freckles shone bright against his skin's pallor. "We were playing, and she hit her head. We tried to—"

Hadley went cold all over. Brushing by the boy, she raced for the door. She reached the terrace, scanning the deck of the kidney-shaped pool. She spotted Brynn facedown in the water. Her heart gave a solid thump.

"Call for an ambulance." Without breaking stride, she scooped up a kickboard and dived in. She reached the unconscious girl in seconds.

With quick moves, Hadley placed the kickboard between them and tilted Brynn's head back, effectively keeping her mouth and nose out of the water. By the time she approached the edge, David had joined her in the water and began mouth-to-mouth.

Numerous hands—she wasn't sure who they all belonged to— pulled Brynn from the water to the deck.

"See if she's breathing," Hadley ordered.

Kneeling beside the child, Cade opened her airway, then placed his ear close to listen for breathing. Hadley went light-headed when he pinched Brynn's nose shut and placed his mouth over hers and blew.

She prayed as she watched Brynn's chest rise. The sheriff's

fingers went to her pulse, then he repeated the breath. "We've got a pulse."

When Brynn began to gag, Cade turned her to one side. She vomited up water, then opened her eyes and began to cry.

It was the sweetest sound Hadley had ever heard. She started to rush to Brynn's side, but sirens sounded and Cade ordered everyone back.

"I'll let them in." Clay, his face an unearthly white, bolted toward the front of the house.

"Tell me what happened." Max's voice, dangerously calm, landed on his twin sons now huddled against their mother. "Make it quick. We need to tell the EMTs how Brynn ended up in the pool."

Callum and Connor looked at each other.

"Now." Max, normally one of the most easygoing guys Hadley had ever met, barked the command.

"We were playing tag," Callum began.

"We were splashing each other first," Connor reminded his brother. "There was water around the edge of the pool. It was kind of slippery."

"We were playing tag," Callum repeated. "She was chasing me and Connor."

"Get to the point." Max's eyes softened as he saw his son's distress, but his tone was firm.

"She slipped and fell into the water." Connor glanced at his brother as he spoke. "She hit her head on the side. We thought she was playing, pranking us, when she first started floating."

"We came to get you." Callum's blue eyes were wide, freckles standing out against pale skin like newly minted pennies. "Is she gonna die?"

"No," Hadley heard herself say, her voice sounding as if it came from far away. "She'll be fine. You did the right thing in coming for help. Your quick action likely saved her life."

Connor's gaze dropped to his feet. "We shouldn't have been running by the pool."

"No," she said. "Next time, you won't."

The crowd parted like the Red Sea for the EMTs and their gurney. Cade gave them a quick report as they did their assessment. After sliding a backboard under Brynn and stabilizing her neck, they loaded her on the gurney.

"I want my daddy." Brynn's voice rose then broke.

Hadley heard the attendants tell David he could ride with his daughter to the hospital. She didn't move, couldn't move. Instead, she stood there, alone, dress soaked, shoes still somewhere in the pool.

She waited for David to turn, to ask her to ride with them.

He climbed into the ambulance without a backwards glance.

"Hadley."

She turned at the gentle voice and saw Lynn, her beautiful face streaked with tears.

"Thank you for saving my granddaughter."

Before she could protest that it had been Cade who'd resuscitated Brynn, Lynn's arms were around her, holding her close.

"You're going to ruin your dress." Hadley attempted to pull away.

"Thank you," Lynn repeated, tightening her hold.

"I couldn't do anything but try to save her." A sob caught in Hadley's throat as the enormity of what had happened hit her. She began to shake. "I love her so much. If anything happens to—"

"Shhh." Lynn stroked Hadley's wet hair as if she was a small child. "It will be okay. She'll be fine."

Hadley let herself be comforted, wondering if this was what it was like to have a mother. Someone to soothe, someone you could count on to be there for you.

Greer touched her shoulder. "I've got clothes in my old room that should fit you."

234 | CINDY KIRK

When David's mother released her hold, Hadley realized she felt steadier.

"I can drive. I just need to find my purse." Lynn gaze darted all around, as if expecting to find her bag at the edge of the pool.

"It's okay." Steve's arm slid around her shoulders. "I'll drive."

When Lynn opened her mouth, prepared to protest, her fiancé shook his head. "If I drive, you can call David and concentrate on what he has to tell you."

Before heading to Greer's bedroom, Hadley walked over to Cade and gave the sheriff a fierce hug. "Thanks for saving my girl."

"We all had a part in that rescue." Cade gave her arm a squeeze. "Now get going. Your daughter will want you there."

Your daughter.

Hadley hurried to the stairs, praying with each step that Brynn would be okay.

CHAPTER TWENTY-FOUR

"The CT was negative for bleeding." The doctor glanced down at his clipboard then up at David. "She's got quite a bump on her head. That will take a while to go away. The nurse will give you a sheet detailing signs and symptoms we want you to look out for in the next few weeks."

The physician had a calm, efficient manner and appeared to know what he was doing. But he looked about twelve, a fact that didn't inspire much confidence.

"Brynn insisted I call my ex-wife. In fact, she was almost hysterical." Reaching out to Whitney hadn't been at the top of David's to-do list, but he had to admit that speaking with her mother had calmed Brynn.

"Brynn may be more emotional for the next few days, but that's normal and to be expected." His gaze met David's. "It's usually a good idea to notify the noncustodial parent anyway when something serious occurs."

Something serious.

This had definitely been serious. Brynn could have died. Bile rose in his throat as the adrenaline pumping through his body dipped.

David cleared his throat. "When can I take her home?"

"Tomorrow morning."

"Why keep her overnight? You said the CT was clear."

"Mr. Chapin, your daughter nearly drowned. There are occasionally complications from those near misses. Most problems usually arise within the first seven hours." The doctor listened as his name was paged overhead. "I don't anticipate any issues, but we can't be too careful."

He turned to leave, then paused. "Brynn is a very lucky little girl."

David watched as the boy, man, strolled off with brisk strides. While the nurse got Brynn settled, he tried to settle himself.

The walls in the pediatric unit displayed an ocean scene, with brightly colored fish, a friendly looking octopus and bright orange seahorses. The mural looked like something Good Hope artist Izzie Deshler might have done.

Staring down at his hands, David saw they trembled. They mirrored how his insides felt at the moment. He closed his hands into fists and told himself to stay strong. Brynn counted on him to stay strong.

He might have had a chance of convincing himself this was no big deal, if not for the movie that kept replaying in his head.

The twins bursting into the parlor, their words tumbling out.

Hadley, racing through the door and diving into the water.

Brynn, his precious child, floating facedown in the water.

The terror of breathing life into his daughter's lungs.

Clay, performing CPR on the deck of the pool.

What had taken only minutes had felt like hours.

If the boys hadn't run into the house for help, if Hadley, if he, if Cade…

David closed his eyes as the what-ifs pounded against his aching skull. He pressed fingers against his eyes.

"David." It was his mother's voice, trembling and filled with fear. She gripped his arm. "Is she okay? Did something—?"

His mother began to sway.

David reached out, but Steve was closer and faster. His arms closed around his fiancée.

Only then did he see Hadley standing with his sister.

"Brynn is fine. I spoke with the doctor." David knew they needed reassurance more than specifics. "He's going to keep her overnight as a precaution, but she's great."

Okay, so *great* might be laying it on a little thick, but it seemed to work. His mother sagged against Steve, relief in her eyes.

Hadley didn't move or speak.

"Can we see her?" His mother eyed the closed door.

"The nurse is in there with her." David kept his tone easy, but his gaze was on Hadley. "As soon as she comes out, we can go in."

"Why don't we grab a cup of coffee from the vending machine?" Steve suggested.

"I don't want to—" Lynn paused when Steve's gaze shifted pointedly from Hadley to David.

"Yes. A cup of something hot would be nice." Lynn smiled, the movement of her lips not reaching her eyes.

"I'll come with you and Steve." Greer gave her brother a pointed glance. "C'mon, Clay."

Steve glanced at David and Hadley. "Can we bring something back for either of you?"

Hadley cleared her throat and finally spoke. "Nothing for me, thank you."

David shook his head. "I'm good."

Then they were alone. David wanted desperately to take her into his arms, but feared if he did, he might break.

"Is she really okay?" Hadley stepped close. Her voice remained low, as if concerned it might carry.

"Yes. It's a miracle. We could have lost her, but we didn't."

Without him quite realizing how it happened, she was in his arms and they were clinging to each other.

"I was terrified."

Without seeing her face, he heard the tears.

"Me, too." His voice caught. "If-if anything would have happened to her, I don't know if I could have gone on."

Her fingers wrapped around the fabric of his shirt as she rested her head against his. Her entire body quivered.

"She's going to be okay. Nothing else matters."

David stroked her hair. "I should have insisted you ride in the ambulance with us."

"You had other things on your mind."

"I'm sorry." When she said nothing, he added. "You saved her."

She shook her head.

"You were in the water and pulling her to safety—"

"*We* pulled her to safety," she insisted. "Cade—"

"He's getting those house plans for free."

The comment brought a choked laugh from Hadley.

"So lucky," she murmured, holding him with a fierceness that steadied him.

"I love you."

She lifted her head, inclined her head.

"I love you," he repeated and tucked a stray strand of her hair behind one ear, wondering why he hadn't said it before. "I've known it for a while."

A look of wonder filled her eyes. For a second, David thought —hoped-she'd say the words back, but his family returned and the nurse stepped out of Brynn's room.

"You can go in." The RN, an older woman with salt-and-pepper hair and a warm smile, gestured toward the door. "She's eager to see her family."

"We'd like to spend the night," David told her.

"Parents are allowed to stay with their child, but I'm afraid you'll have to use the sleep chairs."

Hadley stepped forward. "I want to stay."

The nurse's gaze was cautious. "You are...?"

"She's Brynn's mother," Lynn advised before David could reply. "She saved her daughter's life."

Three days later, David strolled into the kitchen, a bounce in his step. Each day, his daughter seemed more like herself. "How's Brynn doing today?"

"We baked banana bread. While I cleaned up, she built a monster Jenga tower." Hadley smiled apologetically. "Now, she's watching a movie. I know we're supposed to limit screen time, but this is the first time she's had any since leaving the hospital."

He glanced into the other room where he could see Brynn sprawled on the sofa, one arm around her stuffed monkey. She looked relaxed, content and—praise God—healthy. "Tuesday night seems like a bad dream."

"I'd say more of a nightmare with a happy ending." Hadley cocked her head. "How are the surgery center plans coming?"

David had spent the morning in his upstairs office, first on a conference call, then digging into a surgery center project that required a quick turnaround.

"I made excellent progress." He gestured toward the loaf. "That smells wonderful."

"I'll get you a slice." She slanted him a playful glance. "First, you have to do something for me."

David slid his arms around her and pressed his lips to her neck, sending shivers of delight traveling down her spine. "Anything."

His breath was warm and arousing.

Hadley reminded herself Brynn was in the next room. Still, she kissed him lightly. "You can pour us each a cup of coffee."

The eyes that stared down into hers were dark with desire. "You should have asked for more. I'd have given it to you."

A home? A family? A lifetime with the two people who mattered most in her life?

Hadley doubted that was what he meant. The knowledge didn't stop the yearning. Keeping her tone light, she lifted a hand to his cheek, then gave it a brisk pat. "Coffee will do for now."

Once they were seated across the table, Hadley brought up the subject she knew he didn't want to discuss. "Brynn asked again about the performance tomorrow."

David swore. "I wish her teacher had simply said if she didn't practice this week, she couldn't perform. She doesn't even like dance."

"The teacher is being nice." Hadley brought the mug to her lips and studied David over the rim. "She understands what Brynn went through and doesn't want to penalize her."

David expelled a breath. He hadn't been sleeping any better than she had since the accident, tossing and turning, then getting up and pacing.

Hadley knew because she'd been up and heard him. Last night, she couldn't take it any longer. Hadley had eased open his door and, without a word, slid into bed beside him.

After making love, they'd fallen into an exhausted slumber. She'd hopped out of bed at nine and found Brynn still sleeping.

"Brynn seems less restless at night," Hadley told David over coffee. "Yesterday, she didn't cry once."

Though the little girl had been emotional since the accident, Hadley had seen a marked change over the past twenty-four hours.

"Max texted me this morning."

Hadley cocked her head. "What about?"

"They want to bring the boys by today, just for a few minutes." David expelled a breath. "He'd like the twins to see for themselves Brynn is okay. What do you think?"

He'd been doing that more and more often, Hadley realized.

Asking for her input on decisions, like they were a team, like they were a family.

I love you.

Did David remember saying the words? Perhaps he hadn't brought it up again because he regretted saying it in the emotion of the moment.

"Hadley."

She looked up and blinked, realizing he was waiting for her reply. "That's fine with me. We could have them over for dinner? It's no trouble to whip up—"

"Let's wait on that. Brynn's still recovering, and the boys can be a bit...intense." He smiled. "We can have them over once all this Founder's Day craziness is behind us."

It sounded as if he expected them to continue living together but Hadley refused to read anything into his words. But when they were finished with their snack and he pulled her close for a kiss, she let herself dream, just for the moment, of a life with the man and child she loved.

Good Hope hit the Founder's Day jackpot on Saturday. The day dawned clear and sunny with a high temperature forecast in the mid-seventies. A perfect day for Brynn to dance on the bandstand stage.

Instead of heading immediately to the town square for the festivities, they'd decided to spend a relaxing morning at home so as not to overtax her.

The doorbell rang midway through breakfast.

Ruckus barked and raced to the front door.

Hadley paused on her trip to the coffeepot. "I'll get it."

Brynn looked up from the blueberry French toast casserole. "Who is it?"

Hadley smiled. "That's what I'm about to find out."

David, who'd already had one helping, spooned out another, then stood. "I'll refill our coffee. Would you like more OJ, Brynn?"

"Yes, please." The little girl lifted a piece of brown-sugar streusel from the top of the casserole and popped it into her mouth.

Hadley smiled. Getting up early to make the casserole had been the right move. By the time David and Brynn had risen, the enticing aroma of cinnamon, brown sugar and vanilla filled the air. Not to mention the heady aroma of freshly brewed coffee.

She practically skipped as she made her way to the front door, tempted to take a note from Brynn's playbook and burst into song.

Upon reaching the foyer she hushed Ruckus. The dog quieted but his keen-eyed gaze remained focused on the door.

Hadley smiled. The day was planned out. They'd perform their greeter duties, then Brynn would dance. The afternoon would be spent at home, giving Brynn a chance to rest and recharge for the fireworks display that evening.

Yes, Hadley thought as she reached for the knob and opened the door, it was going to be an absolutely perfect day.

The smile remained on her lips for a full five seconds before disappearing. Her heart pounded. Perspiration slicked her hands. "Whitney."

If possible, the woman was even more beautiful than she'd been the last time Hadley had seen her. Instead of burgundy highlights, gold streaks had been woven through thick mahogany hair worn in a long bob.

Without waiting for an invitation, Whitney brushed past Hadley, leaving the sultry scent of her perfume hanging in the air. She set a red travel case on the floor, swaying a bit as she straightened.

"Your food is getting cold." David came to an abrupt halt.

His ex-wife's lush lips curved in a feline smile. "Hello, David."

"Whitney. What are you doing here?"

The coolness of his welcome seemed to amuse his ex. "I've come to see my daughter. I want to see for myself that Brynn is okay."

Whitney's words held a slight slur, as if she'd enjoyed one too many cocktails on the flight from Florida.

"Mommy." Brynn must have heard her voice, because she came running and barreled into her mother.

Whitney raised her hand to smooth Brynn's hair, but her right arm jerked then jerked again when she tried to lower it.

Hadley exchanged a glance with David.

"You've got your suitcase." Brynn's brows pulled together as she noticed the red case. "Are you going somewhere?"

"No. I'm staying right here with you." Whitney slanted a glance at David. "At least for a few days."

At her ex-husband's raised brows, Whitney bristled. "It's Founder's Day. The decent hotels are all booked."

"We don't want you to stay in a hotel." Brynn looked at her father for support. "Do we, Daddy?"

David's smile didn't quite reach his eyes. "Of course not, Sweet Pea."

"I'd better head to the square." Hadley forced an easy, conversational tone.

Brynn's gaze whipped to her. "I thought you wanted to see me dance."

"I will see you dance. I wouldn't miss that for the world," Hadley assured the child. "But Mrs. Rakes needs someone to greet visitors. While I'm doing that, you can spend time with your mom."

Appearing mollified, Brynn nodded.

Hadley gave the child a hug, closing her eyes briefly as love surged.

David followed Hadley out the door and onto the porch. "You

don't have to leave. We had plans. Just because Whitney decided to show up doesn't—"

"She's not some stranger who stopped by. She's Brynn's mother. She flew all the way from Florida to see her." Hadley lowered her voice. "She doesn't look well."

"She's lost weight."

"Did you see her arm? The way it jerked?"

"Those involuntary movements are the hallmark symptom of Huntington's." Sadness washed over his handsome face. "It appears Kim was right to be worried."

"I'm sorry." Hadley wrapped her arms around his neck in an attempt to comfort and soothe.

David pulled her close. "I was really looking forward to today."

"Me, too." She pressed a kiss against his lips, loving the taste of him. "We'll have other days. Lots and lots of other days."

Still, as Hadley left the house, she couldn't help wishing that Whitney hadn't picked today to arrive in Good Hope.

CHAPTER TWENTY-FIVE

David resisted the urge to check the time. The day he'd looked forward to all week was dragging. He knew the reason. Whitney.

Listening to her inane chatter was exhausting. She talked about herself the entire time Brynn performed. Told him how she'd lost interest in the party scene. Told him her friend Kim was *worried* about her.

"Silly bitch." Whitney spoke the words loud enough to have several people turning to look. "Did I tell you she's *worried* about me?"

It was the sixth time in five minutes she'd asked him that same question.

He frowned, but this time said nothing. Whitney and Kim had been best friends as far back as David could remember. They were two peas in a pod in terms of interests. Or had been.

As his gaze scanned the crowd, he spotted Hadley seated off to the right, her gaze riveted on Brynn. As if she felt his eyes on her, Hadley shifted her gaze. When they exchanged a brief smile, David felt his spirits lift.

When the performance ended, he looked for Hadley, but couldn't find her.

"She's probably at the climbing wall." Brynn tugged on his hand. "I want to climb, too. Please, Daddy, please can I?"

"You just finished dancing. That's enough strenuous activity for one day."

Brynn opened her mouth as if to argue, then shrugged good-naturedly. "At least I got to dance. And I'm glad we saw the family tree. Lots of people were looking at it."

"You did the Chapin family proud with that tree." David had been relieved when Whitney begged off going to City Hall where the "history" was displayed. He wasn't sure how she'd have reacted to seeing Hadley's family history displayed under Brynn's maternal side.

When David had agreed to let Brynn interview Hadley, he never expected Whitney to show up this weekend. While he'd initially worried someone might mention Hadley's relationship to Brynn before he had a chance to tell Whitney, he shouldn't have been concerned. He'd yet to see anyone outside of close friends and family speak to his ex.

Whitney continued to tap bright red nails against her thigh in an erratic rhythm. "I want a drink."

Brynn pointed, eager to help. "There's a lemonade stand right over there."

Whitney dismissed the suggestion with a flick of the wrist. "I was hoping for something stronger."

Brynn appeared puzzled, but David understood. "The truck shaped like a beer keg also serves cocktails. The cherry vodka limeade is especially popular."

"I'll catch up with you." Whitney turned in the direction of the truck without saying good-bye or setting a place to meet.

"We'll be at the cakewalk," he called to her back, frowning at her slow, unsteady gait.

The first strains of a Michael Bublé hit filled the air as Prim and Max joined him.

David had known the couple were nearby when he'd spotted Callum and Connor in the cakewalk circle.

Prim glanced around. "Where's Hadley?"

Before David could respond, Whitney appeared. Despite her slow pace, red liquid sloshed over the rim of her plastic cup.

"Why are you talking to them?" Whitney shifted her gaze from David to Prim, her eyes shooting sparks of fury. "Your boys should be in jail."

Prim blinked twice. "Pardon me?"

"Your boys should be in jail."

In one easy movement, Max put himself between Whitney and his wife.

"I heard they said they were playing tag." Whitney drawled the words, her upper lip curved in a sneer. "That's quite a story."

"Whitney." David gripped his ex-wife's arm. "That's enough."

"Get your hands off me." She jerked her arm from his, then had to fight for several seconds to regain her balance. "Their brats could have killed my daughter. They should be in jail not—"

At Callum's shout of triumph, Whitney paused for a second, then finished, "Winning cakes."

Max's eyes had gone hard and flat. "I'm going to cut you a break because it appears that drink isn't your first. You can ask anyone who was there what happened. They'll tell you it was an accident."

"Your boys should be in jail," Whitney repeated.

A muscle in Max's jaw jumped.

"Whitney." David stepped forward and forced a conciliatory tone. "We can talk about the boys all you want once we get home."

Whitney's eyes flashed. "I want to talk about them now."

David's eyes must have transmitted an SOS, because Max rummaged in his pocket, pulled out a set of keys and tossed them to David. "Use my office."

Max's gaze shifted to his wife, who had their baby clasped

protectively against her. "We'll keep an eye on Brynn until you get back."

"Thanks." David lowered his voice. "Sorry about this."

By promising her another drink, David managed to coerce Whitney into accompanying him to the small building on Main Street where Max's CPA office was located. On the short walk, David gritted his teeth as she ranted about redheaded boys and devils.

Whitney had never been good at seeing any side of an argument but her own. This was different. Adding delusional thinking to the mix practically ensured this conversation wouldn't go well.

Once inside, Whitney commandeered the plush leather visitor chair. Under the fluorescent lights, David noticed the red stain from her drink on the front of her dress. The former Whitney would have been horrified. This woman didn't appear to care.

He set a glass of water next to her, which she ignored.

Whitney leaned back in the chair, then straightened. She leaned forward, then sat back. It was as if she couldn't get comfortable.

Fidgeting. Irritability. Lack of restraint.

David's heart twisted. All behavioral symptoms of Huntington's. He forced a calm tone. "Why are you so focused on the twins?"

"I don't want to talk about them." Whitney's right arm jerked up and down. Holding it down with her left, she speared him with razor-sharp eyes. "I want to talk about you."

The comment caught him off guard. Whitney had lost interest in him and his life long ago. David rested one hip on the edge of the desk. "What about me?"

"I read about you and Blondie in the Good Hope newsletter." Whitney stood, then sat back down. Seconds later, she stood again. Her right arm continued to jerk. "I know her secret."

David kept his face expressionless. "What secret is that?"

"She's stupid in her choice of men."

His lips quirked. "I take it you're referring to me."

Whitney laughed long and lustily.

"Not you." She plopped down in the chair with the grace of a drunken elephant. "That Justin guy."

David froze. How had Whitney learned Justin's name? Even when speaking with family, he and Hadley had been careful not to mention Brynn's birth father by name.

"The woman deserved more than she got." Whitney was back on her feet now and swaying. "Kim agrees."

"Where does Kim fit?"

"Kim?" Whitney cocked her head as if having difficulty placing the name. After several seconds, her lips curved in a sly smile. "Oh, she helped me dig. She can find dirt on anyone, even if it's well hidden."

Of that, David had no doubt. Despite her partying ways, Kim was a successful businesswoman, owning a profitable cybersecurity business in Boca.

David shrugged. "I'm not interested in what you found."

"You will be when you hear it. She—" Whitney paused when the bells over the door jingled and Hadley walked in.

Hadley's gaze slid from him to Whitney. "I'm sorry to interrupt. I wondered if you wanted me to take Brynn home. Or—"

"Perfect timing. We're discussing you and your buddy Justin. You really should have told David about your criminal past." Whitney made a tsking sound. "He has the right to know that your lies sent a man to jail."

Hadley stared in obvious confusion. "His actions sent him to prison."

"I bet you didn't know any of this." Whitney turned to David, then cursed as her arm began to jerk again. "Goddamn arm."

"Actually, Hadley told me all about the incident."

Surprise, swiftly followed by disappointment, flashed across Whitney's face.

"I'll take Brynn home." Hadley hurried from the office without a backward glance.

"Kim is my daughter, not yours." Whitney called after Hadley, seemingly unaware she'd gotten her child's name wrong. She murmured something unintelligible before whirling on David, her eyes glittering. "What are you looking at?"

She fumbled with the glass of water. When her arm continued to jerk, Whitney swept the glass off the desk and began to cry.

Compassion filled David's voice when he spoke. "You need help, Whitney. I'm taking you to the hospital. Now."

Brynn chattered happily on the drive home. Hadley let the child do most of the talking. Apparently, after the cakewalk, Callum had presented her with a toy Raphael, who was a Teenage Mutant Ninja Turtle.

"Callum said Raphael is smart and super strong." Brynn held up the green action figure that wore a red mask. "He told me I'm like Raphael."

Hadley slanted a sideways glance as she pulled the car to a stop in the drive. "That's a nice compliment."

"Callum can be selfish sometimes." Brynn unbuckled her seat belt, her tone matter-of-fact. "Under all that swagger, he's very nice."

Swagger. Hadley hid a smile, wondering where Brynn had come up with that word. The crazy thing was, it fit. "Have you thought where in your room you'll put Raphael?"

Hadley had no real interest in ninja turtles, but discussing Raphael was better than thinking about Whitney and David. He'd called her on the drive home to inform her he was taking Whitney to the hospital.

Brynn paused at the base of the front steps. "Raphael is only visiting. He won't be staying long."

"Oh?"

"He belongs with Callum."

"If you feel that way, why take him in the first place?"

"Callum felt bad I hit my head and fell into the water. He thinks it was his fault because I was chasing him." Brynn lifted her shoulders and let them fall. "It was an accident."

"What does that have to do with Raphael?"

"It made Callum feel better to give him to me." Brynn sounded more like a psychologist than a nine-year-old. "Tomorrow, I'll tell Callum my dolls don't like him and it's best if he takes him back."

"That's kind of you." Sometimes Brynn seemed like a little girl, and other times, like now, Hadley caught a glimpse of the woman she'd one day become.

When they started up the front steps, Brynn put her hand trustingly in Hadley's.

Hadley squeezed Brynn's fingers and found herself wondering about Whitney. She hoped the doctors could help the woman. Though Whitney had disappointed Brynn many times, the little girl loved her mother. If something happened to her, it would make Brynn sad.

Shoving aside her fears, Hadley made a light dinner, then helped Brynn get ready for bed. Once the child was in her pink pajamas, Hadley braided her hair.

She let her gaze linger as her fingers moved expertly on Brynn's silky hair. When she'd arrived in Good Hope, Hadley had thought getting to know Brynn from a distance would be enough.

Along the way she'd fallen in love.

With Brynn.

With David.

Now, she wanted more. She wanted it all.

"Know what?" Brynn covered her yawn with her fingers.

"What?" With the braid completed, Hadley tucked in the child. "I'm a lucky girl."

Thinking of the incident at the pool, Hadley nodded.

"I have two mommies." Brynn murmured the words in a sleepy tone. "Some kids only have one."

For a second, Hadley forgot how to breathe. She brushed a light kiss across Brynn's forehead, then stroked a wisp of golden hair back with the palm of her hand. "I love you, sweetie."

"I know." The sleepy words had her smiling. "I love you...Mommy."

Mommy. Brynn had called her *Mommy.* Tears threatened, but Hadley held them at bay until her daughter drifted off into sleep.

Over the past few days, Hadley had been granted a glimpse into how life could be. Her pie-in-the-sky dream of happily ever after had been shaken by Whitney's comment about her role in Justin's incarceration.

Though David had stood up for her, she'd seen the puzzlement in his eyes.

Heck, Hadley had been puzzled, too.

How could Whitney think she was responsible for the crimes Justin committed in Chicago? While Hadley didn't doubt Whitney could spin a convincing tale, she had to believe David had seen through the woman's bullshit.

He wasn't like her father. Her dad had been one of those guys who thought the worst until you convinced him otherwise. But she and David hadn't come this far to be pulled apart because of crazy accusations.

Casting one last look at their sleeping daughter, Hadley headed down the hall toward the living room.

The doorbell rang just as she reached it. Ruckus let out a loud woof, which she silenced with a hand signal. A quick glance through the peephole had her unlocking the door and pulling it open.

Lynn and Steve, along with Clay and Greer, stood on the porch.

Hadley stepped aside. "Please come in."

"Is David back from the hospital?" Lynn glanced around the room as if expecting her eldest son to materialize. "We heard he took Whitney into Sturgeon Bay."

"Apparently, she was acting really crazy." Greer said it loudly, then seemed to remember Brynn and clapped a hand over her mouth. When she spoke again, her voice was a whisper. "Where's Brynn?"

"She's asleep." Hadley kept her own voice low as she waved them into the living room. "She was exhausted."

Steve gave her arm a comforting squeeze as he strolled past. "How are you holding up?"

"Hanging in there." Hadley waited to speak again until everyone was settled. "How did you know David took Whitney to the hospital?"

"Max told us," Clay said. "David and Whitney had gone to his office to talk—"

Clay paused, and Hadley could see him weighing his next words.

"I know she was out of control." Hadley offered Clay an encouraging smile. "I spoke with both of them there myself."

"Well, on his way to the car with Whitney, he ran into Max and gave him back the keys to his office." Clay shifted uncomfortably in his seat, glanced down the hall in the direction of Brynn's bedroom. "Max said Whitney was agitated and not making sense."

Greer's gaze pinned Hadley. "Do you know what's wrong with her? Is she using?"

"I don't know if Whitney does drugs," Hadley told Greer, "but I think she may have...some condition. David should know more what's going on with her once he talks to the doctors."

"When do you expect him?" Lynn sat on the sofa, Steve's arm looped casually around her shoulders.

"He called about an hour ago. They were still running tests." Hadley lifted her hands, let them drop. "He wasn't sure when he'd be home."

"I told you we should stop and grab a burger on the way." Clay cast a pointed glance at his sister.

Greer rolled her eyes. "It's not like you're going to starve."

"I was just headed to the kitchen to make something for David," Hadley said. "I assume he'll be hungry when he gets home. How about if I whip up something for all of us?"

Hadley ignored the chorus of protests. "Seriously, it's no trouble. I enjoy cooking."

Brushing a kiss across her fiancé's cheek, Lynn lifted a hand. "I'll help."

Greer turned to her brother. "You want to get everyone's drink orders?"

"We have both red and white wine, as well as beer," Hadley called over her shoulder.

"Happy to be of service." Clay gave her a mock salute. "And what will you be doing, dear sister?"

Greer smiled at her soon-to-be stepfather. "I've got some ideas about our mother's upcoming wedding that I've been dying to run by Steve."

On the way to the kitchen, Lynn looped an arm companionably through Hadley's. "Now, tell me. How are *you* holding up?"

It was after ten by the time David left Sturgeon Bay. He'd called Hadley to tell her he was on his way home. She told him his family had just left.

He arrived home to find Hadley sitting on the porch, a glass of wine in hand. A bottle of merlot sat on a wicker table, along with another glass.

"You look exhausted." She gestured toward the chair. "Come sit for a few minutes. Have you eaten? Your mother and I made meatloaf and scalloped potatoes for the family."

A startled look crossed his face. "My mother cooked?"

Hadley gave a little laugh. "She said something about going back to her roots. We have plenty of leftovers. It won't take much to warm up."

"Thanks, but I grabbed something at the hospital." He glanced toward the door. "I should—"

"Brynn is sleeping." Hadley's eyes, sharp in the dim light, remained on his face. "She went to bed early. I think the day took a lot out of her."

David frowned. "Is she okay?"

"Just worn out." Again, Hadley gestured toward the chair. When he sat, she sipped her wine. "What's going on with Whitney?"

"The doctor is keeping her overnight for observation." David splashed wine into the empty glass Hadley had set out.

"What do they think is wrong?" she prompted when he simply stared out into the darkness.

Hadley listened intently, waiting to comment until he finished. "That's why she was off-the-wall with Prim."

"You heard about that?"

"Prim called. Your mother had also heard all about it from Max." Hadley shook her head. "I didn't say anything about the Huntington's to either of them. I believe once they know about the disease, they'll understand and forgive."

"Whitney laid into you pretty hard, too." David studied her over the rim of his glass. "She was out of control tonight."

"What happens now?"

"Unless she's a danger to herself or others, they won't be able to keep her." David blew out a breath. "The psychiatrist started her on medication for underlying depression."

Hadley cocked her head. "How did you get her to agree to go to the hospital?"

"The involuntary jerking is recent. It worries her." David stared into the darkness. "I told her they might have medicine at the hospital that could help her."

"*Are* there medicines?"

"Doctors used to prescribe a specific type of antipsychotic." David rubbed the bridge of his nose with his thumb and forefinger, as if fighting off a headache. "I assumed that's what they'd put her on, but the doctor in Sturgeon Bay put her on a drug recently approved by the FDA specifically for Huntington's."

"Well, that's a positive." Hadley sighed. As much as she didn't care for the woman, she wouldn't wish this disease, or disorder, or whatever it was, on anyone.

"We're not married anymore, but she is Brynn's mother. I couldn't walk away from her."

"Of course, you had to look out for her." Hadley spoke matter-of-factly. "She's family."

"Thank you for understanding." David reached over and took her hand, bringing it to his lips. "I told Whitney that you're Brynn's birth mother."

Hadley inhaled sharply. "What did she say?"

He shrugged. "She's distracted right now with her health problems. She'll deal with it at some point."

"How long do you think she'll remain in Good Hope?"

"She's itching to get back to Boca." David shook his head. "I predict she'll be on a plane to Florida the day she's released."

Hadley twisted the stem of her wineglass back and forth between her fingers. "Did she happen to say any more about Justin and why she thinks I had something to do with his sentencing?"

"She said something about you being arrested, too?" There

was no condemnation in his tone, no look like her father would give, the *you'd better not be lying to me.*

"I've never been—" Hadley began, then stopped. She gave a little laugh. "Do you know what a catfight is?"

"Two women fighting." When David's lips twitched, everything tense in Hadley went smooth.

"Justin and this guy, the same one who'd texted me, got into a fight." Hadley sat back in her seat. That night at the country fair seemed a lifetime ago. "While they were punching each other, the guy's girlfriend attacked me. I only defended myself, but the police arrived and hauled in all of us. We were charged with disorderly conduct. The girl and I paid a fine. The guys each got a week in jail and community service, since it wasn't their first offense."

"Fun times."

"Not really." Hadley took in air, expelled it slowly. "Thanks for standing up for me to Whitney. I didn't mean to keep this from you, but Justin's behavior and the resulting pregnancy are what I think of when I remember that summer."

"I'm sure there's a lot you don't know about me yet." He cupped her cheek and kissed her softly. "But I know all the important stuff about you."

"Such as?"

He grinned. "You're able to share a kitchen with my mother without strangling her."

CHAPTER TWENTY-SIX

"This place is amazing." Hadley gestured with her cup of punch to the newly renovated Blooms Bake Shop.

"Even with the delays, we're still only reopening a week later than planned." Ami smiled happily. "The shop is just as I envisioned it."

Though the It's Cupcake Time clock remained, as did the pink and blue tables with their mismatched chairs, there'd been lots of changes to Blooms Bake Shop. With more room, other tables in equally pretty hues had been added. The trim around the windows and doors sported a fresh coat of paint in a soft mint green. That color was echoed in the large cabinet behind the bake case. Or bake *cases*, as there were now four running the width of the shop.

A recently acquired three-tiered round table, painted a soft rose, held various prepackaged bags of treats, while chalkboards provided patrons with the pricing for all the bakery items.

The result was a quaint shop that reflected Ami's bubbly personality and love for her customers. Today, the bakery was filled to capacity with friends and family invited to celebrate completion of the project with sweet treats, including a Bloom staple, lavender cookies with rosewater icing.

Friends and family, Hadley thought, catching sight of David across the room speaking with Cade. Since moving to Good Hope, she'd been blessed with both. She and Brynn grew closer every day, and Hadley's relationship with the Bloom sisters had blossomed.

The fanciful thought made her smile.

If only…

Hadley pushed the thought away. How many times in the past two weeks had she waited for David to once again tell her he loved her? She'd finally accepted that the declaration had been simply something said in the heat of a moment when he'd been worried about Brynn.

But, oh, how she wished it was true. Not because it would be nice for Brynn to have a mother and father under the same roof, but because she loved David. Heart and soul. As in wanted to spend the rest of her life making him happy.

Though David hadn't mentioned her moving out, now that the bakery had passed inspection and the second-story apartment was ready for occupancy, there was no reason for her to remain at his house. Especially now that Brynn was back in school and no longer needed a nanny.

"How's Brynn liking fourth grade?" Ami set down her cup and waved at Cassie, then picked up a lavender cookie.

She needs a mother. She needs me.

For a second, Hadley feared she'd spoken aloud, but Ami only continued to smile, an expectant look in her eye.

"She loves it." Hadley's lips curved the way they always did when she thought of her daughter. "She's so smart and social."

"I bet she's loved having you around."

Loved, Hadley thought, *as in past tense.*

"It's been wonderful." A lump formed in Hadley's throat. "The time I've spent with her and David is a dream come true."

Ami's green eyes softened. "I knew it'd work out."

Hadley blinked and realized she'd given her friend the wrong impression. "But—"

"There's our girls."

"Dad." Ami popped the rest of the cookie in her mouth and gave her father a hug.

To Hadley's surprise, Lynn gave her a quick hug. It really shouldn't have been a surprise, since David's mother had started with the hugs right after they'd made meatloaf together.

Hadley didn't mind. She liked the closeness. Liked Lynn.

She'd be the perfect mother-in-law...

Stop it, Hadley told herself. Things were the way they were, and wishing wouldn't make them different.

"Brynn is going to love this shop." Lynn glanced at Hadley. "You and I will have to bring her here some weekend."

Hadley knew she'd likely be working, but summoned a smile. "Sounds like fun."

The four of them chatted for a few minutes. Every so often, Hadley would cast a surreptitious glance in the direction of the cupcake clock, where David was having an intense discussion with his brother.

Without warning, David turned and caught her staring. He smiled, then shot her a wink.

Hadley returned his smile as her heart swelled with love. David was simply the nicest and the best. The best guy. The best friend. The best father.

"We're going to mingle. We'll see you ladies later." Steve brushed a kiss across his daughter's cheek. "The lavender cookies taste just like the ones your mom used to make."

High praise indeed, Hadley thought when she saw Ami blink back tears.

"Are you okay with them being together?" Hadley asked Ami as the two strolled off.

"I am." Ami's lips tipped up. "They're good together. Not like him and the piranha."

"I saw Anita earlier with Tim." Hadley lowered her voice to a confidential whisper. "I was surprised you invited her."

"How could I not? Lindsay is a good friend, and Anita was a personal friend of my mother, which is still something I find hard to understand." Ami gave a little laugh. "Fin still calls her I-Need-a-Man."

Hadley chuckled. "To her face?"

"No, though I wouldn't put it past my sister if Anita pushed the wrong buttons."

"Your dad was decent about his breakup with Anita. I mean, whenever I've seen them at the same event, he's always gone over to speak with her."

"He wants them to still be friends." Ami picked up another cookie from her plate. "I remember when he decided to break it off. No ghosting for my dad. He did it face-to-face. He was so nervous beforehand."

"Because he was worried how she'd react?"

"That was probably part of it," Ami conceded, "but I think it was more that he's such a nice guy and didn't want to hurt her."

The tightness in Hadley's chest grew with each word. David had been nervous and secretive these past few days. Could *he* be planning to break it off with her?

She had no doubt he'd be willing to let her be part of Brynn's life. The problem was, *he* wouldn't be in her life.

"Are you okay?" Concern filled Ami's voice. "You look pale all of a sudden. Are you feeling okay?"

"I feel great." Hadley put some enthusiasm behind the words. "You've got a nice place here, Ami."

"I agree." That voice and his hand on her shoulder had Hadley turning. The love of her life stood smiling at her.

She smiled back. "Hey, you."

The look in his eyes was as warm as the clasp of his hand.

"David." Ami flashed a bright smile. "I'm glad you and Hadley could make it."

David gestured wide with an arm. "This is a first-rate remodel. It looks good."

"Kyle and his crew did a fabulous job." Ami glanced over to where the contractor stood, his wife at his side. "We hoped to be open by Labor Day. But this worked out. I'm sure you and Brynn didn't mind having Hadley under your roof for an extra week or so."

David grinned. "It was difficult, but we made it work."

Ami laughed. "Speaking of Kyle, I haven't had a chance to say hello to him and Eliza."

"Go." David slung an arm around Hadley's shoulders. "I'll keep this one company."

Ami wiggled her fingers in good-bye, then disappeared into the crowd.

"I haven't seen much of you since we arrived." Hadley winced. What was she thinking? It wasn't as if they were joined at the hip.

He cocked his head. "Will you take a drive with me?"

Her heart stuttered. "Where to?"

David put his palm against her back. "Somewhere more private."

"Sure. Great." Hadley forced herself to breathe in and out as they said their good-byes.

By the time David turned into the drive leading into Peninsula State Park, Hadley had to resist the impulse to urge David to simply spit it out. She'd rather he just told her he wanted to be friends, rather than making small talk about the changes to the bakery and then the weather.

The weather.

A clear sign this little trip to somewhere private wouldn't end well.

By the time David pulled into an empty parking lot next to

the recently reopened observation tower, Hadley felt numb inside.

He hurried around the front of the car to open her door. It figured he'd be solicitous. David was like Steve in that respect, a true gentleman, no matter what the circumstances.

David took her hand when she stepped from the car, and Hadley didn't pull away.

If he could be polite, she could do no less. Besides, this might be one of the last times that she would be able to touch him, other than in the most casual manner.

They walked to the base of Eagle Tower, originally built as a lookout for forest fires. The new structure rose high over the Bay of Green Bay.

Hadley inclined her head back. "I've never been up here. They closed the old one shortly after I moved here."

"The wood had deteriorated, plus it had been determined the load-bearing weight wasn't adequate for public use." David cast her a sideways glance. "Feel like doing some climbing?"

"Sure." Since exercise was supposed to reduce anxiety, Hadley figured a bunch of steps were just what the doctor ordered. "Want to race me to the observation deck?"

David laughed. "Maybe another time."

The breeze off Green Bay riffled his dark hair. In jeans, a blue polo and sneakers, he looked more like a man on vacation than a prominent architect.

With great effort, Hadley pulled her gaze from him. She began to climb, feeling like a condemned prisoner on her way to the gallows.

"We'll be able to talk privately once we reach the top." David fell into step beside her. "We'll be alone and undisturbed."

"Not necessarily. The tower is open to the public."

"Obviously, you didn't notice the sign Cade put up."

Hadley saw no reason to mention she'd been too busy looking at him. "What did it say?"

"The tower is closed, by order of the sheriff's department, for the next hour."

Hadley stopped suddenly. "Can Cade do that?"

"He did." David grinned. "An extra thank-you for the plans I drew up for him and Marigold."

"You could have just done this at the house," Hadley muttered.

"What did you say?"

"Nothing." Hadley picked up the pace. Cade had deliberately given David the privacy he needed. Did everyone but her know this was going down today?

Ami didn't. Hadley was sure of it. Her friend wouldn't have let her walk into this blind. She would have given her a heads-up.

Hey, Hadley, the man you love is going to tell you today that he just wants to be friends. Hadley winced at the thought as she stepped onto the observation deck.

"I used to climb up here in high school when I had thinking to do, or when something was gnawing at me." David's sheepish smile had her stomach clenching. "I know it sounds crazy, but this place always helped put things in focus."

The best Hadley could manage was a nod. She moved to the rail and gripped it tight. Gazing west, she stared, unseeing, at the Upper Peninsula of Michigan in the distance.

"Like I said, there's something important I need to say to you."

The serious dip in his tone had Hadley releasing her death grip on the rail. She wasn't a coward. She would face him and hear what he had to say with her head high. But she turned too quickly and stumbled.

David was there, the way he always was for her, hands on her arms to steady her. The fragrant woodsy scent from the cedar trees mixed with the familiar citrus of his cologne.

"You're trembling." Concern filled his voice, and he pulled her tight.

"Just say it." She stiffened and pushed him back, resisting the overwhelming urge to burrow into him. "I want this over with."

He stepped back, and his lips twitched. "I believe it's customary to drop to one knee first."

Hadley stared. "Dr-drop to one knee?"

"When you propose to the woman you love." As if needing to touch her, he tenderly brushed back a strand of hair. "I believe it's common to say a few words, too. If you don't mind, that is."

It took several erratic heartbeats for Hadley to find her voice. She waved a hand. "I don't mind. Talk away."

Amusement mixed with the tenderness on David's face. He took her hand, caressing the palm with his thumb. "Hadley Newhouse, I believe we were destined to find each other when the time was right. In addition to being the love of my life, you're my closest friend. With you, I can be myself. You bring out the best in me."

The impact of David's heartfelt words washed over Hadley.

This man knew her.

This man loved her.

Her heart leaped to her throat when he dropped to one knee and pulled a ring from his pocket. The emerald-cut diamond in an ornate platinum setting flashed fire.

"I want you to marry me, Hadley. I want us to build a life together. You, me, Brynn and any other children we might have. If there are hard times, we'll get through them. I firmly believe there isn't anything you and I can't face as long as we're together."

Love swirled, filling her to bursting, while blood flowed like warm honey through her veins.

David shot her a questioning glance as he continued to hold the ring between his thumb and forefinger. "Want to try it on? You don't need to give me an answer right away, if you're not sure."

She extended her left hand. As he slid the sparkling diamond on her finger, she remembered him telling her once that Whitney preferred to buy her own gifts, because none of his was ever exactly right.

Hadley gazed at the ring, then back into the face of the man who was the right one for her. "I don't need to take time to consider. It's absolutely perfect. You're absolutely perfect for me. You are the man I love, the man I want to spend the rest of my life with. Only you. Now and forever. So, yes to everything you asked, and more."

With a whoop of delight, David sprang to his feet and gathered her close. He covered her lips with his in a sweet kiss of promise. "I'm going to make you so happy."

She planted a kiss at the base of his neck. "If I was any happier, I'd explode."

He chuckled, a low pleasant rumbling sound. Gently tucking a lock of hair behind her ear, he murmured, "Tonight, after Brynn is in bed, we'll celebrate. Just the two of us."

Anticipation skittered up her spine. Winding her arms around his neck, Hadley kissed him softly on the mouth. Off to her right, a bird landed on the rail.

As if reluctant to give up the intimacy once the kiss ended, David moved his arm so her hand slid down to his. He gently locked their fingers together.

"Do you think Brynn will be surprised?"

He flashed a grin. "Not a chance."

Still holding David's hand, Hadley moved to the rail. She expected the bird to fly off, but the grosbeak simply cocked its head and watched her through sharp brown eyes.

Gazing over the rail, Hadley took in the beauty that was Door County. Fall colors were expected to peak early this year, and already, the trees were turning shades of rust, yellow and orange.

This was home.

A lump formed in her throat. Tears sprang to her eyes.

David frowned and tugged her close. He wiped the tears away with the pads of his thumbs. "What's wrong?"

Hadley gave a little laugh, feeling foolish. "I'm just happy. So very happy."

David stepped behind her and wrapped his arms around her waist. His breath was a soft caress on her neck.

As she reveled in the love of a man who knew all her secrets, the bird with the black head and bright red breast spread its wings and soared off.

David's mouth moved up her neck, scattering kisses and making her shiver.

"No more cages," she murmured.

He lifted his lips. "Did you say something, my darling fiancée?"

Hadley turned and wrapped her arms around him, holding him close. "Kiss me again, then let's go home and tell our daughter the good news."

Thank you for coming along on David and Hadley's journey. If you've read very many of my books, you know I love adding children wherever I can (especially little girls). Probably because I have a wonderful daughter and three amazing little granddaughters. David protected and loved his daughter fiercely which makes him a true hero in my book.

Many readers tell me they'd love to live in Good Hope. So would I! Never fear, we'll be coming back here again and again.

The next book in the series brings Lindsay and Owen together, two characters that very much deserve their happily ever after. Grab a copy of this uplifting story today (or continue reading for a sneak peek) Tie the Knot in Good Hope

Chapter One

Lindsay Lohmeier set down her fork. Normally, the interior of Muddy Boots café made her smile. She loved the cobalt blue splashes of rain, er paint, on the white walls and adored the mural of a happy girl in a bright red raincoat kicking up water.

Today, as lunch progressed, finding her happy place had become increasingly difficult. Though her lunch hadn't yet had a chance to settle, Lindsay knew the words would choke her if she didn't get them out.

"I finally did it." Nerves had Lindsay speaking more loudly than she'd intended. "I quit."

Lindsay's friends, who'd been arguing about something to do with the upcoming Harvest festival, paused the debate to focus on her.

Eliza Kendrick and Ami Cross sat directly across from her in a booth overlooking Good Hope's Main Street. They'd scored a primo spot by the window because Muddy Boots was owned by Ami and her husband.

"*What* are you quitting?" Eliza's grey eyes narrowed. She was a beautiful woman with shiny dark hair cut in a stylish bob and lips of bright red. "You better not say the Cherries, because no one leaves the Women's Events League. Not under my watch."

The frostiness that invaded the Executive Director of the Cherries' voice made Lindsay smile. Many on the Door County peninsula were intimidated by the woman's forceful personality. But she and Eliza had been friends for as far back as she could remember.

"I sense a story here." Ami leaned forward, resting her arms on the Formica tabletop, her green eyes dancing with curiosity. Her blond and brown sun-streaked hair shone in the glow of the fluorescent lights. "Tell us."

Eliza glanced at her phone's display and checked the time. "Don't keep us in suspense, Lin."

"I believe," Ami shot Eliza a warning glance, "what Eliza is trying to say is we know Shirley is a stickler about your lunch breaks."

"You have something to tell us." Eliza pointed a long, elegant finger at Lindsay. "Just say it."

Lindsay told herself she should be scared out of her mind. But compared to the news the doctor had laid on her this morning, not having an income was the least of her concerns.

"Yesterday," she paused, not so much for dramatic effect as to still the tremble in her voice, "I quit my job."

Ami's eyes grew wide. "Seriously?"

A slow smile lifted Eliza's red lips. "Well, hallelujah."

"If you're happy," Ami reached across the table to give Lindsay's hand a squeeze, "we're happy."

Eliza nodded then cocked her head, her sleek hair falling like a dark curtain against her cheek. "What made you decide to take the plunge?"

Lindsay understood their surprise. She'd worked as a floral designer at the Enchanted Florist for nearly ten years. She'd lived in her apartment for nearly that long. She'd never been one for change.

Now, looking ahead, she saw a future that held nothing *but* change. Lindsay swallowed against the bile rising in her throat.

"Was it that hideous uniform Shirley insisted you wear?" Eliza chuckled. "Or did you finally get sick of her bullshit and snap?"

Ami turned to Eliza, a smile tugging at the corners of her lips. "Why Mrs. Kendrick, I don't believe I've ever heard you say bullshit."

"Blame it on my husband." Eliza flashed a sly smile. "Kyle is a bad influence."

Lindsay and Ami looked at each other and burst out laughing. Everyone in Good Hope knew Kyle was the best thing that had ever happened to Eliza.

Eliza knew it, too. Her happiness shone as brightly as the diamond on her finger.

"Your ex-boss never gave you the credit or the freedom to create that you deserved." Eliza studied Lindsay. "I wouldn't have lasted a week. How you lasted ten years is beyond me."

"You're not Lindsay." Ami told Eliza then refocused on Lindsay. "What made you decide to leave now?"

Ami added an encouraging smile to the question.

"Shirley informed me the twins would be taking over my design work." Anger that she couldn't quite control licked at the edges of Lindsay's voice.

"Her daughters?" Eliza's brows pulled together in puzzlement. "They're in high school."

"They graduated last May," Lindsay reminded her. "After one class, they are now officially floral designers."

Her friends appeared as stunned as she'd been when Shirley delivered the bombshell. Lindsay had completed a two-year program in floral design, had ten years of experience and received numerous accolades. The twins' only education was the recent completion of a six-week online course.

One online course, Lindsay thought bitterly, then shoved the anger aside. She would not dwell on the negative. She told herself this change in circumstance had been a blessing, the shot in the arm she needed.

"I didn't go to school to ring up sales and schedule deliveries." Lindsay didn't mention Shirley had simpered that *unfortunately* she'd have to cut her salary since her job duties would be changing.

"I wish I could have seen Shirley's face when you quit." Eliza's lips lifted at the thought. "Mark my words her business will take a nosedive. I only sent Cherries' business her way because you worked there."

Ami nodded. "She's taken advantage of you and your talent for years."

"I let her," Lindsay admitted with an embarrassed smile.

"The job worked for you." Ami's tone had a matter-of-fact-ness, but sympathy filled her eyes. "Now that it no longer does, you quit."

Lindsay nodded, still embarrassed by the number of years she'd let Shirley trample over her.

"If you need a job while you decide your next step, I can always use help at the bakery." Ami's voice radiated reassurance and told Lindsay she wasn't in this alone.

It was a generous offer, but with Labor Day in the rearview, they'd officially entered the off-season. And Bloom's Bake Shop was fully staffed for the winter months.

Eliza, not to be outdone, met Lindsay's gaze. "There's always a place for you at the General Store."

Lindsay's heart swelled with love for these two women who would always have her back. In high school, they'd dubbed themselves the Three Musketeers. Over the years they'd weathered many tough times, including a horrific car accident the summer before their senior year.

Though Ami had been driving, Lindsay had been the one seriously injured. Now, the only reminder was a scar across her cheek. What had hurt most was the chasm between Ami and Eliza that had lasted for years, with Ami guilt-ridden and Eliza blaming Ami for Lindsay's injuries.

That was behind them now. They were a united front. For that, Lindsay was immensely grateful. She needed their love and support more than ever. Especially after the news she'd received barely two hours earlier.

"I appreciate the offers, but I've got some savings." Lindsay hoped saying aloud the plan circling in her head would make it real. "I've decided now is the time for me to follow your lead. I'm going into business for myself."

Excitement skittered across the table like the leaves dancing in the outside breeze. Before Lindsay could catch her breath, Eliza offered space in her store and Ami mentioned giving her several commercial refrigeration units.

"I have no need of them," Ami insisted. "We went with all new when we remodeled the bakery."

Lindsay found herself touched by the offer, but unwilling to take advantage. "I'll buy them."

"Absolutely not." Ami lifted her hands, palms out. "The units work, but they're old. You'll be doing me a favor by taking them off my hands."

Lindsay bit her bottom lip. "If you're sure…"

"I'm positive." Ami smiled. "I'm happy I can help."

Eliza glanced around the café, known for its comfort food and warm ambience. "If Muddy Boots had a liquor license, we'd open a bottle of champagne and toast your new business."

"I'm afraid the bottle would be wasted on me." Ami's hand dropped to her abdomen, reminding Lindsay her friend's second baby was due in February.

"It would be wasted on me as well." Lindsay clasped her fingers together to still their sudden trembling.

"I know you're not a big drinker." Eliza offered an understanding smile. "But this is a special occasion."

"I'm afraid the drinking door is solidly closed."

Ami shot her a quizzical glance.

Eliza circled a hand in a get-to-the-point gesture.

Lindsay took a deep breath then exhaled the words. "I'm pregnant."

Grab your copy of this uplifting book that will warm your heart and keep you turning the page! Tie the Knot in Good Hope

ALSO BY CINDY KIRK

Good Hope Series

The Good Hope series is a must-read for those who love stories that uplift and bring a smile to your face.

Check out the entire Good Hope series here

Hazel Green Series

Readers say "Much like the author's series of Good Hope books, the reader learns about a town, its people, places and stories that enrich the overall experience. It's a journey worth taking."

Check out the entire Hazel Green series here

Holly Pointe Series

Readers say "If you are looking for a festive, romantic read this Christmas, these are the books for you."

Check out the entire Holly Pointe series here

Jackson Hole Series

Heartwarming and uplifting stories set in beautiful Jackson Hole, Wyoming.

Check out the entire Jackson Hole series here

Silver Creek Series

Engaging and heartfelt romances centered around two powerful families whose fortunes were forged in the Colorado silver mines.

Check out the entire Silver Creek series here

Silver Creek Series

Engaging and heartfelt romances centered around two powerful families whose fortunes were forged in the Colorado silver mines.

check out the entire Silver Creek Series here

Made in the USA
Monee, IL
21 March 2023

30316055R00154